D1447251

Enchantment

OF A

Highlander

MADELINE MARTIN

DIVERSIONBOOKS

Also by Madeline Martin

Deception of a Highlander
Possession of a Highlander

Diversion Books
A Division of Diversion Publishing Corp.
443 Park Avenue South, Suite 1008
New York, New York 10016
www.DiversionBooks.com

For more information, email info@diversionbooks.com

First Diversion Books edition January 2016.
Print ISBN: 978-1-62681-922-1
eBook ISBN: 978-1-62681-921-4

To Hillary Raymer, my wonderful critique partner—through everything life has thrown at us through the years, you've always been there with your positive encouragement and support. This book, and many others, wouldn't be what they are without you. Thank you.

Chapter One

Isle of Mull, Scotland, August 1608

If he was to die, Alec MacLean would take a couple of thieves with him.

The sharp scent of pine mingled with the thick odor of blood. His blood.

He edged back against the jagged rock wall and lifted his sword to the six advancing men. Blood flowed freely from the wound at his chest. The bastard had sliced him somewhere below the collarbone. His right arm was weakening.

At least the boy had gone ahead to the village and couldn't do anything stupid to get himself killed. With any luck, the woman Alec had rescued was there by now as well.

The largest man of the group lunged forward, but this time Alec was faster. He crouched low, gripped the sword between both hands, and thrust, using the power of his left arm to compensate for the weakness of his right. The black polished steel slid deep into the man's gut, a lethal wound.

Eventually.

Alec jerked his blade free. If he hadn't been so travel-weary, the fight would have been over minutes ago.

But Alec was not the kind of man who surrendered. Not while outlaws roamed the woods, not while innocents were subjected to their abuse, not while he was the new laird.

A charge of energy spiked through him. He would fight this battle and he would win. For his people.

The ones he'd abandoned so long ago.

The force of his resolve roared from his throat in a battle cry. His muscles swelled with crazed determination.

The semicircle of men stopped their advance and their blades dipped. Alec held his at the ready.

But they were not looking at Alec.

Their gazes crept up the rock wall behind him.

"*Bana-bhuidseach*," one of them murmured.

Witch.

The men's eyes went wild and they scrambled back with their wounded man clutched between them. A gust swept around Alec so viciously it sent his kilt slapping against his knees and thighs.

Alec jerked around and looked up, but found only the rock wall and gray sky.

"Are you as foolish as those men?" A voice came through to him, soft, feminine, and impossible to locate with all the damn wind. It seemed to come from everywhere and nowhere at once.

His heart slapped against his ribs.

A witch? On his father's lands—on *his* lands?

Impossible.

His gaze combed the forest in long sweeps. Naught was there but the trees bowing their limbs to the wind and the grass bending to its wrath.

"Who's there?" The words came out strong and gruff.

The other men had been afraid.

He would show no fear.

He licked his lips. "Reveal yerself."

"Perhaps you are foolish, then." The voice was behind him now.

He spun around, and his body pumped with a fight he resisted.

A tall, willowy woman stood before him with her hands clasped at her narrow waist, serene and eerily beautiful. Her long, silver-blonde hair blew loose behind her, like a cape rippling in the wind. That same wind flattened her pale blue dress to her body, hugging the curve of her breasts and the roundness of her hips.

He stared at her, fascinated. This was the witch? *This* was what had caused the men to run?

She stepped—nay, glided—toward him, and he had to stand firm to keep from staggering backward.

"Do you need so much comfort from your sword?" She nodded toward his blade. "Surely a strong man like you isn't afraid of one unarmed woman."

He grunted and slid the blade into the scabbard between his shoulder blades. Pain burned across his chest and a fresh stream of warmth ran down his torso.

Her careful, calculating gaze lowered to his chest, to his wound.

He wanted to stand there, to stare longer, to see if she was real.

Perhaps she was a nymph come to tempt him from his path.

She beckoned him with a gentle curl of her finger. "Follow me."

Perhaps she was an angel and he was dead.

"Come with me and I will heal your wound."

He flexed his shoulders out in a motion he'd used before to intimidate men on the battlefield. "It isna more than a nick."

Her brow lifted. She reached out one long, delicate finger toward him and hooked the hole in his blood-soaked leine. His flesh was torn beneath, the muscle glistening red and exposed.

"Aye." She peered into his shirt. "A nick." She released his clothes and her hand fell away like a sigh. "Do what you want, but be warned—if you try to walk home, you will lose strength."

Alec forced himself not to take a step back. "Do ye curse me?"

She rolled her eyes. "You've already lost a considerable amount of blood. If you don't have enough in your body, you will die." Her words were slow and measured, as if she were speaking to an errant child.

"Why do ye aid me, witch?" He watched her carefully, marking the way the wind ripped against the trees, yet did little more than brush the length of her hair.

Her pointed chin jutted up and her eyes sparked. "I'm a

healer, not a witch."

Alec kept his gaze fixed on her willowy frame and bent to retrieve the pack he'd thrown at the onset of battle. The forest pulsed hot white and spun.

Perhaps the wound was more than a nick after all.

He hefted the thick leather strap to his good side, but the torn skin on his chest still wrenched against its weight. A low grunt slipped from his throat.

She did not move to aid him with his bag, and for that he was grateful.

He didn't want the woman's pity.

"The villager you saved was with child," she said. "That was kind of you, to offer her your protection."

"How do ye know I saved a villager?" he asked.

She turned and glided away. The wind caressed her pale hair, sweeping it aside to blow like a tendril of linen caught in a breeze. Her waist was so narrow he could probably span it with his hands.

"Are you coming or not?" Irritation laced her tone. "I won't drag you."

Alec stumbled after her then, focusing on keeping his footing sure in a world where everything had begun to tip and rock. Certainly he was in no position to refuse her offer.

Even if she very well might be a witch.

• • •

Celia closed the door of her cottage against the push of wind. A stark quiet filled the room.

Gray light filtered in from the open shutters and highlighted the warrior's massive form. She studied him now in the privacy of her own home. His hair was black as peat and pulled into a braid long enough to graze the sheath he wore between his shoulder blades. Blood stained his shirt, a violent splash of color against otherwise muted tones.

Even with the wound, the man stood upright, his broad shoulders pulled back with the pride of someone who never bowed.

His eyes were pale blue, the color of a cloudless sky on a cold winter day, and his unwavering stare left her skin tight with awareness.

She pointed to a chair by the hearth. "Go sit by the fire."

His pack fell to the floor with a *thunk* that rattled the shutters.

She pulled open the plain wooden box of thread. Her back faced him, but she kept her ears strained for any sounds of his approach.

Bringing the injured man to her home by invitation was imprudent. She knew nothing of the stranger aside from the assistance he had offered Bessie when the woman was attacked.

He'd angled himself between the outlaws and Bessie so the young woman could escape. Only then had he backed against the rock wall to keep from being surrounded. Surely his valor spoke something of his morals.

The chair by the fire gave an aged groan. She dug a needle from another box and glanced over her shoulder. He watched her still with those cool blue eyes.

Rescuer of women he might be, but she would be keeping her dagger at her waist.

"Where was the woman's husband?" His voice was strong, commanding. The kind men obeyed without question.

But Celia wasn't a man.

She took her time pulling a bundle of thyme from the rafters. His gaze drifted to her naked ankles.

"Dead." She readjusted the hem of her dress with a snap.

She didn't typically know much about the people who sought her aid, and preferred to keep it that way. But Bessie had always taken Celia's silence as an invitation to chatter nonstop.

It had been impossible not to listen.

The stranger's gaze slid up to her face. "Where's yer husband?"

His inquiry was more than most men asked.

Fortunately, the rumor of her being a witch kept the men fearfully at bay. Ironic that the dangerous slur shrouding her life was the very thing protecting her.

Such had not always been the case.

"You should take off your leine so I can see your wound," she said. She shifted her gaze to the dried thyme in her hand to keep from watching him undress.

The dusky green leaves crackled against her palm and released a smooth, clean scent.

"Do ye always ignore questions or is it just me?" His sheath clattered to the ground followed by the slick peel of wet fabric sliding off skin.

"Do you always ask so many questions?" She dragged the extra chair toward the fire and sat upon its hard surface. "Or is it just me?"

The water had begun to boil, bubbling low in the pot, yet she did not pull it from the flames.

Her gaze fell on his bare torso and any comment she might have made died in her throat. She'd seen men without their shirts before—in fact, she'd seen men naked. Some were fleshy with inactivity or age and some were hard and sculpted like the one in front of her.

But never had she seen one with so many signs of past hurt.

"It's just ye."

She lifted her eyes and found him staring at her again. "What?"

He didn't reek of stale sweat and sour cloth as some of the other warriors she'd tended had. She drew in a long, discreet breath through her nostrils. No, he smelled like sun-warmed grass and leather.

"Ye're intriguing." His eyes searched hers.

She looked away, focusing instead on carefully removing the pot from the flames.

"Who are you?" she asked.

"Alec MacLean."

She knew that name. What resident on the Isle of Mull did not? Alec MacLean was the name of the laird who had recently died. Finally died. But not before destroying the land and breaking his people.

And this warrior bore his name.

"Our former laird had that very name, the one who just died."

He made a noncommittal sound.

"He was not well liked." Celia stated baldly.

"I've heard something of that."

"He ran this land into ruin and let its people starve."

The skin around his eyes tightened. "I've heard that too."

"Are you…?"

"Aye." A muscle flicked in his jaw. "I'm his son and I've returned home to claim my inheritance."

Chapter Two

"Are ye regretting having saved me?" Alec had come home expecting a similar response from everyone, yet her reaction bothered him. The intended jest fell flat with the long look of consideration she cast in his direction.

She lifted the jug and pushed it toward him. "Drink this."

No reply.

Again.

The woman was maddening.

Maddening and altogether too enticing.

The robust floral scent of elderflower liqueur wafted toward him. He tensed against the offer.

"I'm no like my father." Alec's breath hissed through his nose. "Once I'm settled, I will restore Duart Castle and the lands to what they were in my childhood. There is much to cleanse. The people need protection."

She turned away to pour the boiled water into a bowl of green flaky leaves. He rested his elbows on his knees and leaned toward her.

"You're making yourself bleed again." Her voice came softer this time, barely audible over the wind knocking against her cottage. "This wash will clean your injury and keep infection away."

The yellow-green water released a curl of moist heat and scented the air with a rich, spicy aroma.

She dipped a white cloth in the mixture and blew at the tendril of steam rising from it. "It shouldn't be too hot."

The warm cloth pressed not to his chest but to his lower stomach, just above the waist of his kilt. His muscles bunched instinctively and the breath hissed between his teeth. Her gaze trailed the heated path of the cloth, sliding up his torso to the tightness of his nipple.

The cloth passed over the sensitive flesh, warm as a mouth, her careful ministrations dangerously close to a caress. There was an edge of pain when she dabbed his wound, but for the most part, he had never enjoyed being injured more.

She pulled the cloth away and his skin immediately cooled. "Are you sure you don't want some of the liqueur? It's nothing fine, but it will help take the sting—"

"Are ye a Lowlander?" he asked. He didn't want to talk about his wound or fighting or his land and certainly not his piss-poor example of a father.

He wanted to know about her. Why a woman from the Lowlands happened upon his father's land, how long she'd been in the cottage, what she expected of him as laird.

He wanted the caress of her gentle hands on his body and the calming tone of her silky voice in his ears.

She did not answer him. Of course.

Instead he answered for her. "Aye, ye are no from here. But what made ye come to the Highlands? Did ye no find Lowland men to yer liking?"

She lifted the needle. "A Lowlander would never stare at me as you do." Only when she passed a thread through the eye of the needle did he notice a slight tremor to her fingers. "It's rude."

He couldn't help the grin tugging at his lips. She'd said it without malice, but it was enough to let him know she was aware of his interest.

The woman was full of pride, full of fire, and he wanted to sample every tasty morsel she had to offer.

Her fingers swept across his chest like an angel's kiss, sweet and whisper soft.

"I want ye," he said.

She pinched the corner of his wound together and the sharp edge of pain cut through Alec's awareness. "We'll see if you still feel that way after I've stitched you together." The point of the needle pressed to his skin. "Now be quiet until I've finished."

• • •

Celia examined the row of pale white stitches against the golden tone of Alec's skin. They were neat and steady, a miracle considering the way her hand had trembled. She'd never been so out of sorts before, so distracted.

No doubt it had to do with all the man's questions.

"You'll need to be mindful of these or they will tear out." She set the needle aside and placed the soiled cloth in the bowl.

The corner of his lip lifted. "If they tear out, I'll have an excuse to see ye again."

"If you let them tear out intentionally, I'll let you bleed to death for your own stupidity." She rose from the chair.

He caught her fingers and held tight. His palm was warm and callused like weathered bark. She turned to him in exasperation and found his eyes burning into hers with icy heat. "What I said about wanting ye hasna changed, healer."

Her cheeks went hot beneath a pulse so strong she could scarce catch her breath. "You would force yourself on me even after I have aided you?"

He rose from his seat and stood over her—no, towered over her. She craned her neck back to look up at him.

"I wouldna have to force myself." The commanding tone had not left his voice, but it was softer now, more intimate.

Her nipples tightened beneath her homespun gown and warmth swirled eddies in her stomach. "Wouldn't you?"

"I havena misread the way ye reacted to me, the way yer hands shake." His jaw tensed.

One large finger slid under her chin, a delicate touch for a man so intimidating. Her head fell back of its own accord, her body obeying what her mind stubbornly fought.

"The way yer nipples grow hard for me." The skin around his eyes tensed and his gaze slipped toward her breasts, where his effect on her stood proud against the fabric.

His hand cradled the back of her neck and he leaned closer. "The way yer eyes keep drifting to my lips, like ye want to know how I taste."

She swallowed and found herself staring at the Cupid's bow of his top lip. He was inches from her mouth. Her heart sputtered.

"No." She stepped back, pulling herself from his touch. "You misread me." Even she could hear the lie in her breathy words.

He narrowed his eyes, but did not move to touch her again. "I dinna think so." His gaze trailed down her body before coming to rest on her face. Her skin sizzled beneath the path of his observation.

"Be my mistress."

Celia blinked. "What?"

He closed the distance between them, the heat of his hard, naked chest touching the tips of her breasts. "Be my mistress. Stand by my side as I purge the land of the ruin my father created."

His fingers combed through her long hair. Chills of pleasure tingled across her scalp and raced down her spine. "I want ye warming my bed."

She arched away from the promise of his embrace and tried not to stare down at his muscular torso, at the way the sinewy muscle flexed and shifted beneath such scarred flesh. "Your wound is tended to as promised. I suggest you leave and not return."

The corner of his lip lifted with a hint of arrogance as if he sensed her inner battle. "Ye are on my land. Of course I'll see ye again."

She pulled the door open and wind gusted into the cottage. Herbs rustled against one another from where they swung wildly on their threads, and the curtain strung around her bed sucked toward them.

Alec pulled a fresh leine from his bag and tugged it over his head. "I'll leave only if ye tell me yer name, healer." He hefted his sack to his shoulder with an almost imperceptible grimace and stared at her where he stood.

"Celia," she said, loud enough to be heard over the howl of the wind. "Now be gone with you."

The line across his brow eased with his small victory. He strode to the door and paused beside her. "I'll see ye again, Celia." He said her name slow, purposeful, as if he were savoring the way it rolled off his tongue in that soft burr of his.

The wind fluttered his leine and flattened his kilt to the tops of his muscular thighs, but he did not waver against its insistent push. He stood stoic in its wrath, unfazed by the wet cold. Celia's legs trembled beneath her and she had to fight the part of herself that wanted to sway against his powerful body.

Neither of them moved for a moment, both staring with a mix of intimidation and curiosity. Finally, he strode out the door. She slammed it shut behind him and rested her forehead on the rough wood.

She had known the man was nobility by his fine dress, but she hadn't expected him to be Laird MacLean. Nor had she expected the son of the former laird to be so just, so powerful.

So dangerous.

The law did little good from what she'd seen, from what she'd experienced. Innocents were sacrificed under the guise of "law".

A scratch sounded at the base of the door where the wind mewled. Celia pulled the latch and held the door wide enough for the red fox to slink inside before bolting it shut once more.

"Is he gone now, Ruadh?"

The fox stared up at her with his golden eyes and flicked his bushy tail in aggravation.

"Good riddance to that one." She tossed the remaining thread into the fire and watched the remnants of the laird's blood sizzle and curl into ash. "For the time being we are safe."

She glanced at the door once more. Her skin still tingled where he had touched her. Unwanted, a thrill wound down her spine and blossomed in goosebumps across her skin.

He would be back and she would need to keep her secrets locked away, the way she had managed to do thus far.

Her life depended on it.

Chapter Three

Alec stepped over a pile of refuse and glanced around the alley's corner to the sea of faces crowding the market. An aging merchant argued with a woman over the price of something bundled in linen, but aside from their bickering, all appeared peaceful. It was better than he'd expected.

A tall, thin lad of twelve with straw-colored hair stood near a pastry cart. His head drooped lower, toward the outstretched hand of the young cart owner. She handed him a pastry with a wink and returned her attention to her cart.

Alec leaned against the pitted wall of a building and watched from the shade. The boy stepped from the stall and bit into the pastry. Duncan might be an awkward youth, but his shy smile won him a considerable amount of favors.

He nodded to a woman dressed in a blue silk dress and wove his way ever closer to Alec. The woman did not belong among the other villagers. Her dress was too rich, her chin angled with an edge of entitlement.

The boy waved to Alec before trotting over to him. The musk of sweaty boy filled the air.

Duncan's eyes widened and seemed to fill half his face. "Is that blood?" he asked, pointing to Alec's shirt. "What happened? Where did ye go?"

Alec glanced down to the thin line of blood over his wound. "After ye headed to the village, I happened upon a woman being attacked."

Duncan's brow furrowed beneath spikes of sweaty blond hair. "I shoulda been with ye."

Alec sighed. "Ach, I dinna take ye because I couldna afford

for all the coin to be lost if we were found out." The petty excuse seemed to placate the boy well enough. Truth be told, most of the coin was with Laird MacKinnon in Angus, but Duncan didn't need to know. What mattered most was that the boy was safe.

"And what about this?" Duncan pointed to the wound. "Did they cut ye?" He nodded toward Alec's chest. "Was it a dagger or a sword? Do ye think it was poisoned? Do we need to get a healer to look at it for ye?"

Were Duncan any other person, Alec could have shrugged off the questions and remained quiet. Time and experience, however, had taught him the boy did not let the fine details go.

Ever.

"I've already seen a healer." An image of her rose in his mind like a flower pushing up through the ground.

Duncan's mouth opened and Alec put a hand up before another string of questions began. "Have ye learned anything from the villagers?"

Sometimes the lad could be distracted with his own stories. Alec hoped this was the case now. His energy thinned and his wound burned like a demon. Perhaps he should have taken a swig of the liqueur Celia had offered.

Duncan looped his thumb in his belt. It was an action Alec had seen him do when the boy didn't want to answer a question. "I havena heard much more than the rumors we already found on our own. The land has been so long without a good laird that it's become filled with outlaws. Homes have fallen to ruin, but they dinna have the means to repair them. Everyone is scared and hungry and there's no anyone to help." He scuffed his foot on the ground.

"What else, Duncan?"

The boy stared down at the pastry braced within the cage of his long fingers. "Yer castle was ransacked right after, ye know…" he cast Alec a sidelong glance. "After yer da's death." He said it softly, as if he were afraid of brushing an unhealed wound.

Obviously the boy didn't understand what an arse Alec's father was. *Da* indeed.

"We can have more furniture built," Alec said.

Duncan pursed his lips and squeezed his eyes as if he were in pain. "It's more than ransacked. I dinna think it can even be lived in."

Alec uttered an oath and gazed in the direction of Duart Castle. "We'll find out soon."

"Alec?" A woman's voice sounded in the crowd.

He turned to find the woman in the blue dress coming toward him. Her black curls gave a little bounce with each dainty step.

"Laird MacLean." She curtseyed and met his gaze with eyes that sparkled like sapphires set in sunlight.

He studied her upturned nose and the wide set of her mouth. This woman who knew him was wholly unrecognizable to him.

"My lady," he said politely, and inclined his head.

He'd be damned if he was going to bow like some courtier in the middle of his own market square.

This did not appear to please her. The full bottom of her pink mouth puffed out in a pout. "Do ye no recognize me?"

The question set him up for failure and would without a doubt lead to her disappointment. Irritation drew tight across the back of his neck. He didn't have time for such childish games.

She turned her face toward him just so and a small scar became visible under her left eye.

Then he remembered.

She'd been struck there by a rock when they were children, playing some nonsense rescue-the-princess game.

"Saraid."

Her smile widened and brightened up her face considerably. "Ye remember after all," she said.

A little girl ran from behind Saraid and upset the delicate pouf of her skirts.

"Watch it, brat," Saraid snapped at the girl, who paid her no heed.

Now Alec remembered Saraid with such clarity, it was a wonder he'd ever forgotten her in the first place.

Bossy, impatient, and prone to tantrums when her way

was not met.

"I dinna forget ye," she said pointedly. Her stare swept over him, polite yet appreciative. "And now ye've grown into a man, and I a woman." Her deep sigh swelled her full breasts against the tight cut of her gown.

Alec wanted to roll his eyes, but averted his gaze instead. Duncan, however, leaned forward for a better view.

Her gaze shifted to the boy for the first time. "Is this yer son? Where's yer wife?"

"He's no my son," Alec said.

"Oh." She swirled a curl of dark hair around her finger. "And yer wife?"

Alec suppressed a long-suffering groan. "I'm no married." The words gritted from his teeth, low in the hopes she wouldn't hear.

But she'd been listening very attentively and her eyes brightened. "Oh? Aren't ye, then? And ye've returned home?"

Again, he didn't want to answer. Again, he knew he had to. "Aye."

She shifted closer. "Well, I'm no married either. I've had many suitors, but none have been what I've been looking for." Her gaze was full of suggestion.

An aging woman stood behind her, watching the conversation with intensity. Saraid's lady's maid. Neither she nor the guard loitering nearby admonished their mistress for being too close.

Alec would have no help.

It was time to fall back onto social tact.

"Good luck to ye then," he said. "Duncan, get the bags." He nodded toward her. "Good to see ye, Saraid."

Her mouth fell open and her cheeks colored a brilliant red. She nodded and her ringlets bobbed around her face. "And ye, Alec." She recovered with a sweet smile. "I do hope to see more of ye."

Alec grunted and nudged the boy forward.

Together they strode from the ridiculous conversation and toward Duart Castle to see how very unlivable it truly was.

• • •

Rain dripped like bitter tears down stone walls gone black with age, and a part of the curtain wall was missing, gaping darkly like a missing front tooth.

Where fields of soft green grass once grew, now weeds twisted against one another in a thorny battle for dominance.

A door once meant to keep armies out hung on only the bottom hinge, a chunk of wood nicked from its rounded top.

Alec stood before the neglected remains of his childhood home. He glanced at Duncan, unsure if the boy would be safer waiting outside or walking through the bowels of the castle with him.

"What'd the villagers say about people living here?" Alec asked.

Duncan tossed his head to the side to clear a lock of wet hair from his eyes. "They dinna say. Just that..." He rolled up on his tiptoes before rocking back. "They said the castle's haunted."

Alec groaned. "Ghosts, my arse. Ready yer dagger, boy, and stay close, aye?" He tugged his sword free of the scabbard behind his back and paid for the sharp action with a searing jolt along the expanse of his chest.

His muscles tightened against the offending wound. The damn thing would prove cumbersome in battle.

He pushed the heavy door open with his good side and slipped inside ahead of Duncan.

A somber light filtered through broken windows in the distance, but did little to brighten the entryway shrouded in darkness. The steady leaking drip of rain echoed from an unseen source.

"Do ye think there's really a ghost here?" Duncan came up beside Alec and cast a nervous glance around them.

Alec caught the tip of the boy's blade with his thumb and forefinger and tilted it upward. "Mind yer weapon, lad. I dinna teach ye to hold it like that."

Duncan gave an eager nod and corrected his grip. "Are daggers good against ghosts?"

"I can promise ye, the only ghosts here are ones that bleed." Alec stalked forward cautiously. Debris and dirt crunched beneath the soles of his boots.

The narrow hall was empty, starkly so. Vacant sconces scorched black from years of fires lined the walls and a cold, musty dankness hung in the air.

They stepped into the great hall and stopped. The room had been something to marvel at when Alec was a boy. Now the walls that had once been draped with gold- and silver-threaded tapestries stood naked. The benches and tables were gone—even the massive sword that had once hung impossibly high over the fireplace was gone.

Where opulence had resided, now gray rushes rotted on the floor with things moving within their depths.

A raindrop splashed against the top of Alec's head.

He jerked his head upright to see the gray sky visible overhead in a hole no bigger than a man's fist.

Repairing the high ceiling of the great hall would not be an easy feat.

"Do ye think they were right?" Duncan asked. "Is it unlivable?"

Truth be told, it wasn't as bad as Alec had anticipated. Aye, some of the stone had been smuggled away, most likely by villagers needing to repair their own homes, but most of it remained, and completely intact.

Most likely he wouldn't even need to seek the aid of a master builder to complete the tasks he'd seen thus far.

"We've no seen all of it yet," Alec said in a low mutter. There was an edge to his voice he knew even Duncan would not counter.

They passed through an empty archway where two great wooden doors used to close off the entrance to the kitchens. A fat black rat darted in front of them, scuttling away from the yawning doorway.

An uneasy feeling crawled over the skin on the back of Alec's neck. There was a shift in the still air, a scent, a slight grind of dirt against stone, something he could not quite name.

But he knew exactly what it meant.

They were not alone.

• • •

No matter how much the villagers tried to hide it, Celia knew they stared. Their gazes bored into her like needle pricks.

A flicker of red fur showed through the thick brush on the outskirts of the village. Ruadh was near. He always was. Even in the populated areas he hated, he lingered on the edge, waiting for her to emerge.

She tightened her grip on the basket and approached the home set off from the others.

A voice sang from the other side of the door, sweet and gentle. Celia rapped her knuckles against the splintering wood and the song abruptly stopped.

Bessie's face appeared in the doorway, lit with a smile that made her nose wrinkle and her eyes crease. Freckles spattered her cheeks, making her appear younger than her eighteen years.

No evidence from the attack was apparent on the woman's face, thankfully.

"I'm sorry." Celia thrust out the parcel of bundled herbs she'd prepared only minutes before. "You forgot the rest of your tea."

Bessie glanced down at the linen-wrapped items and stepped back for Celia to enter. There was little more to the small cottage than the bed, a table with a couple of chairs, and a cradle in the corner, but it all appeared tidy and in good repair.

The spicy sweet aroma of brewing herbs wafted from a pot on the fire, a scent Celia recognized as the very tea she held in her hand.

"I thought I'd gotten it all," Bessie said. "I appreciate ye making it for me. This sickness is getting worse as the babe grows."

"I'm glad it's eased your nausea." Celia set the extra bundles on top of the table and carefully eyed the girl. The swell of her pregnancy was almost invisible despite being four months along.

Celia saw no perceptible limp or wince as Bessie walked, but she wanted to ensure no injury had been sustained in the attack. "I'm glad you made it home safely," she said.

Bessie's eyes widened. "I almost dinna make it home at all," the young woman said. "There were men in the forest. So many men. Celia, they shoved me on the ground and demanded coin." Her cheeks went red. "Ye know I dinna have coin. I told them as much and they grabbed me up by the arm and held a blade to my throat."

Her gaze turned distant and her fingers pressed protectively over her little stomach. "Then this man I've no ever seen came from nowhere, a verra large man, and he told me to run. I should have stayed close, to help if I might. I shouldna have left him to die with them, but I…I…"

Bessie's eyes glazed with tears. "I was so afraid. I've been so afraid since Connor died." Her face glistened with falling tears. "And now I may have gotten a man killed."

A soft sob broke from her lips and tugged at Celia's heart.

"He didn't die." Celia was grateful to offer the woman solid reassurance. "He came to see me not long after you left, with a cut on his chest." The image of the new laird's powerful chest rushed into her mind, as did the way those light eyes watched her with such burning intensity.

Bessie straightened. "A cut? Was it deep? How do ye know it was him?"

"It was but a nick," Celia fibbed, using the man's own words. Alec. Alec MacLean.

She turned the cold side of her emotion to the memory. "He told me about the battle and he scared them off before they could do any real harm."

Bessie nodded and her shoulders hunched forward once more, cradling her own small frame in frailty like her sharp hipbones cupped the babe in her womb.

"You did what you had to do to protect your baby, as any mother would have done." Celia spoke in a gentle voice and moved her hand over the woman's shoulder, where it hung with hesitation.

A decade and a half had passed since Celia had touched someone without the intent to mend a break or stitch a wound. Her hand withdrew an inch, as if of its own volition, the act of touching someone in comfort so foreign a concept, her hand did not want to comply.

But this was a form of healing, was it not? To comfort an aching heart.

One could comfort without love, couldn't one?

She lowered her palm to Bessie's trembling shoulder. It was an awkward attempt, unnatural feeling in such a way it left her cheeks hot with embarrassment. She quickly withdrew and clasped her hands together lest she make so foolish a decision again.

Bessie did not appear to notice the failed attempt. She pulled the sleeve of her chemise up to her elbow. "One of them grabbed me," she said miserably, and lifted her arm.

Three deep gouges showed where fingernails had raked across her skin. Angry red skin already swelled on either side of the wound. This was what Celia knew how to handle and why she'd made up the flimsy excuse of the teas in the first place. She might not be able to comfort, but she would keep the pregnant woman as healthy as was possible.

"I have my things here with me." Celia looked up at Bessie. "May I?"

Tears shone bright in the woman's eyes. "I can't afford to—"

"It's fine," Celia reassured her.

She cleaned the wound with more of the thyme infusion and rubbed a plantain and agrimony infused salve across the torn flesh.

When she was done, Bessie gave her a shy smile. "Thank ye for helping me. I know I dinna have coin, but perhaps…" She pursed her lips with obvious hesitation. "Perhaps I can share some information with ye," she said in a soft voice. Her breath smelled like peppermint from the tea. "But ye canna tell anyone. We've all been warned to keep it quiet, aye?"

She rose abruptly, closed the shutters, and snapped the latch into place.

Celia wanted to press her for clarification, but knew she must be patient.

"Something happened on MacDougall lands two days back," she whispered. "Women were burned to death on the lawns before Aros Castle."

A chill slipped over Celia's shoulders and trickled down her spine.

"They were accused of witchcraft. There were three of 'em." Bessie's brows furrowed. "I hear Laird MacDougall is starting the trials again. Ye need to be mindful."

"Me?" The word came out like a gasped exhale.

Bessie nodded solemnly. "There are some who say ye heal so well there is more to ye than just herbs."

Celia's stomach twisted in a hopeless coil of knots.

"I dinna think ye need worry much, though," Bessie continued with her positive cheer. "I suppose the one good thing of being without a proper laird is that ye dinna have to fear the law, aye?"

But Bessie's bright smile did little to quell the unrest churning in Celia's gut. She knew too well how close the law lay and how that law dealt with witches.

It was only a matter of time.

Chapter Four

Alec and Duncan edged along the walls of the castle. The weight of being watched had not abated, yet no one emerged from the shadows. And so they'd continued on.

They'd tried to move quietly, but it was impossible in such a vast, empty space. The crunch of their footsteps echoed around them. At least the boy's incessant chatter had dwindled down to occasional whispered comments.

Alec recognized the hall before them as the one housing the main bedchambers. His father's, his own, and his mother's.

Something twisted inside him, something he thought he'd freed himself of when he left ten years ago. Yet being in the familiar layout of the hall, even with debris scattered on the floor and all the fine trappings gone, memories rolled frantic through his mind like a broken strand of pearls.

He stopped in front of his mother's door. The wood had gone dull with age. His palm ached to press against the cool, worn surface.

The sweetness of jasmine lingered in the stale air, so faint he had to breathe in deep and slow to find it. His heart squeezed at the thought of his mother and suddenly he had to see her room. Even if it was empty, as devoid of furniture as the castle was devoid of her life, he had to see it and let himself remember. Her love, her kindness. Her dire, unhappy situation.

He reached for the handle and a high-pitched squealing rang out, long and loud.

He spun toward the noise as something soft and thick and warm slammed into him.

He careened backward beneath the massive sack of a

person, all massive arms and legs and that awful, awful noise.

Duncan shouted and appeared at Alec's side, but only succeeded in tangling their feet, which sent them both crashing to the hard floor.

A massive woman slammed on top of Alec's chest, her red hair flying in all directions. Bright blue eyes glared at him, wide with rage and insanity. Her hands slapped against his forehead, his left ear, his right temple, his neck.

And damn that noise she was making.

Alec caught her hands in his and spoke in a level voice. "I demand ye stop."

The sound ceased and his ears hummed with relief.

The woman struggled and her red face twisted with the effort. Breath huffed from her chest as if she'd run to the other coast of Scotland in a day. Then she stopped. Her face smoothed.

She gasped and leaned forward. Beading sweat left puddled dots along her flushed skin. Gone was the crazed look and in its place was the gentle face of kindness, the corners of her eyes crinkled.

A face he recognized.

"Wynda?" He stared at the woman in disbelief and recalled the many comfits the cook had sneaked to him as a boy.

Her eyes went glassy and her hands pressed into his cheeks, damp and warm. "Ach, my wee lad has returned home after all these years and what do I do? Beat him like he's one of the outlaws come to steal the fortune."

She stayed where she straddled him and jerked his torso upright, hugging his face into the overly generous swell of her bosom. "Welcome home, laird. It's been too, too, too…" She rocked her body, and him, with each word. "Too long."

"I see now I should have come home sooner." Alec's words were muffled against her massive chest.

Wynda dropped him backward and clambered upright. "Come on then, let's look at ye." She grasped his hand and hauled him to his feet.

Her critical eye swept over him and her mouth puckered. "Oh, lad, ye've grown." She waggled her eyebrows at him.

"Ye're rather fine."

Alec's cheeks went hot in spite of himself. Duncan peered around from behind Wynda with a hand over his mouth, smothering a laugh.

"Surely a man so braw as ye has a bonny wife." Her eyes lit up. "And wee ones? Do ye have wee ones?"

"No wife or bairns." His voice was intentionally gruff. "Where are the others, Wynda?" he asked. "What's happened here?"

The light faded from her eyes. "Most of the servants dinna wait for yer father to die before they left. Most left after ye. The ones who remained stayed for the memory of yer mother, but loyalty only lasts so long, especially with the way yer father treated them." Her gaze slid away, as if she had a hard time looking at him. "He got much worse after ye left."

Guilt pressed hard on Alec's shoulders. He'd thought if he could escape, everything would be better. And it had been.

For him.

He'd been selfish.

"The castle fell into neglect," Wynda continued. "And yer da stopped listening to the tenants. With no one standing trial or being punished, the land became flooded with outlaws." She shook her head and the top of her fluffy hair wavered. "After he died, the remaining servants took their pay in the form of tapestries or silver, whatever yer da hadna already sold off himself."

Wynda wiped her hands on the dirty apron she wore. "I dinna stop them. No one had been paid in so long. But when the outlaws started coming, I locked the treasures in a room to make sure they dinna get in."

"Treasures?" Alec repeated. Perhaps all was not lost after all.

A wide smile spread over her lips and he noticed for the first time she'd lost several teeth since he'd seen her last.

Wynda pulled a tarnished key from her pocket. "All in yer mother's room."

She stepped over a brownish-red stain on the floor and slid the key into the lock. The door groaned open and the musty odor of disuse hit Alec's nostrils.

He caught no scent of the jasmine perfume he'd smelled earlier.

His mother's room lay exactly as it had when she died.

He could see the ghost of her long, slender back in front of the dressing table. The bottles on the surface lay gray with dust now, but he remembered how they'd gleamed in the sunlight like jewels and how her fingertips would skim over the smooth surfaces.

A long chest at the base of the bed most likely still contained all her gowns. His gaze caught the bed. The place he hadn't wanted to look, but could not avoid. It was dull and faded now, but once the velvet had been a brilliant blue.

She'd lain against those fine coverlets, her brow dotted with sweat and flushed with fever. Her pale blue eyes darting everywhere, seeing things unseen by anyone else, before finally meeting his and locking there.

I love ye.

It'd been a whisper, but he'd heard it—the last words she'd spoken with the last breath she'd breathed.

He sucked in a deep gasp of air in an effort to ease the rending pain in his chest.

A hand rested on his shoulder, heavy and warm. He tore his stare from the bed and found Wynda's sad smile on him.

"Is this all of it?" he asked, looking for the first time at a pile of goods in the center of the floor. His words came out tight and hard.

A silver candlestick and several tapestries lay among various plates and cutlery. Three sacks of grain sagged in a folded sigh surrounding the small pile. While the room lay shrouded in a dark layer of dust, these items appeared to have been wiped clean. They'd been well cared for.

"It isna much." Wynda's dirt-creased hands twisted anxiously against one another.

No, it was not.

But it was more than he'd expected.

For the first time he noticed a brownish-red stain smeared

across the expanse of her apron and dress. A similar color to what he'd seen on the floor.

It almost looked like dried blood.

Alec put his hands on her shoulders and she straightened a little taller.

"Ye've done verra well, Wynda. I canna thank ye enough for what ye've endured for my family and will ensure ye are properly rewarded for everything." What had not been spared could be repurchased, save the tapestries made by his mother's hand.

Alec's ventures around Scotland with Kieran MacDonald and Colin MacKinnon had made him a wealthy man. He hadn't wasted it on drink and pleasure as other men would. Never had he been more grateful for his prudence.

Wynda's round cheeks flushed with obvious pleasure at his gratitude. "Now that I see ye standing here before me, I'm happy to have done it. Besides…" She shrugged and looked around the room. "I've been here my whole life. Where else would I go?"

Alec patted her shoulder. "I'm home now and I'll set things to rights. If ye know some able-bodied men who might be willing to help, we'll have the castle restored in no time."

Wynda folded her arms over her wide chest in the take-charge way she had when he was a lad. "Aye, I think I know a few."

For the first time since entering the castle, Alec had hope. Duart Castle would be restored to its former glory.

• • •

Golden streams of sunlight lit the floors of Celia's home and filled the small cottage with cozy warmth. The sweet stalk of agrimony she'd been grinding lay half churned in the mortar.

Her mind was on the dream. The same one she'd had every night for the last fortnight.

Ever since she met the new laird.

Each morning she awoke tangled in the sheets, her heart racing, her body on fire for something she'd never before craved.

The dream played out in her mind. Alec MacLean standing before her, bare-chested and powerful, bidding her to sate her curiosity and taste the very mouth she'd watched so carefully.

In her dreams, she was bold, leaning into him and sucking his lower lip into her mouth. He'd tasted the way he smelled—clean and fresh and wholly wonderful.

The rest happened in a heady rush. Clothes were stripped off with trembling hands and fingers raked across naked, glistening flesh. His lips sampled as much as hers did, his tongue teasing each moan, each sigh…

Celia rubbed her thighs together. She was slick and swollen, feverish with a lust that hadn't waned even hours after waking.

A knock at the cottage door pulled her from wanton thoughts in a dizzying mix of relief and irritation. She patted the dagger at her waist to ensure herself of its presence before opening the door.

A woman in a brilliant red silk gown pushed her way into the cottage, a feat not easily done for one with so many skirts. Celia moved aside to let the woman flounce in. It was never in one's best interest to offend nobility.

The woman looked side to side at the room, setting her black curls bobbing around her face. Her nose peeled up with disdain before she faced Celia. Her smile did not touch her eyes. "Ye're the witch, correct?"

Nobility typically meant a fair amount of coin, but Celia suddenly found herself wishing for a randy drunk to contend with over this woman. At least those she knew how to handle.

"I'm a healer," she specified. "Not a witch."

The woman peered into a jar containing bits of betony and jerked her head back. She placed a gloved hand under her nose. "I need a love potion, so see it mixed for me." Her chin jutted upward so high Celia could see into her pointed nostrils. "I'll wait, but ye best no make me wait too long."

Celia did not move from the door. "I'm sorry, my lady, but I do not make potions."

The woman's black eyebrow rose and she took a menacing step toward Celia. "Of course ye make potions. Stop wasting my time and give me the exorbitant price. I'll see it paid." She lifted a heavy purse at her side where the bulging leather was suspended from a silk cord. There was probably more money in there than Celia had made in her entire life.

She turned away from the woman and the pouch. "Forgive me, my lady, but for all the coin in the land, I cannot make you a potion."

Hard footsteps stomped across the floor and Celia spun around as the woman came face-to-face with her. "Do ye know who my father is?"

Celia clenched her teeth to keep from backing away. Of course she didn't know who the chit's father was.

"Laird MacDougall of Aros Castle." She spoke the name like a threat.

Ice prickled through Celia's veins. She wanted no part of MacDougall's witch trials and now this unwanted visitor brought the threat right to her home.

"I still cannot help you. I do not do potions or spells as I am not a witch. I only offer healing with herbs I grow." Celia hoped her voice sounded strong. It certainly did not feel such.

The woman gave an over-wide smile, displaying a mouthful of crammed teeth. "I willna forget this slight."

She shoved past Celia in a bustle of her massive skirts and stalked across the small front yard, a grown woman in full tantrum.

No escort waited beside her horse, but then one was most likely unnecessary. Obviously the woman would be able to handle herself against the most unruly of outlaws.

Ruadh slinked in through the doorway and nudged Celia's hand with his moist black nose. She managed to scratch behind his ear once before he scampered to the pile of old cloth she'd laid down for his bed.

Unrest churned in Celia's stomach.

The woman's visit was a stone in her mind.

The witch-burning fires in Aros singed too close for comfort.

Why did she now feel their flames lick ever closer?

Chapter Five

Light filtered through the trees and dappled the ground with flecks of gold. Celia tilted her face toward a gentle breeze and breathed in the sun-warmed scent of the forest. The earthy, clean scent had been her home longer than home ever had.

It was nice to be outside. Her cottage was still tinged with the expensive perfume the noblewoman had worn.

MacDougall's daughter.

The memory of the malice in the woman's eyes slipped into Celia's mind like a nightmare. Suddenly she was glad to be gone from her cottage and out in the open of a beautiful day.

Her basket of herbs was already laden with her harvest from the forest, so she had nothing more to do than enjoy the stroll back home.

She gazed out at the loch through the trees, at the sunlight twinkling off the surface, at the rocky bank with stones worn smooth, at the man standing before it.

Her body went stiff.

She had no desire to run into anyone, especially not a man. Lone or not, most men on MacLean land were dangerous.

A stroke of recognition swept over her—those broad shoulders, the black hair tied back in a braid, the power he exuded.

Alec.

She shouldn't stand there watching him. She should move on.

He jerked at the leine and tugged it over his head.

Celia's breath snagged. Her tongue licked between her suddenly dry lips.

She'd seen the power of his chest before, but never had she glimpsed his naked back. Nor had she been able to admire the fine way it tapered down to a trim waist and narrow hips.

Every bit of his exposed flesh rippled with the muscles of a well-trained warrior.

Memories of her dreams flooded through her mind and captivated her body with a lusty fire. She imagined touching his back. Soft, scarred skin over powerful muscles flexed tight with desire, tensing and straining as his hips pushed against hers.

As he fit himself so perfectly inside her.

Her breathing went long and slow.

She should move on, she knew, but everything in her body demanded she stay and watch.

• • •

Alec breathed in the scent of the forest around him—heather and pine with the undercurrent tang of the sea. The smell of his home.

Loch Linnhe stretched before him, its mirrored surface reflecting all the greatness around him—the swell of lush green hills, the craggy shore, the open sky above.

He felt as open. As free.

At least in this one moment.

The previous two weeks had passed in a mix of hard labor and speeches made to the people in villages, all foundations for the greatness he intended to restore.

And God, was he paying for it. His back ached and popped, his arms groaned in protest every time he moved, and his head swarmed with the buzz of hundreds of voices and faces.

The villagers didn't trust him, he knew, and while their suspicion was disappointing, he didn't blame them. Not after the stories he'd heard of his father.

A part of it lurked in Alec, a larger part than he cared to admit. No matter how much he tried to deny its existence, no matter how many times Alec declared he was not the same man as his father, he knew it was there within him. The darkness. It lay dormant, waiting for a chance to emerge.

A breath of angry determination hissed through his teeth, as if the act could push the darkness down deeper.

He kicked the heel of his right boot and slipped his foot free. His father would not haunt his thoughts now, not when there were more pleasant thoughts to focus on. He kicked off the left boot likewise.

Here he was alone, without ghosts, without burdens, with nothing but silence caressing his ears and the great loch stretched in front of him. The water lapped at his toes, cold and teasing.

He stretched his arms over his head in a ripple of overused muscles and let the sunlight press warmth against his bare skin. No longer did the wound on his chest ache. The stitches had come out clean. He glanced at the thin pink line running over his skin.

Celia.

He shoved her from his thoughts, not wanting to think of how he hadn't seen her despite seeking her face out in crowds, not wanting to think how he couldn't get her off his mind.

He tugged off his kilt, tossed the heavy wool on the bank behind him, and stepped into the chilly water. The clear water slicked over his head and body, stroking him in a long sweep of sweet icy refreshment, washing away the strain and stress of the last fortnight as well as a fair amount of sweat and grit from his labors.

He came up for air and braced his weight on the rocky bed beneath him. The aggravation and stress along his back eased to a manageable tension. He pulled the leather strap from his braid and raked his fingers across his scalp, freeing his hair.

A movement on the shore caught his eye—the subtle sway of a tree branch.

He stilled.

The bushes at the edge of the clearing gave a great rustling shake. Whatever had caused the motion was bigger than a squirrel, yet nothing emerged, nor did it rustle again.

His first time alone to relax and now it appeared he had to deal with someone hiding in the damn bushes.

• • •

Celia bit her lips to keep from making a sound, a feat difficult to do when extricating oneself from a bush.

She'd leaned forward to get a better view and had clumsily fallen into the bushes. He faced her direction now, but he wouldn't be able to see her through the trees.

At least she hoped he wouldn't.

His thick black hair hung past his shoulders and his powerful torso reflected in the smooth surface of the loch. He looked savage. Beautiful.

"Get yer arse out here, Duncan," he called.

She startled at the sound of his voice and jerked free from the foliage.

"Ye might as well come get yer own bath if ye went to all the trouble of following me to the loch," he continued. "I'm done anyway."

A flicker of hope eased the clutch of fear. He thought she was someone else. Such knowledge could work to her advantage. She could sneak beneath the cover of the trees and slip away before he realized she wasn't Duncan.

"C'mon, boy. Dinna be a lass about it. Ye're past due for a bathing and it isna that cold."

Her gaze trailed over his sculpted flesh and she remembered when he'd been in her cottage, how he'd felt beneath her fingertips—soft skin stretched taut over hard muscle.

Everything in her pulsed hot with longing, pounded with the exquisite torture of raw lust.

The laird swam toward the shore, his gaze sharp. If she was going to leave, now would be her prime opportunity.

Or…

She swallowed.

Or she could stay.

Her nipples tightened at the audacious thought. She could stay and taste what she longed for, what haunted her dreams.

If her lust were slaked, she could be done with it. The frustrated rub of her fingers between her legs at night only seemed to exacerbate her wanton need.

But Alec was powerful, virile. Her stomach tightened. Surely he could drive the desire from her.

Celia straightened and pulled the leaves from her hair. Then, without letting herself think on it further, she pushed her way through the bushes, her thoughts swirling with nervous anticipation.

• • •

The bushes rustled once more and Alec swam closer to the shore where he'd left his sword. If Duncan were in the bushes, he would have called out by now.

But it wasn't Duncan who emerged from the forest.

Leaves and branches bowed aside beneath the graceful press of a slender, white hand, unveiling a woman whose beauty could be rivaled by none.

Long silver-blonde hair fell past her slender waist and wide blue eyes met his from across the grassy shore.

"Celia." Her name slipped between his lips in a whispered exhale and his body went hot despite the cold water wavering at his hips. She stepped forward, her feet appearing and disappearing from beneath the long hem of her homespun gown.

His quickened breath expanded his chest.

She sauntered toward him, her eyes dark and determined, her pace impossibly, teasingly measured.

She reached behind her back and, in a smooth motion, the tight bodice around her waist loosened and fell away. Her hand reappeared by her side with a long white string clutched between tapered fingers.

She continued her easy gait forward and the simple overdress slipped to a pool of coarse brown fabric at her feet. Only a linen chemise separated his ravenous gaze from the naked curves of her body.

His cock had gone hard somewhere between her appearance from the wood and the loosening of her bodice and continued to grow harder with the removal of each garment.

Sunlight danced through the thin fabric of her chemise. It played against the shadowed outline of her rounded hips and the narrow gap between her thighs. She caught the tie at her throat and pulled it free. The neck of the underdress widened.

His mouth went dry and he strained forward, every muscle in his body locked tight.

He'd thought about this too damn often.

The linen slipped from her shoulders and bared her smooth, fair skin. The gown lowered further still, revealing her body inch by slow, delectable inch.

His gaze trickled down the graceful curves on display—her incredibly long, slender legs and narrow waist. He gritted his teeth against the singe of desire. She was even more beautiful than he'd imagined.

Her breasts stood proud on her chest, big enough for a handful, her nipples small and pink and tempting.

The water licked at her slender toes and she stopped. Alec's chest rose and fell with each ragged breath. She needn't join him in the icy water, not when he could easily meet her on the shore.

But he never got the chance before she stepped into the loch. Her nipples drew tight against the shock of cold. Each careful step brought her closer, until she stood directly in front of him.

She stared up, hot and full of enough promise to make his cock ache.

He wanted to reach out to her, to stroke the side of her perfect breast and follow the curve of her waist, her hip, down to the strip of blonde hair covering her sex. He wanted his lips on hers, his body against hers.

But he would not make the first move.

He swallowed before trying to speak. "Are ye—"

Her finger pressed to his lips and he fell silent. She stared at his mouth, the way she had done in the cottage when they first met. Her fingers threaded through his hair, her palms warm against the coolness of his scalp.

"You were right," she whispered.

Her body swept closer to him and a slight wave washed

against Alec's stomach before the heat of her breasts pressed to his chest. She tilted her chin up toward his mouth, her lips parted, her eyes fluttering closed.

He needed no further invitation.

With a groan, his lips closed over the softness of hers.

He would take all his healer was willing to give.

Chapter Six

Water lapped against Celia's stomach, cold in contrast to the blazing heat of her skin. The hair on Alec's chest rasped her already sensitive nipples and she arched herself harder against him.

Alec's lips were warm on hers, intoxicating. He moved his mouth with such slowness she found herself lifting her chin in encouragement.

Men had kissed her in the past and she had been repulsed. Their lips had been hard and prying, their tongues like great slimy slugs.

But not now, not with Alec.

The touch of his soft lips to hers, the bump of his hardness against her belly, all of it stoked the ready flame of her desire into an unbearable heat. She wanted him to lift her into his arms and ravish the need from her body.

His tongue stroked hers and sent a shock of excitement raking across her flesh. Her fingers tightened in his hair. She copied his actions and swept her tongue against his. His arms came around her, solid and strong, yet his touch was tender.

She didn't want tender. She didn't want the feelings that tender might warrant.

There were to be no emotions involved, just the sating of lust.

His cool palms pushed up her waist and cupped the swell of her breasts. She pressed into him and explored the lines of his body. Every part of the man was hard, save his lips.

He slipped his free hand down her back and over the curve of her bottom. "Celia," he groaned.

An excited chill raced down her spine.

He remembered her name.

The cool water did little to ease the pulsing heat between her legs. She needed release. She needed him.

There would be pain at first, she knew, but she'd heard enough women discuss the intimate details of their lives to know that what followed would bring incredible pleasure if done right.

She let her fingers skim lower, down the ridges of his stomach, the hard, flat bands of muscle there, and brushed the tip of his cock.

Alec sucked in a mouthful of air between their lips and his body jerked.

He grasped her bottom tighter, pushing her closer against him. The tips of his fingers swept the seam between her legs.

A gasp slipped from her lips this time and her nipples tingled. She wanted to grind herself against him, to encourage the probing of his curious fingertips, to get him to touch the greedy little bud between her legs.

A frustrated whimper strangled from her throat.

She curled her hand around his cock. The skin there was impossibly silky, the firmness of it impossibly hard.

His finger dipped inside her. Finally. Gloriously. Prickles of pleasure tingled around his hand and cleared all thoughts from her mind.

She moaned and arched her back, readily exposing herself for his exploration.

Her body ached for him, the steady pulse of desire now an insistent hammering. Everything in her demanded what only he could provide.

She stepped backward, toward the shore, and tugged him with her in silent plea.

He ceased his play and slid his hands down over her, cupping her bottom and lifting her toward him. She instinctively opened her legs and wrapped them around his waist.

Finally, blissfully, the length of his cock settled against her, insistent where it bumped against the center of her heat.

He held her against his body and carried her to the shore.

She felt herself lowered to the sun-warm grass on the bank.

He stretched his body on top of hers in their haven that smelled of sunshine and nature. His skin was still cool from the loch—a delicious contrast to the sizzling need inside her. His hand moved between them and something hot and blunt rubbed against her slick center.

Celia leaned her head back and moaned until he captured her lips once more.

His sweet torment was more than she could bear. Her nerves were strung tight and her body trembled. She widened her legs and lifted her hips toward him, silently demanding what she wanted.

What she needed.

What she intended to get.

• • •

Alec stroked the tip of his cock against Celia's ready entrance. She moaned beneath his mouth and caught his bottom lip between her teeth.

For a woman so guarded and cold not two weeks prior, she certainly burned hot with passion now.

A passion he planned to sample again and again.

He slid a hand up one smooth thigh and curled her leg around his waist. He wanted her in one thrust, hard and deep.

Her other leg slid over his body so her heels rested against his buttocks. He stared down at her face, eager to see the passion flutter her lashes closed.

In one move, he shoved inside her slippery sheath.

Her eyes flew open with shock and his body locked tight, freezing him within her.

Had he gone too deep? Had she been…

His stomach clenched.

"Were ye a maiden?" he asked.

She closed her eyes and flexed her hips against him. "Don't stop."

He gritted his teeth against the painful pleasure of

her tightness.

He had his answer and he wasn't proud of what he'd done. Disappointment for himself at his misdeed swept at the haze of his lust.

His hands fisted in the soft earth and the scent of warm soil mixed with the heady perfume of their coupling.

Then she squeezed around him, trapping him where he hovered inside her.

Something primal inside encouraged him to stroke deep within her. He knew what that something was—his darkness, the one encouraging of rapacious acts.

Her heels pressed into his buttocks, pushing him deeper inside her, closer to the edge of surrender.

"Don't. Stop." She opened her eyes and regarded him with a heavy-lidded gaze.

"Ye know I want ye as my mistress." He searched her glassy stare, hungry for her to say something. Aye, he wanted this, but he knew he'd want her again. He knew he wanted so, so much more from this mysterious woman.

She tucked her lower lip into her mouth and nodded.

Her hips ground against his in a show of helpless frustration. The muscles along his back knotted against the incredible pleasure of her movements.

Everything in him ached to move within her, to give her what she asked for.

"And ye want this still?" he asked in a tense voice.

She knew what he asked—he saw it in the way her eyes searched his.

He tensed, waiting for her agreement to become his woman, waiting for the permission to claim what would be his and no other man's.

She arched her back and her breasts thrust forward. "Yes," she said in a breathy moan.

That was all the permission he needed. He slid one hand beneath the curve of her bottom and pushed inside her. His body shook with the exertion of restraint.

With each gentle thrust, her shoulders relaxed more

and more until her body gyrated in time with his, matching his rhythm.

Her legs tightened around him and she pulled him closer against her. His lips found the tight pearl of her nipple and closed over it gently with his teeth. She cried out with such pleasure his cock drew tight with the need to release.

He groaned and slowed his pace.

Not yet.

He wanted to kiss her more, taste her more, touch her more.

After the tension of impending release lessened, he kissed his way up to her small, lush mouth and quickened his thrusts. She was so wet, so tight, it was almost more than he could bear.

Her breath came in short gasps and her body flexed beneath him. This time he knew it was not a virgin's pain that caused her to squeeze against him. The soft cries of her climax sounded against the press of his mouth and he drank them in with greedy desire.

Her sheath tensed around him, milking him toward his own surrender. His hips flexed hard and sharp, once, twice, and then a final time, burying him deep in the warm, moist flesh of his woman.

His own release burst within her and euphoria flashed white, dancing stars behind his closed lids.

He waited until the final tremors of his powerful orgasm tapered before opening his eyes. He found her staring up at him with cheeks pink from their lovemaking, her chest rising and falling with a rapid breath that matched his own.

He lowered his head and kissed her once more, savoring the lushness of her mouth, before pulling himself from her. A sharp breath sucked from between her lips.

Happy, accomplished exhaustion tugged at him. A hard day of labor and a clean, sated body—if he had a hearty slab of venison in his stomach, he might sleep until winter.

He rolled over to lie beside her and slipped an arm across her shoulder, pulling her down against his chest. The softness of her body cradled against his as if she had been made solely for him.

His fingers brushed her naked shoulder. Her skin was like silk. All of her was.

He'd taken her maidenhead and would never forget the gift she had so willingly given him. She would have the finest gowns, the softest mattresses, the most exquisite furnishings.

He would break down her defenses and find out her past, learn why she was so guarded.

He swept his cheek against her hair and breathed deep the clean scent of rosemary, eager to start his new life back on the Isle of Mull with his beautiful mistress.

• • •

Gentle waves from the loch licked lazily against the shore like a rhythmic shushing. The warrior laird's skin was warm against Celia's naked body where they lay. Warm and strong and incredible.

He'd pleased her well physically.

Yet he expected too much.

The strong beat of his heart bumped a steady rhythm beneath her ear. But she could not give into its soothing lure.

Not when her own heart pounded with such frenzy.

The encounter did not go as she'd planned.

The caress of emotion wasn't supposed to be so welcome, the need for acceptance wasn't supposed to be so palpable, and the desire to love was never supposed to exist.

The way he'd touched her, looked at her, taken such great care with her—she knew without a doubt he would protect her no matter the cost.

No matter the cost.

She knew all too well how high the price could go.

The very thought left her skin too tight against her nerves and her mind screaming.

She would not see another person die for her sake.

Never again.

She'd only ever let one person know her, care for her.

Fiona.

The name wrenched at Celia's heart.

She'd been stupid to come to the laird like this, to think sating her need for pleasure could be without emotion.

Her throat constricted.

She hadn't expected to *feel* so much.

Alec's thickly muscled leg draped over hers and his arm flexed, pulling her tighter against him. He gave a lazy groan and nuzzled his prickled jaw against the top of her head.

It hurt too much to want this too badly.

Her breath came faster and her heart pumped so quickly it left dots of white in her vision.

She never should have done this, never should have come here.

The ache of loneliness in her chest squeezed, but loneliness was better endured than loss.

She slipped from his arms, scuttling away on shaking legs, and gathered her clothing. The sun left the cloth hot and scratchy where she balled the bundle against her belly. She crept past him and should not have looked down one last time.

Yet she did.

Alec's brow was smooth, his lips more sensual when they weren't pressed so tightly together. Powerful muscle carved his body, even in his sleep.

It was just a glance, but the image would forever stay in her mind.

And then she did the only thing she knew to protect herself and those who might love her.

She ran.

Chapter Seven

Alec hovered in the languid state between asleep and awake. He drew a deep breath and let out a slow groan. The scent of crushed grass filled his nostrils.

And rosemary.

But he did not feel the heat of a body curled around him.

He sat up, but saw nothing more than the flat lake in front of him and the shadow of his horse tied to a tree in the forest.

He pushed himself up to his feet and stalked over to his clothes. Irritation bristled along the back of his neck.

She'd left for some reason he did not see.

He knew he hadn't hurt her, not when she'd encouraged him to move inside her when he'd tried to stop.

Alec groaned at the memory.

There had been many women in his past and he'd done many lusty things with them, but never had a one come to him like a water nymph.

He wrapped his plaid around himself and tugged on his leine and boots.

The only way to understand a lass sometimes was to talk to her. Though he'd stayed away from her cottage thus far, he would be damned if he'd stay away after she loved him better than any woman and then immediately left once he'd fallen asleep.

Though two weeks had passed since he'd last been to her cottage, he found the small home with ease. The entire ride, he'd tried to figure out what to say, how to reassure her of her decision to be his mistress.

She had agreed to be his mistress, hadn't she?

Still unsure what to say, he approached her door and rapped

upon the rough wood with his knuckles.

Nothing.

His blood surged in his veins.

Again he knocked and again Celia did not come. Surely she was not avoiding him.

His muscles seemed to swell with impatience. He did a swift walk around the small building, confirming all the shutters were tightly locked.

Tension grated the edges of his nerves.

He stalked to the front once more and heaved the door open. The cottage was dark inside.

The clawing, gnashing frustration inside him went wild. He rushed in and threw the shutters open so sunlight glowed brilliant inside the cottage, exposing the empty tables and stripped bed.

Even the bundled herbs once hanging from the rafters had been cleared away.

The home was empty.

Celia was gone.

• • •

The rocky coast did not provide much in the way of shelter, but the crude cave offered Celia more than most other locations had in the last three months. Sea water dripped from the jagged ceiling and echoed around her with a rhythmic *plink*.

MacDougall's witch hunt was on the rise. People were being accused and subjected to fantastical, humiliating tests.

Innocents were being burned.

She'd heard the horrible tales from the few souls brave enough to speak to her.

Everyone was wary of strangers, of Lowlanders. Of healers. *Witch*.

She knew too well what they did to witches.

She'd been subjected to their cruelty during the North Berwick witch hunt of her youth.

Her body had absorbed the cold, wet dungeon, her ears had borne witness to animalistic screams, her heart had suffered the suffocating loss of love.

The bitter November wind whistled outside the cave, but could not enter, not when the swell of the cliff wound to the side. It was not only far enough to block out the worst of the gusts, it was near enough to let moonlight filter through, to keep the black of night at bay.

Celia huddled deeper into her cloak. The proximity to the savage sea left everything wet and stiff.

She cupped her hands against one another and breathed hot against them. Warmth blossomed against her palms and fingers for one blissful second before fading to aching cold once more.

Ruadh crept into the cave and curled into a tight ball at her feet. Her toes tingled to life against the heat of his belly.

"What would I do without you?" She scratched the back of his ear, but he flicked his head away irritably. Affection always came on his own terms.

The wind screamed a high-pitched wail outside. The fox tucked his black nose beneath his tail and squeezed tighter against himself.

Had she ever been as warm as he looked?

An image of her cottage back in the forest flashed in her mind. The softness of her dry bed, the quiet chatter of leaves outside, the perfumed spice of her herb garden. Sunlight had always seemed to fill the room with warmth and the small fireplace gave off any extra heat she'd needed.

Alec had sat near the hearth the day they first met.

Her heart weighed down in her chest, its beat labored and painful. She wouldn't think of him.

She couldn't.

Yet no matter how much she told herself this, his memory seeped into her thoughts daily. His touch, his smell, the incredible pleasure they shared, the feel of his arms around her. That one last image of how he'd looked in sleep.

The days were terrible and long, despite the shorter periods of light. Terribly long and painfully filled with too many thoughts.

Her stomach loosed a ragged snarl. The loaf of bread she had bought three days prior was now gone. She was out of food and money with no hope to get enough of either to sustain herself.

The people on the road did not trust her enough to purchase her herbs and no one dared take her in for fear of being called witches themselves.

After over eighteen years of living in her quiet cottage, life outside was more difficult than she'd ever imagined. How had she survived this when she was only seven?

Her shoes were shredded from the sharp rocks she passed over every day and her clothing was soiled and torn. Her body ached with hunger and everything was rigid with cold.

Never had she been more miserable.

She'd tried several times to leave the island, but had encountered battle after battle and had returned back to the little cave as far from Duart Castle as was possible.

Resignation settled hard and indignant in the pit of her empty stomach.

Regardless of the danger she faced, she had no choice—she must return where people trusted her. Where she could earn coin enough to buy food.

She needed to return to the Isle of Mull.

Chapter Eight

Alec stared down at the murky concoction swirling in the narrow bottle against his palm. Rowan berries and a pregnant heifer's piss, or so the aging woman had said.

"He's supposed to drink this?" He gave the vial a shake. Threads of gray slime unfurled from the bottom and floated upward.

The old woman sucked her lips deep into a mouth devoid of teeth and nodded.

How the hell was Duncan going to swallow this when he couldn't keep anything down as it was?

Already the boy was too thin, too weak. Worried thoughts nipped at the forefront of Alec's mind.

"And if that doesna work, I've got a charm I can make for ye." She patted Alec's arm with a withered hand. Her fingernails were gray-yellow and varying in length.

He nodded and handed the woman a purse with more coin than she deserved for the foulness she'd given him.

She slipped the payment into a hidden pocket in her cloak and disappeared into the crowd.

Alec curled the vial in his hand, protecting it as if it were something that might actually work, and wound his way through the busy market.

More people attended this week than last. They felt safer, more protected, now that Alec had a force of men behind him—even if it was a small one.

But the shell of security was fragile and Celia's disappearance had caused a level of unease among the villagers. Many had relied on her for relief from their ailments.

He'd heard their rumors and how they feared she'd been swept up in the witch fires burning across MacDougall land.

Alec knew better.

His gut twisted with guilt. The blame sat squarely on his shoulders.

And now the boy paid the price with his illness left untreated. Alec looked down at the vial once more and cast it into an empty alleyway.

He wouldn't make the boy drink such filth, especially not when he was already so sick.

Duncan's illness had come fast and unexpected. His cheeks flushed with a burning fever and he woke only to beg for water. Wynda had checked his slender body for marks of the plague. Fortunately, none were apparent.

Still, the boy did not rise and each day saw him weaker.

Alec's chest squeezed tight. Duncan would not last much longer.

Something between the pastry cart and a luckenbooth of colored ribbons caught his attention.

His heart lurched.

Had he truly seen Celia's proud posture standing out against the crowd?

He dashed across the dirty street, his feet splashing through the watery puddles of mud. His gaze darted through the throngs of people.

A ripple of pale blonde hair disappeared around the corner.

His breath came faster now, fueled by raw desperation.

He raced through the crowd, darting and dodging to keep her quick pace.

The back of her straight, glossy hair shone bright against the sun. She glanced over her shoulder and met his gaze with a deep blue stare.

Air pushed from his chest and a strange stirring shifted inside him.

It was her.

Celia had returned.

A large cart rolled past, obscuring his view for just a

moment, but that was all it took. By the time the cart had rolled away, she was gone.

No.

Damn it, he would *not* lose her again.

Alec angled his shoulders and sidled through the masses. He moved too slow.

He must find her.

He had to, or Duncan would die.

• • •

Celia's heart fluttered in her chest and left scant room to breathe. Had she really just seen Alec?

She stopped a moment and looked back, but saw nothing more than a mass of faces.

The market swirled around her and carried her forward into a maze of merchants and all their wares. It had become significantly more populated since she'd last visited. Obviously Alec had been doing good for the people as he'd promised.

She'd not seen any overthin children as she had in the past, and most faces were smiling or intent on their purchases, not turning over their shoulders with unease.

No one except her.

Stares settled on her with the tickling unease of an army of ants marching over her skin.

Something warm and dry clasped her hand and held firm.

"I've had enough of ye running from me." Alec's voice spoke next to her ear.

His tone stroked over her, tempting and dangerous all at once.

It commanded the hairs on the back of her neck to rise and the insides of her stomach to swirl.

She spun around to face him and pulled in a sharp breath. He was larger than she remembered—taller, more muscular, more imposing.

She wanted to believe her reaction came from anger or fear or even disgust, but she knew with sickening certainty it was desire.

His hand was almost hot against the iciness of hers. Hot and intimate in the way he gripped her with firm tenderness. The same way he'd held her before.

She wanted to wrap both her hands around him and savor the sensation, but she pulled herself free. Her goal in leaving was not to come back into the same situation.

"I wasn't running," she said.

His eyes were even more ice blue than she remembered and the shadow of a beard stood out against his sharp jaw. Had he always been so angular and hard?

"Why did ye leave?"

She should have prepared herself for the possibility of meeting him here. Truthfully, she'd thought about it, but in her mind, there was nothing to fear, nothing to consider.

"I wasn't running from you, I was leaving the market." Her voice was small.

"Why did ye leave me at the loch?" The lines around his eyes tightened.

That day surfaced in her mind. The heat of the sun, the chill of the water, the incredible pleasure their bodies had elicited together. "Because I couldn't stay."

He scrubbed his palm over his jaw. "I dinna understand ye. Ye willna talk to me, then ye happen upon me bathing and ye seduce me, then ye leave and I see ye now and ye act as though we've no ever shared—" He straightened and regarded her with a level expression. "I think ye're scared."

Her face went cool as the blood in her body rushed to her staggering heart. "I'm not afraid of you." The word came out as a thread of a whisper.

Alec stepped forward and she caught the scent of outdoors and leather. His scent. She wanted to close her eyes against the burn in her chest.

"Ye were scared because ye dinna understand what to expect and all ye knew of me was the shite legacy my father left behind." Something dark flashed in his eyes and his hand squeezed into a fist at his side.

Celia didn't answer—she couldn't, not with the way her throat thickened.

How could she give him an honest answer while maintaining the secrets she refused to share? What might he say if he knew she'd been in a dungeon as a girl? Or that she couldn't sleep without a source of light to block out her nightmares?

Or that she'd been responsible for the death of the one person who ever gave her kindness and love?

She pressed her lips in the silence.

Alec sighed. "No matter why ye left, I'm glad to see ye back now. There are many who need ye, including me." His gaze swept down to her waist and his jaw hardened. "I confess I worried ye might grow with my child and I wouldna ever know."

"There is no child." A pennyroyal tea that day had ensured his seed did not take root in her womb.

His lips thinned in a hard line and he nodded slowly, as if it pained him to do so.

Was he actually disappointed?

"I don't know if I intend to stay or not," she said.

He reached out and touched her wrist with three fingertips. "Stay, Celia."

The stares from earlier now weighed upon her like stones.

Too many people watched.

Too many people knew she'd come back.

"I must go," she said in a sharp voice. She tried to push past him, but he caught her at the waist gently and pulled her back toward him.

Back against his chest.

He was hard and warm despite the chill of the day.

"Listen for one moment, aye?" His breath was warm, the subtle spice too familiar for comfort. Her pulse ticked a languid, sultry rhythm.

"I dinna do this often, but I beg ye to stay. My people need ye." His lips brushed her neck. "I need ye."

She stiffened. "People are watching. I'm not—"

"Please, Celia," he said in a softer voice.

Her traitorous body wanted to melt against him. Deep

down was a part of her needing him too. It craved the attention he'd paid her and reveled in the memory of the intense pleasure they'd shared.

He nuzzled her neck and a soft sigh escaped her lips. "Will ye stay and keep yer promise to me?"

She stepped back from him and this time he did not stop her. "Promise?"

He stared hard at her. "Aye, to be my mistress."

• • •

Alec reached for Celia once more, but she shook her head and her gaze darted to those around them.

"I made no such promise to be your mistress."

Her proximity made his body ache to feel her body against him again. "Aye, that day on the shore, ye agreed to be my mistress."

"You asked if I knew you wanted me to be your mistress and I did. Then you asked if I still wanted you." Her slender throat squeezed around a swallow. "I did."

He watched her carefully. "And now?"

Her cheeks tinged a delicate shade of pink and she looked around the crowd once more. Fewer people stared, their interest lost when the conversation went quiet enough for only Alec and Celia to hear. "I must go," Celia said.

"Ye canna go." He put his arms up once more. She couldn't leave, not without at least looking after Duncan first. Alec refocused his attention where it should have been the whole time. "There's a lad at my keep. I need ye to look at him." Alec lowered his arms, but she did not move. "He's verra, verra sick."

Hesitation crossed over her face. "It's not a safe time to be a healer." Her eyes were even larger in her narrow face than they'd been before she left. He could see himself in them, the oval of his face framed by mesmerizing deep blue.

"Ye mean the witch trials?" he asked. "I dinna allow that on my land."

She studied him carefully, as if weighing his words, his

appearance, for the truth.

The same as he'd done to her.

"Please," he said. "The boy is verra sick."

The strained tension of her shoulders relaxed.

She was considering it.

"If ye dinna do this…" Alec squeezed his fist, hating the words he had to say, "…he will die."

She swept an errant strand of hair from her forehead. "I'll stay under two conditions. The first is that you promise to keep the witch trials from your lands."

"I've already said I would."

She nodded. "And the second." Her gaze slipped down his body once more. "You have to promise not to touch me ever again."

Her words were harsh and snapped him like the sting of a whip. Indignant protests rose in his mind, burning with the urge to be hurtled at her.

She'd enjoyed his touch, enjoyed their coupling, enjoyed the way he'd brought her release.

An urgent reminder blared in the back of his mind.

Duncan was more important than pride.

The rest could be handled later.

"Verra well," he said in a slow huff. "Ye have my word I willna touch ye."

Celia nodded. "Then show me the lad. I'll see what I can do."

Chapter Nine

The sweet, musty stench of sickness and sweat filled the small room.

Celia knew Alec had spoken true. Death was close. A boy no older than thirteen lay immobile under a pile of blankets with hair plastered to his scalp.

She pressed a hand to his scalding cheek. If she was going to help him, she would have to work quickly.

"Get a pot of water boiling, but not here. He can't take any more heat." She crossed the room and drew aside the heavy curtains.

Her eyes narrowed against the glare. She flicked the latch on the shutters and pushed the wooden screen open. Fresh, icy air immediately rushed in and she drew a deep, cleansing breath.

"Are ye mad?" Alec charged across the room and slammed the shutters closed. "He canna handle air blowing at him."

"He needs fresh air," she said patiently. "The air in here is tainted with sickness. You wouldn't drink from a stagnant pool any more than he should be breathing this in."

She pushed the shutters open once more and a refreshing gust filled the room.

Alec cast an anxious glance to the boy lying in the bed. She knew the fears he did not voice.

"Alec." She waited for him to look back at her. "You have to trust me."

He gave a grunt she took as acquiescence.

A shriek came from the doorway and a woman with a puff of bright red hair ran into the room, her finger pointed at the open window. "Ye canna do that—"

"It's fine, Wynda." Alec's tone suggested the statement was more of an order. He put his arm out in front of the woman, blocking her.

Wynda stopped obediently and twisted her hands against her apron. Her nervous glance darted to Celia.

"Are ye Celia?" she asked.

Celia nodded. "I am."

Wynda's worried blue gaze swept once toward the window and then toward the boy. "Ye're sure about this?"

"I am."

Tears shone glassy in the woman's eyes. "And ye can help Duncan live?"

Celia stepped toward Wynda and gave her most confident nod. "I can."

It was a wild claim when the boy was so ill, but Celia was determined. She would not rest until he was better.

Wynda cried out and caught Celia in an unexpected and exuberant hug. Celia stiffened against the contact, unsure how to respond. The woman did not notice her obvious discomfort and rocked her several times before finally letting go.

The aroma of freshly baked bread surrounded Wynda, giving her a homey, comforting feel. A snarl of hunger emanated from Celia's stomach.

Wynda released her. "Ach, ye're hungry, lass. I'll get ye some food—"

"No. Please, I need water boiled for Duncan. Also several bowls, clean strips of linen, a sponge…" She looked down at the sorry state of her dress. "And an extra apron."

Wynda gave a nod and bustled from the room. Silence fell once more. Celia rolled up her sleeves and dug through the massive pack she'd carried across the western tip of Scotland.

Within minutes, Wynda returned with an armload of the required supplies and no breath. "I've got…" she panted, "… the water…in the next…room." She stood upright and wiped the back of her hand across her slick brow. "Ye just call…if ye need more."

Celia waited until Wynda left before peeling back Duncan's

heavy blankets. Alec opened his mouth, but she quieted his protests with a glance. "Trust me," she said in reminder.

The boy's lips were dry and cracked.

"Does he relieve himself frequently?" she asked.

Alec stared at her with a blank face. "I dinna..."

"No," Wynda said, coming back into the room with a pot dangling from a thick cloth in her hand. "Mayhap once per day, twice at most."

Celia nodded. "That's what I thought." She tied the apron over her filthy clothes and scooped a bowl from the kettle of boiled water. To it, she added meadowsweet and blackthorn bark to bring down his fever, blackthorn berries to increase his appetite when he woke, and some skullcaps, just a pinch, to ease the ache in his head from lack of proper liquids in his body.

The water turned a murky, brownish green with bits of dried herbs floating at the top. "Set this by the window to cool while it steeps," Celia instructed.

While Celia waited, she wiped the sweat from Duncan's flushed face and carefully prodded various parts of his body where sickness such as his could originate. Organs sometimes went bad. If this were the case with Duncan, her claims were for naught.

Fortunately, he did not appear to wince at any of her delicate presses. A good sign.

"It's ready," Wynda said, and set the bowl onto the small table beside the bed.

"You may close the window now," Celia said, and pushed the sponge into the tea. "Keep the room the same temperature as you would for a well person, but try to air it out once per day."

The sponge darkened and swelled in the mixture. Celia pinched it from the liquid, then, with a hand under it to keep drips from landing on the sick boy, she brought it to his lips and gently squeezed. A thin line of murky liquid dribbled into his mouth and trickled from the corner of his lip.

Alec hovered over her shoulder. "He'll choke."

But the boy did not choke, not with the careful amount she administered. His throat flexed and the sharp knot of his

Adam's apple bobbed.

Celia ignored Alec leaning so close and focused on the slow method of getting Duncan to drink the tea, stream by careful stream.

This process repeated through Alec's impatient grunts and the shifting of his feet.

Perhaps his close observation should have bothered her, but concern did strange things to people. Experience had taught her asking for more space was only successful for several moments and wasn't worth the effort.

When the tea was finally gone, Celia rubbed a salve made with plantain leaves over Duncan's cracked lips and wiped her hands on the apron. "That is all I can do for now. He'll need to be fed this tea every four hours with water in between, the same as you've seen me do."

Alec frowned. "Ye dinna bleed him."

She glanced down at her patient's thin face and understood Alec's concern. With the exception of glossy lips, Duncan looked no different than he had when she arrived. "Correct, I didn't bleed him. I've never seen the process help anyone heal. Blood gives you strength. Bodies already weakened by illness need their strength."

She sank to the floor and began separating the herbs into tea-sized portions for future use. "You'll have to be patient—he will heal in time. I can speak to his parents if you like."

Alec looked toward the boy and though he kept his face hard, there was affection in his stare. "His parents are dead, killed long before I met him."

Celia stared up at the massive warrior. "You took him in?"

Not many people would take in an orphan.

She knew that better than most.

"Ach, the lad would've gotten himself killed, what with the way he chatters on and on. I couldna just leave him." He shrugged as if what he'd done were some small deed. As if Duncan held no place in his heart.

The concern lining his brow said otherwise.

"Duncan will heal with time," she said softly.

Alec's gaze fell heavy on her, the way it had when he first came to her cottage.

"I want ye to stay here." It was a command more than an invitation.

Celia stood and handed him the pack of dried herbs. "No."

The muscles along his neck stood out, a clear indication of his feelings on her rejection.

"I need to return to my cottage and see to the herb garden." It was a partial truth.

How could she stay under the same roof as Alec, tortured by his alluring scent and the memories it evoked? How could she see him every day and keep from touching him?

How could she live among people again and not let herself care?

No, she was better off alone, depending only on herself.

• • •

Alec held the reins of his horse loosely to accommodate Celia's slender body in the saddle in front of him. He rode slower than was necessary, to prolong their closeness.

She'd sat the entire way with her back stiff—every part of her keeping from touching every part of him.

Unbeknownst to her, tendrils of her hair swept across his arm as they moved, caressing him, enticing him to run his fingers over the glossy white-gold strands.

Her tattered dress hung loose on her body and made him all the more grateful he'd insisted she eat with them before leaving the castle.

She had dined slowly, her bites delicate and careful, but her shaking hands gave her away—the anxious, greedy tremor of a person who had not eaten in days.

The pale walls of her cottage came into view. She leaned forward. "Stop," she said in a sharp whisper. "You must turn around."

"Have ye changed yer mind?" he asked. A shot of hope flared through him.

"Someone else lives here." The stiffness of her back sagged.

His horse continued to saunter forward at a leisurely pace. His chest bumped in a slight rhythm against her back with the steed's gait, but Celia did not appear to notice.

"Why do ye say that?" he asked.

Her shoulders lifted and rose with a deep sigh and he knew she was gathering her strength to speak. "There is a new door, a new roof, and the garden has been tended to." She shook her head. "I will not remove someone from their home when I abandoned it in the first place. Please, turn around."

This time Alec did stop the horse, directly in front of the home. A red fox slipped from the woods and sat beside a nearby tree with his tail folded across his paws.

Alec slid off the horse without disturbing Celia and raised his hand to help her down. She stubbornly stared at him from up high.

"'Tis just a fox," Alec said. "He willna hurt ye."

Celia shook her head, ignoring his attempt to calm her. "I am not going in there. It belongs to someone else. I'll...find somewhere else to go."

Alec suppressed a smile and pulled the iron key from his pocket. "That willna be necessary."

Her brow furrowed.

"This is yer home. I've been repairing all the tenants' properties." He held the key out toward her. "No just yers, aye?"

She slid from the horse finally, her fingers warm against the palm of his hand. Her mouth opened and closed, wordless. She pressed her fingertips to her lips as if she could hold in the emotion sparkling bright in her eyes. "It's so lovely," she exhaled.

Alec's cheeks burned with barely restrained excitement.

If she was surprised by the outside of the cottage, she'd be even more thrilled with the inside.

But he wouldn't stay to see her face, not when doing so would appear as if he wanted more in return.

And the assumption wouldn't be wholly incorrect. He wanted more, he wanted all of her, but not in repayment for what he'd done and only if she would let him. Only if she asked.

Her eyes shone glassy with unshed tears. "I can't pay you for this."

"It isna to pay back. This is what my father should have done all these years—maintain the land and the people."

A pink blush tinged her cheeks and paired beautifully with the way her eyes sparkled. Her smile was broad and unhindered and it made him realize he'd never seen her look genuinely happy until this moment.

He also realized then, he wanted to see that expression more often.

She stepped slowly toward the front step and let her fingertips brush the metal lock, an amenity her previous door had lacked. "This is so much. Surely it was expensive."

He shrugged off the comment. "Ach, dinna worry, the rents ye've paid cover the cost."

She turned back around to him and the smile faded.

He'd said the wrong thing.

"I never paid rent. None was ever required." She glanced to the cottage at her back. "But I will, if not with coin, then with my healing."

"Say ye'll come by the castle tomorrow." Sunlight filtered through the leaves overhead and glowed against her smooth cheek. "To check on Duncan."

God's teeth, it was so hard not to reach out and touch her, especially when he knew how soft and smooth she'd be against his fingers.

He hadn't known another woman since her. Fool that he might be, he hadn't wanted to. Not after she'd emerged from the forest and stripped down with the grace of a nymph before offering herself to him.

No man could go back to a common woman after such an encounter.

Not when she was so provoking, so enigmatic.

He wanted her secrets whispered against his skin, he wanted her to gaze up at him with unquestionable trust, he wanted her to be as consumed by him as he was by her.

Her tongue flicked against her lips. How he wished it'd flick against his own, or perhaps against his flesh, or even lower, to the source of his heartbeat.

"You can't stare at me like that," she breathed. Her gaze, he noticed, did not leave his eyes.

He clenched his hands into fists at his side to keep from grabbing her against him. "Ye said I couldna touch ye." She was already close enough to tempt him with the warmth of her body. "Ye dinna say I couldna look at ye."

She pulled a shaky breath between her parted lips. Her gaze slid down his chest, leaving warmth in its wake.

He braced a hand on the wall behind her head and leaned over her. The rough exterior bit against his fingers, keeping him focused on his promise. "I'll no ever forget that day, Celia."

He waited for the sharp side of her tongue and found it had melted into silence. Her breath came faster and brushed over his skin like a caress.

His body strained toward her. Everything in him bellowed in his head for him to kiss her, to take her.

He pressed harder against the wall so it scraped into his palm and kept his wits in place.

"I'll see ye tomorrow then?" he asked. "At the castle. For Duncan."

His own breath was coming faster now. Damn if his skin didn't feel alive in its tangible awareness of her.

She watched him anxiously, as if she were afraid he would kiss her. Then her gaze slid to his mouth, as if she hoped he might.

"Tomorrow." There was a huskiness to her voice that shot through his body like wild fire. "After the midday meal."

"Before."

She licked her lips again and left her lush mouth wet and tempting.

"Very well," she said at last. "But don't think to ask me to join you there, because I won't." Her chin lifted with stubborn pride, but the movement wasn't a hard jerk. It was a soft gesture, one that exposed the creamy expanse of her neck.

The temptation was more than he could bear. He pushed

off the cottage and strode toward the horse, not bothering to look behind him as he spoke. "We'll see."

• • •

Celia remained against the wall until Alec and his horse had long since disappeared into the forest.

It had taken that amount of time for her heartbeat to slow, for the bones in her legs to harden again and support her weight.

He hadn't touched her.

As he'd promised.

As she'd made him promise.

Warmth hummed between her legs. What she'd thought to sate with his body months ago awoke anew, the hunger and intensity only exacerbated by hot, slick memories.

But standing idle against the wall while reliving fantasies was not a productive use of her time.

Not when there was so much to do.

Not when resisting him would be hard enough as it was.

The herb garden had to be inspected, harvested, and replanted, her meager stores she'd brought back had to be put away.

She curled her hand around the key until it pressed cool and hard into her palm.

A locked door.

It was security she'd never had. The leather sling and wood toggle latch mechanism she'd used before had provided little resistance between her and everything outside. Now she'd have a band of steel with her very own key.

She pushed away from the wall and retrieved her small bundle of belongings where Alec had set it beside the door. Her gaze snagged the herb garden.

The bit of soil had been bracketed off with a knee-high wooden fence. Someone had also painstakingly removed all weeds from the bed and apparently had been watering it regularly. The small garden was in good repair for the time of year, as if she'd never left and had tended to it herself all this time.

She smiled to herself, grateful for what Alec had done in her absence. One look at the heavy wood door and she knew she'd need those herbs for making concoctions and healing. There was a lot of coin to be made for her services or she'd never be able to repay him.

The key was heavy in her hand. Solid.

She slid it into the latch and turned until the she heard a metallic *thunk* indicating the locking mechanism had been sprung. She pushed into the dark home, expecting to be hit with the musty odor of disuse.

The sweet scent of new wood greeted her inside.

A sliver of light from one partially opened shutter revealed the source.

Sources.

The tension in Celia's shoulders relaxed in surprise and she pulled in a sharp breath.

A sturdy table and four chairs, all newly constructed, sat in an empty corner and a large chest of drawers and cabinets occupied almost the entire side of the wall next to the door.

The most shocking of all, though, was the massive four-poster bed at the back of the room.

Celia walked toward it carefully, her footsteps soft on the wooden floor lest a loud noise somehow shatter this incredible dream. A thick white blanket rested across the top.

This was too much.

All of it.

She turned abruptly and set her bag on the new table. Ruadh slinked into the cottage and stopped. His tail flicked.

"Too much, isn't it?" she asked.

His golden eyes turned to her and he shrank back to the door, as if confirming her words.

She pulled his tattered blanket from her bag and set it beneath the table so he might feel more comfortable. He dashed across the room and all but leapt into it. He turned several times before settling into a tightly wrapped ball with his nose tucked into the crook of his bushy tail, then gave a great sigh.

She watched Ruadh with a prickle of envy. He carried no

debts on his slender shoulders.

And soon neither would she. Tomorrow when she went to the castle to see Duncan, she would tell Alec she could not keep the gifts he'd bought her.

• • •

Alec took his time returning to the castle. There was much to do, he knew, but he needed time to let his thoughts settle, to let his body cool.

The sun was sliding into the cliffs by the time his castle came into view. The guards he'd hired were not at their sanctioned posts, but milled about in clusters.

Alec narrowed his eyes and nudged his horse toward the easternmost portion where the majority of the men gathered.

Before he came into speaking distance to ask why they'd abandoned their posts, his gaze fell on the chunk of protective wall that had once stood there, which now lay in large chunks of stone and soft mortar. The hole it'd made gaped open, wide and vulnerable.

Duart Castle had been attacked.

Chapter Ten

Alec stared at the costly castle wall now lying in a heap of stone on the ground. With the barrier breached, anyone could enter the castle.

It had been the last of the castle wall to be repaired, as most of it had been missing three months prior.

He swung a leg over his horse and covered the short distance to where the guards stood over the wreckage. His thoughts fell to Wynda, who'd already been through so much, to Duncan, who was in no condition to defend himself, to the families of the guards, who sought residence and employment in the keep.

"Where are the women and children?" he demanded.

"Inside and safe," a man with a thick red beard replied. "The bastards dinna get in."

Alec knelt by the rubble and examined the mass of stone and soft, gritty mortar. "What happened?"

"Damn outlaws," the guard said. "There were too many of 'em for the men stationed here. A couple of 'em with axes made quick work of this part of the wall. Some went through it, but Donnell picked off two with his bow and the others dinna feel much like staying after that."

Alec bit back a curse lest the men think they'd failed. "Ye did well, Donnell." He nodded to a tall, thin man before turning his attention to the other guard. "Ian, get the stonemason and have him seal this again immediately. Ye'll all need to stand extra watch to ensure this dries thoroughly."

The guard nodded. "Aye, laird." He turned and jogged toward the courtyard.

Alec stared after the man, grateful for his eagerness. The

guards recruited thus far were good men, they were just too few.

The other men in the area were farmers or fisherman—men who couldn't fight. Alec had yet to find his father's remaining forces. Those warriors had been fierce, determined, unstoppable.

If Alec had had them at his side, the outlaws would not have even made it to the castle wall.

Someone gasped behind him. Alec turned to find Saraid sitting atop a white horse. Her massive blue cloak spread out over her clothing.

Another woman sat on a small brown horse beside hers and two guards rode several feet behind them.

"What's happened?" She slipped from the saddle in a rustle of fine cloth.

"Outlaws, my lady," said one of the guards.

Alec stabbed a glare in his direction and the man immediately excused himself along with the remaining men who lingered nearby.

"Outlaws?" Saraid stared at the useless door. "Ye havena cleared them off yer land yet?"

Alec's body was already tight with frustration. Her comment only served to cinch the strain across his shoulders.

He glanced at her from the corner of his eye. "Is there a reason for yer visit?"

"Ye havena come to Aros."

He gave her his full attention now. The pout on her lips was a clear indication of her displeasure.

"I'm no on friendly terms with yer da," Alec answered simply.

The MacLeans had no friends nearby. His father had ruined every alliance their predecessors had secured.

She stepped closer to him and swept the hood off her head to reveal a tangle of dark curls. "Ye could be. I could speak with him on yer behalf—"

"No." Alec said the word with hard finality. The last thing he wanted was her pleading with her father to help him. "If I want to speak to him, I'll go to him on my own."

He stared at the pile of disassembled stonework. It'd been expensive. Alec's fortune was vast, but it was not unlimited.

He couldn't afford to continually have his castle rebuilt. Undoing destruction was too costly an endeavor.

As much as Alec hated to admit it, the outlaws were too much for his small guard.

Aye, he could seek aid from Kieran MacDonald, but a war had recently broken out between the MacDonalds and the MacLeods. Kieran would send men if asked, but Alec knew he couldn't afford to do so now.

Edzell Castle was located in the Lowlands and didn't require the amount of men necessary in the Highlands, so Colin MacKinnon wouldn't have the men to spare either.

Alec folded his arms over his chest and settled his weight deeper into his heels with an aggravated grunt.

His other neighboring lairds had sworn to kill any MacLean who set foot on their land. Not that Alec blamed them. Several kidnappings and unwarranted raids by Alec's father long ago had only heightened the savage hatred between the clans.

And Scotsmen did not let past transgressions go easily.

"Laird Stewart spoke with my da yesterday about marrying me." Saraid's voice broke through the barrier of Alec's thoughts.

He grunted and nodded absently. "Laird Stewart has a fine amount of land."

And was one of the neighboring lairds ready to kill any MacLean at any moment. Not a good option for an ally. Not for him, at least.

"He's old." There was a flatness to Saraid's voice.

Alec shrugged and cast her a weary look. "We all will be eventually."

She planted her hands on her hips and cocked her head to the side. It was the same action she'd done when they were children.

"Do ye even care that I'll be wed?" The shrill note in her voice needled his ears.

He stilled.

Something about her made him feel like he was always going to give the wrong answer.

"I thought ye wanted to be wed," he answered.

Hadn't she said she wanted marriage when they spoke at the market?

Or maybe she'd said she'd been offered marriage.

He had been too preoccupied with thoughts of what he'd find at Duart.

She met his gaze and ducked her head in a demure fashion. The action seemed ridiculous after her brash display of irritation. "Aye, I do. But I'm waiting for just the right man."

He nodded and turned back to the ruined curtain wall.

Looking at it again was like another hard punch to the gut.

Maybe Saraid was right about approaching MacDougall. If they could form some kind of alliance, Alec could easily defeat the bands of rogue men and let Duart's rebuild continue uninterrupted.

"I should be going," Saraid said.

Alec turned to her one last time, his mind made up. "Wait."

Her hand rested on his sleeve and she gave a low hum of interest.

"Tell yer da I'll come see him tomorrow."

Saraid's smile grew wide. "As ye wish, laird."

He ground his teeth against the reality of it, but knew he had little choice. This was what lairds did for their land. This was what his father should have done.

And after the way Alec had abandoned the people to handle his father on their own, this was what he had to do.

Tomorrow he would seek the aid of the one remaining laird who could give him aid.

• • •

Celia strode into Duart Castle the next day with honest-earned coins in her pocket and stoic determination. The soft soles of her crude shoes thudded on the floors with her resolve.

She would find Alec and she would have him listen.

A door slammed in the hall behind her, a loud pop of wood slapping hard against stone.

Celia spun around and found Alec standing in front of

a door several paces away. He still faced the closed room, his head bowed.

She knew what she'd say. She'd gone over the speech in her head on the way. Over and over and over again until her main arguments were lodged word by perfectly composed word in her head.

She knew what she would say and yet she didn't go to him. But nor did she turn away.

He faced toward her and stopped.

"Celia." Her name was a hoarse whisper on his lips.

His hair was wet and pulled back in his customary braid. His clothes had been crisply cleaned. The colors of his plaid were more vibrant than normal, the saffron dye to his leine all the more golden.

Those were not all that drew her eye.

He'd shaved the day's growth of stubble he typically wore. It softened his face, easing out the hard lines of his jaw and cheekbones, and left his mouth looking soft, full, and sumptuous.

How would it feel to nuzzle her lips against his clean-shaven face? To let the sensitivity of her mouth caress the smoothness of his jaw before encountering the warm, silky heat of his lips?

His dark brows drew downward. "Has something happened with Duncan?"

"No." The word rasped from her throat and made her pause to clear it as delicately as was possible. "No, Duncan is fine. Uh…that is, I haven't seen him yet today, but I assume he is or I imagine I would have been taken to him without pause."

"Then it's me you seek."

The quiet authority in his deep voice swept across her skin and left a trail of pleasant prickles.

She nodded and again her gaze slipped to his smooth jaw, to the sensual shape of his lips.

The reason she'd come here niggled in the back of her mind.

He let his own gaze wander down her face, her neck, her breasts. Her heartbeat fluttered from steady to erratic.

Though he didn't step toward her, though he hadn't touched her or even spoken, Celia's body heated with wet desire.

"I came to talk to you." Her voice sounded as breathless as she felt.

He raised an eyebrow for her to continue.

That slow, steady gaze of his made the words in her head go fuzzy, all the rehearsed speech now reduced to a blur of ideas. "You see, you've done too much," she said finally.

"I havena done anything at all," he replied in a velvety voice made more for the bedroom than for discussion.

She swallowed around her dry mouth. "You've been too generous."

"No nearly so much as I could be."

"The cottage," she blurted. "It's too much. I thank you for caring for my herbs and giving me a lock, but the furniture, it's too much. The bed…"

The feather bed. It had been the best night of sleep in her life. The pillow fluffiness of it had cradled her into sleep.

"You dinna like the bed?" he asked.

It was too easy to imagine him in the bed, the contrast of the white bed sheets to the black of his hair, the hardness of his body pressing her into the softness of the bed. To think of the bed now with such wicked thoughts, its pillowed surface seemed more of a cloud to shield the tangle of sweat-slicked bodies and muffle the cries of pleasure.

"It's too costly." She forced the words from her dry throat. "I could never pay it back."

He shrugged. "Ye come to see Duncan every day—'tis payment enough."

She gritted her teeth against the thoughts writhing in her mind. "I don't want you to expect anything more from me than has already been discussed."

His gaze narrowed slightly. "Ye've stated yer own expectations."

"Yes. I just didn't want…" She felt foolish suddenly, standing there stammering out a broken speech that had been so smooth in her mind only minutes before.

"Me to break my vow to ye? Do ye think so little of me?" His jaw tightened.

Her cheeks flared with horrified heat. She hadn't meant to question his honor. But what had she meant to do?

Convince him she wouldn't be his mistress?

Maybe convince herself?

Her mind swirled.

"No, I didn't mean—that is…" The muscles along the back of her neck drew tight. Who was this stammering idiot in her place?

She was not this woman.

"You did far more for me than you've done for other villagers," she said finally, focusing on each word. "Unless you put feather beds in every home."

He didn't stop her, but nor did the rigidity of his shoulders seem to relax.

"I'm fine coming to see Duncan. I want to heal him as much as you want to see him well. But I don't want special treatment, because others will see what you do for me and assume I'm your mistress. And I don't…" The last few words stuck in her throat. "I don't want to feel like I owe you anything outside of my rents and my daily visits with Duncan."

There. She'd said it and it was done. She stared up at him, hoping for…hoping for what exactly?

"Ye dinna owe me anything outside coming to see Duncan." His voice was unreadable.

Somehow the conversation didn't hold the completion of a conclusion. "Right," she said. "Which I should probably be doing now. Good day to you, laird."

She spun away then and made her way down the shadowed hallway to Duncan's room.

Wynda stood inside, stoking the fire beneath a small cauldron. "Ach, dinna ye look a sight?"

She got to her feet with a *whuff* and tugged Celia's apron from a peg on the wall.

Celia accepted it and gazed over at the slender form on the bed. "How is he?"

Wynda smiled and all the creases on her weathered face deepened. "He's still no waking, but he's better 'n I've seen him.

He's no as hot as he was."

Celia tied her apron on and approached the bed. Duncan's cheeks were not as flushed as they'd been. She pressed her hand to the boy's brow and felt it warm.

Warm, but not hot.

She pulled in a relieved breath. Now they had to stay ahead of the illness lest he slide backward in his recovery.

"I thought ye'd be here sooner, lass," Wynda said beside her. "The guard told me ye'd arrived a while back."

"I had to speak with the laird."

"He's no in the mood today, lass. I coulda told ye as much." Wynda pushed her hands into her hips so her plump elbows jutted out. "He's on his way to see about an alliance with a neighboring laird."

A chill jagged down Celia's back. "Which laird?"

Unruffled, Wynda grabbed up a stack of linens and made her way to the door. "Laird MacDougall."

Chapter Eleven

Aros Castle was more fortress than anything else. The cold stone had gone dark with age and left an ominous shadow streaking the long stretch of lawn before it.

If Alec had not believed the rumors of witch burning, he did now. Wide expanses of blackened earth scarred the ground in six perfectly spaced patches.

He did not turn his head to examine them more closely as he passed. Instead, he kept his face, and his focus, forward.

He was not at Aros to discuss witches—he was at Aros to seek aid for his people. One issue at a time, and he was barely in a position to ask for what his people needed.

He followed the servant through halls he remembered from his childhood and emerged in the open space of the great hall where Laird MacDougall sat at the head of the table.

Several men sat at the table around him. Men who came from noble families, who had created legends of themselves in battles.

Men who made begging for help that much more cowardly.

MacDougall rose and beckoned Alec closer with a wave of his hand. The old man's hair had gone white since the last time they'd met.

"Alec." MacDougall lifted his hands in the air. "Laird MacLean. I wondered if ye'd return."

Alec locked arms with the old man, but MacDougall pulled him in for a solid embrace.

"I'm glad ye did." He released Alec and indicated the vacant seat at his right. "Join us."

Alec sank into the seat with a grateful nod and immediately

had a mug of frothy ale placed before him.

The welcome was far more than he'd expected. Far more than he deserved, given the tumultuous relationship MacDougall had once had with Alec's father.

"Saraid said ye'd be coming by." The laird winked at him. "She's still got quite a fancy for ye, ye know." Alec sipped his ale. It was cool and wet against the dryness of his throat. "I'm glad ye agreed to see me. My da dinna exactly leave a trail of friends."

MacDougall lifted his hands. "The sins of the father are no that of the son."

Silence settled between them. Heavy silence. One that left the gazes of the surrounding men pressing on Alec.

He didn't want to be in this position, damn it. He hated having to ask for help.

But he was in this position.

"Ye arrived much more quickly after yer da's death than I'd anticipated." MacDougall rubbed the side of his middle finger with the pad of his thumb.

"Aye, I was closer than I expected to be." A fact he was now grateful for lest his people have suffered longer without his presence.

"How have ye found Duart since yer return?"

A hot swell rose up in Alec's gut and he didn't know if he was grateful or irritated the laird was nudging him toward the conversation they needed to have.

"It isna the place I remember," Alec said finally.

MacDougall nodded and the wisps of his thin hair caught against the silver whiskers on his jaw. "Indeed it isna the same."

Alec clenched his jaw.

Damn it.

He drew a deep breath and thought of his people, of the havoc the attacks had wreaked on his land.

"There have been a lot more attacks now than there ever were before," Alec confessed.

"Yer da let a lot of evil come onto his land." MacDougall took a sip from his goblet and set it down again before speaking. "I tried to help, but he threatened war every time."

His hand rested on Alec's arm. The veins were deep blue lines swelling beneath the paleness of his aged skin.

"I want to help ye." MacDougall's sharp gray eyes fixed on Alec. "We can band our forces together. Be stronger together, have more land to clear, more clout with the other lairds to encourage the same. Together we can rise strong and keep our people safe."

Alec's heart pumped faster with the prospect. He had expected to beg, not be offered an alliance.

"We can help each other." MacDougall withdrew his hand. "I've got a problem too, ye see."

The hope that had surfaced so quickly now gave way to the chill of wariness.

"I wasna as lucky as yer da," MacDougall said. "I dinna have a son, but a daughter." He shook his head. "I need a son, lad. I need heirs to inherit what I've built."

The memory of his conversation with Saraid flicked through his mind. "I dinna think she was of the mind to wed."

"Och, aye, she is. She's just a picky lass whom I've indulged too much." MacDougall placed a hand on Alec's shoulder. "She's got it set in her mind that yer the man she wants to wed."

The laird's words shot through Alec's brain.

"Ye need more men, more protection," MacDougall continued. "I need heirs and the power of a strong alliance on Mull."

"What are ye saying?"

The hand on Alec's shoulder squeezed with surprising strength. "I'll give ye all the men and coin ye need, but I want ye to marry Saraid."

• • •

Celia shielded the glare of the sun with her hand and scanned the marketplace for the fabric merchant. She'd purchased a bolt of homespun cloth with newly earned coin just before Alec saw her the day before. The merchant had needed to get more, but she'd forgotten to return to claim it.

Running into Alec had completely swept clear her thoughts that day.

Alec.

A sharp blend of excited attraction and fear shot through her.

If Alec aligned with Laird MacDougall, Celia would have to further distance herself from Wynda and Duncan lest the witch hunt sweep Duart and its lands. She would not have them stand up to defend her and find themselves punished in her stead.

She refused to place them, or anyone else, in danger. If what was said of MacDougall's witch trials were true, she knew how quickly people could be implicated for even having known someone who might be considered a witch.

And she'd seen what loving her had done to Fiona.

She'd seen how those awful men had twisted love, wielded it, to get what they needed.

Never again would she let others sacrifice for her.

Hopefully she'd blundered her strange relationship with Alec with her awkward speech before his meeting.

And yet there was a tightness inside her stomach she did not like when she thought of never seeing him again.

Even if it was for the best.

Her eyes lit on the familiar merchant with long, gray hair. The booth beside him had flaps lifted at the front to reveal multicolored cloth of varying degrees of costliness, from the finest silk to the plainest homespun cloth. The kind of cloth Celia had ordered.

The cloth merchant looked up with the same friendly hazel gaze as he had the previous day. "Ah, the healer returns," he said in a fog of frozen breath.

His gaze trailed down her ruined dress and all the heat in her body went to her cheeks. The cloth had been the most necessary of goods to purchase now that she was near the village once more.

Her palms practically itched with the need to clutch the fabric in her hands and stitch a new overdress. The garment she currently wore was beyond shameful.

"Aye, I have a purchase made for ye." He turned his back to her and rummaged through a stack of bound fabric.

Celia peered around him toward the folds of cloth he focused on. "A purchase made for me? I believe you're mistaken—"

"Nay, lass, I'm no ever mistaken." He pushed a bundle of dark blue silk onto the table and tapped his right temple. "I've got a mind sharp as a battle axe, aye?"

She pulled her hands back from the fine fabric lest she leave it dirty and find herself beholden to pay for it. Silk was far more than she could ever afford. "I purchased the brown cloth, not this."

"Ah, right. That reminds me." He ducked under the booth and popped up with two coins in his hand.

Celia stepped back from the money. "What is this?"

"Yer coin from purchasing the homespun cloth. If I say so meself, the silk will suit ye verra fine. Laird MacLean knew what he was doing when he picked out the color."

Alec.

Her body prickled with uncomfortable heat.

She put her hand up. "I cannot accept this gift. Please keep the silk and I'll purchase the cloth."

The merchant shook his head and a strand of hair caught against his white whiskered cheek. "Canna do that. The laird already told me ye'd say nay and said if I dinna want him to import all his fabrics from another merchant, I'd no sell ye the brown cloth."

He nudged the fabric toward her. The sun rolled over the slick surface. "I'm also the only merchant who sells cloth in town, but ye already knew that, aye?" He gave a sniff and wriggled his cold-reddened nose.

A woman stepped to the edge of the booth with a fat baby in her arms. The infant gave a loud screeching squall and the woman began bouncing him while making a soft clucking sound with her tongue.

Celia refused to touch the fabric. "I spoke with the laird this morning and told him I refuse to accept any more of his hospitality. He understood."

The cloth merchant stared at her without sympathy. "I dinna hear otherwise from my instructions."

The baby's cries pitched higher.

"I don't want this. I'm sorry," Celia said plaintively.

"And I dinna have a choice," the merchant said. "Sorry." His friendly wink took the edge off his mocking tone.

The mother glanced between Celia and the cloth merchant. A grimace puckered her brow. "Are ye done?" she asked in such a hard voice it quieted the startled child for one brief, blissful moment.

Celia stared hard at the merchant's unwavering smile. Alec had planned too well. She stepped forward and pulled the silk into her arms. Her gaze landed on the merchant's outstretched hand.

"Keep those," she said of the meager coins.

The merchant pushed his hand out further to her. "Nay, lass. I'll no take coin from the laird's mistress."

Shock slapped across Celia and for a moment all she could do was sputter, open-mouthed and idiotic. "I'm not—"

The child in the woman's arms loosed a howl. She shifted him from one hip to the other with an exaggerated movement.

The merchant pressed the coin into Celia's hand in a way that suggested there would be no protesting. Especially not over the screech of the child's cries and the way the infant's mother glared.

Celia folded her hand around the coins and clutched the costly silk to her chest. She strode out across the market, eager for the caress of silence against her poor ears.

The fabric in her arms was ridiculous and impractical. With all the time she spent in the forest combing through the foliage for herbs and working in her garden, it would be shredded within weeks.

It was cool under her arm, almost icy in the bitter chill of the day. Surely she'd freeze wearing it.

She'd return the next day and convince the merchant to at least sell her some of the homespun cloth she'd initially paid for.

Her gaze wandered down to where the fabric settled like a sigh over her arm. The color reminded her of the sky at night, deep blue with twilight before fading to black and displaying countless stars.

Her fair skin stood out like cream against the dark, rich color. Surely it would feel like heaven to wear.

But Alec had done enough already with what he'd purchased for her cottage. In addition to the drawers filled with bright new metal needles and true catgut string, there had been new bowls and a seemingly endless supply of linens. And then there had been the bed.

Her cheeks went hot to think why he might have gone to the expense of such a bed. Though he claimed otherwise, she knew what he'd wanted of her, what he doubtless still hoped for.

What the village already thought she was.

Celia glared down at the fabric and wished she could transform it into rough, cheap cloth—the kind no mistress would be seen wearing.

"Healer."

Her hand released the fist she'd made in the silk. Small wrinkles spiraled in a gathered bunch of glossy fabric.

A shadow fell over her and pulled her attention up to a tall man. His lashes were hopelessly, almost comically, long around dark, doe-brown eyes. He gave her a carefree smile, showing a flash of white teeth. That smile had left all the women and girls on the Isle of Mull swooning with desire.

Celia was unaffected.

He leaned against a merchant's booth despite the owner's chastising glare. "It's good to see ye back, healer. Ye look a mite thin, but I'd still enjoy a tumble with ye."

The muscles of his chest flicked alternately beneath his green cotton shirt.

Disgust clenched through Celia and it was all she could do to not take a step back from him. "It didn't take you long to find me, Grant."

"Well, I heard ye were back in town, which meant I needed to see ye." He looked down at her and winked. He glanced around Celia, his attention momentarily wandering. The way his gaze combed downward, she knew it was no doubt a woman.

"Good afternoon to ye, Margot," he said with a wink.

A comely brunette passed them, her gown tied a smidge too tight.

Grant waited for her to pass before craning his neck to watch her go.

Celia set her free hand on her hip and waited without patience. "When you're done…"

"Aye, so…" He slowly turned his gaze from the woman and lowered his voice. "Can I see ye tonight?"

For the first time she noticed how he stood, with his back slightly arched to keep his kilt from grazing any part of his anatomy.

He'd obviously been enduring it for some time if he sought her out so quickly.

"How bad has it gotten? Have you noticed—"

"Tonight." The charm slipped from his face for one cold flash of a second. His gaze darted around the crowd and his shoulder relaxed, his smooth smile showing once more.

She crossed her arms over her chest. "You've followed my rules?"

"Why do ye think I'm so damn desperate to see ye?" The flicker of irritation was back. He truly was miserable if he'd let his charm slip twice in one conversation.

"Fine, but don't be late," she acquiesced with a grate of irritation.

The smile flashed on his face once more. "I'll see ye then. And I hope ye'll be wearing this." His finger slid across the silk in her arm.

This time she did roll her eyes. He shrugged and strode confidently through the market with his hips cocked back in that slightly awkward angle. Two women at a trinket booth stopped and gawked as he passed, oblivious to his altered gait. They turned to one another with flushed cheeks and excited grins.

As much as Grant loved women, the women loved him even more.

If only *they* had engagements planned with him that evening, instead of Celia. She'd forgotten how much she dreaded his late night visits.

Chapter Twelve

Night cast her cloak across Duart Castle's great hall, but Alec paid it little mind. He sat at the head of the table in his seat of authority, alone and unfeeling.

He'd succumbed to his darkness. Nay, not just succumbed. He wore it the way a king wore a mantle of authority.

He couldn't feel his fingers, his legs—hell, his whole body. It had gone numb. His hand hung limp over the edge of the chair.

Every part of him except the areas he'd wanted to quiet. His temples ached from churning thoughts, from the onslaught of emotion that screamed louder with each fiery swallow of whisky.

He'd put his people in this precarious situation—he had left them to his father's mercy. Four months after his father's death and still the people suffered.

Alec had never thought all those years of neglect could do so much damage.

He'd never thought of anyone but his damn self.

Alec cupped his hands and scoured his face. He should have readily accepted Laird MacDougall's offer to marry Saraid.

If Alec were a good man, he would have.

But he wasn't a good man. He was a fraud, a shadow cast in undeserving light.

He was selfish.

He lifted the decanter of whisky from the table. It rose with ease. Empty.

Rage tightened his body.

If he were a good man, he would have taken MacDougall's offer without thought instead of asking for time to consider.

Alec stared bitterly at the fallen bottle.

If he were a good man, he would not have turned to alcohol to assuage his troubles. He'd avoided drinking liquor for ten long years, yet only one taste confirmed his weakness to avoid another.

Just like his father.

"It worked well for ye, dinna it, da?" he shouted into the empty hall.

All his good intentions when he'd left for Aros Castle, all his stoic determination, all his begging at the feet of a man he didn't respect—all in forfeit for her.

Celia.

He closed his eyes against the spinning room and saw her in his mind's eye, rising from the water like a selkie.

His blood bubbled with heat.

Every movement she'd made the day she'd lain with him replayed in his mind. The erotic removal of her clothing as she watched him, the way she'd glided through the water as if she were liquid herself, the way she'd caressed him with the boldness of a whore.

But she'd been innocent, untouched.

He groaned out loud and his hands curled against the arms of his chair until the wood pressed hard and cool into the wet heat of his palms.

She'd had no man but him.

And still she refused him.

Even though she stared at him as if she wanted to devour him every time they met. The deep blue of her eyes burned with the same desire they had that day at the loch. She could deny it all she wanted, but he knew the truth.

Celia wanted him as much as he wanted her.

And damn it, he wanted her.

She filled his thoughts with such insistence it was as though she'd bewitched him.

The thought floated in his mind.

Maybe she had.

A frigid wind whistled through the open windows and

pushed icy cold across his blazing cheeks. The scent of rosemary wafted from the rushes below.

Alec pushed his hands against the table and stood. He would not sit idle and muse over Celia, not when he could see her.

Alcohol sloshed in his empty stomach. He clenched his teeth against the wave of disorienting weakness and strode across the room.

Celia would see him whether she wanted to or not. He would not refuse Laird MacDougall's offer if she truly did not want him.

But, if she did…

He leaned his head against the stone wall and reveled in the cool quiet press of it against his temple.

If she wanted him—God help him, for Laird MacDougall surely would not.

• • •

Alec staggered through the shadowed forest. He'd been foolish to leave without his horse and yet every part of him had long ago memorized the path to Celia's cottage.

The whisky fired through his blood with each step, encouraging the darkness, strengthening his resolve to speak with her.

Lights burned bright in the windows of her cottage and hope spurred his pace. She was still awake.

He caught sight of her profile in the window and stopped. Her sharp chin jutted upward. She shook her head and gestured with her hands.

His breath came faster.

She was not alone.

• • •

Celia turned away from Grant lest she be forced to watch him unlace his codpiece.

"I like meeting ye like this," he said softly behind her.

There was an intimacy in his voice she did not care for.

She opened her mouth to throw a sharp retort at him when the front door burst open and smacked the wall with a deafening crack.

A short, fast scream squeaked from her throat—a mighty pathetic sound for the way her heart knocked into her ribs.

Alec stood in the doorway with the black of night behind him. His massive arms braced either side of the door frame and his chest rose and fell with a frenzied breath. His pale eyes were glassy in the firelight.

Glassy and wild.

An edge of fear scraped down her spine.

He stared first to Grant, whose hands were frozen on his gaping codpiece, then to where Celia stood in front of the pestle.

"What. Is. This?" He bit out each word in a low growl.

Celia stared at him a moment, her mind still spinning with a lack of understanding. "What are you doing here? You can't just come in."

He stalked inside and stopped in front of Celia, his face red. "I own this cottage."

Her cheeks flamed with the offense. "And I pay my rent to you by healing Duncan. It was the agreement we settled upon. This is *my* home and you cannot enter whenever you please."

The scent of whisky stung her nostrils and there was a slight waver of his stance.

The long, slow breath he drew seemed to do little for his patience. "I can do whatever I damn well please. I'm laird of this land and if I dinna want men in yer home in the wee hours of night, ye will do as I say."

Grant had already laced up his codpiece and crept behind Alec toward the door. His movements were quick and silent, a master of sneaking out undetected.

Still, he was a customer and Celia would ensure he came to no harm. She thrust her chin up at Alec with intentional defiance. "I don't belong to you. I thought I'd made that clear."

Grant slipped silently through the still open door and out into the night.

"Ye claim ye're no witch, but since I met ye, I havena been able to sleep for thinking of ye. Especially after ye came to me. Like ye've cast some spell upon me, and left me. No warning, no explanation, just left."

"I did not cast a spell," Celia said, but then stopped herself from saying more.

He was angry.

And he was right, at least about her seducing him and leaving. But there was too much to explain.

Too much she did not want to tell him.

"I thought of ye every day ye were gone. Wishing ye'd be here. Wishing ye'd come back to me. Then ye return and ye dinna let me touch ye, but yet let him…" He thrust a hand toward the empty space where Grant had been, his stare never leaving her face. "Him. Of all the filthy men ye could bed, ye let *him* touch ye?"

Unexpected tears stung Celia's eyes.

"I'm not a witch," she said in a strong voice. "And I'm not a whore."

He braced his hands on the wall behind her and leaned forward. "Did ye strip away yer clothing for him like ye did for me?" His voice broke, "Did ye come upon him like a goddess and let him love ye?"

The unguarded emotion tugged at her heart.

"I refuse to listen to your insults and I refuse to have a discussion with you like this when I'm damned no matter what I say." Her gaze darted toward the door. "You need to take your leave."

• • •

Alec heard her ask him to leave, but how could he when she stood so close?

There was a rift somewhere in his mind, torn between his anger at finding her with another man and stupidly wanting to still touch her. To possess her.

Her rosemary scent hovered around them both, baiting him.

"You're drunk, Alec. You need to go home."

"And leave ye alone. With him?" Alec spun around to address Grant and found naught but an empty room.

The darkness inside him welled beyond his control. It pounded through his chest and roared in his ears until his muscles strained against the tightness of his skin.

"Ye let him leave?" He turned a hard glare on Celia.

She stood with her back straight and regarded him with a calm that made him want to break something. The alcohol churning in his gut lashed at his insides like whips of fire.

"How could ye let him leave? Is he coming back later to finish what I interrupted?" He put his hands on the wall on either side of her once more.

Her eyes flashed with matched anger. "If you don't leave this cottage, I will."

She ducked under his arms and shoved past him, making good on her threat.

Alec's heart swelled with a frenzy of panic. If she left, he might never see her again.

His hand shot out and caught her arm, his grip firm to keep her from leaving.

She jerked away from him, eyes wide.

Just like his mother.

Alec dropped her arm as if she were made of flames and stared down at his hands. "Celia…" he started. "I dinna…"

She lifted the dagger from her waist and held it between them.

He did not fear her cutting him. The tremble of her hand told him she would not.

No, it was his own loathing chasing him from her cottage and into the black, black night where he belonged, where he could be alone with the demons who shrieked in his mind what he already knew.

He was just like his father.

Chapter Thirteen

The savage wind howled off the coast. It swept through Alec's clothes to the deepest part of his bones, where a chill settled. He forced one foot in front of the other and fought off the fatigue pulling at him. Sleep promised a place where his head didn't ache and his insides didn't squeeze with painful regret, but he couldn't give in.

The nearer he drew toward the village, the more he cursed his own weakness.

Celia would be arriving at Duart Castle soon to wait upon Duncan. He should have waited for her, to explain himself. But there was nothing to say that could make any of this right.

Several people milled around on a dirt road between rows of simple cottages when he arrived. The wariness on their faces had long since given way to gratitude and most smiled in his direction.

He nodded in greeting, sober enough now to acknowledge etiquette. His gaze scanned each face with great care.

He found himself always looking through the faces of the men and seeking out the familiar ones from his memory, the warriors his father once held in his employ.

If he found the soldiers he sought, his force would be strong enough to defend the villagers. He would not need the marriage to Saraid. He couldn't, in good conscience, marry her with his thoughts fixed on Celia.

Even if she *had* taken a lover, Alec could not ease her from his mind.

Not yet.

Alas, none of the men he saw were the ones he needed.

No doubt the villagers knew where the men hid, but they still did not trust him enough to divulge the whereabouts of his father's former soldiers.

Never before had he needed them as badly as he did now.

All he had to do was convince them he was a better man.

His chest ached so badly it squeezed the breath from him.

His actions the previous night made him just like his father, the very man he'd tried to convince everyone, including himself, he was better than.

He never should have had the whisky. It let the darkness come too quickly and left him too weak to fight it off.

A powerful lack of control.

He thought back to his father, to how the man drank without shame and raged without mercy.

And Alec thought back to how many times he'd sat in front of his mother's door through the night, ready to protect her. He flinched from the sting of the memory.

The scent of fish mingled with briny ocean in the whipping gusts. New roofs showed light against the dinginess of the homes. There was still much to do in the way of repairs, but those would come another day. Nothing would sway Alec from his mission.

Two people leaning into one another along the side of a building caught his attention.

Almost nothing.

All the energy he lacked earlier swirled up in him like the red hot embers of a fire. He stalked across the worn road to where Grant propped himself against a building with one arm while he whispered to a comely redhead. The woman giggled behind her hand.

Alec wasted no time with speech. He cocked his elbow back and smashed his fist into Grant's high cheekbone. It connected with a dull slapping sound and Grant staggered backward.

The ache in Alec's hand was one of the most gratifying pains he'd ever felt.

A gasp hissed from the woman and she pressed herself back against the wall. Alec turned to her and found her mouth hanging open in shock.

He nodded toward the street. "Go."

She ran from him. He did not watch her depart, but heard the steady splash of her feet connecting with the wet ground.

He turned toward Grant, who was once again standing. A growl rasped from Alec's throat and he rushed forward, pinning him to the wall with a forearm against his neck.

Questions ripped through Alec. Ones that had plagued him through the night, ones that erupted on the quiet ride to the village. Ones that started the minute he saw Grant with the woman just now.

Grant squirmed between the wall and Alec's arm.

"Why were ye in Celia's cottage?" Alec asked with barely tethered patience. He pressed harder with his forearm.

The throat was a fragile thing, and could easily be crushed beneath the force of a man's elbow.

He made damn sure Grant was aware of that.

Grant's eyes bulged. "It's no...any of yer...business..." he choked out.

Something cold flipped in Alec's gut. "Was that the first time ye went there?" He eased off the man's throat so the coward could answer.

"I've gone before. She only ever sees me at night." His eyes turned up toward the sky and the gray clouds overhead reflected across his brown stare. "My request, no hers."

He made a choking sound and only then did Alec realize he'd pushed his arm harder. "I should kill ye for touching her—"

Grant shook his head rapidly. "...didn't..."

Alec removed his elbow and wrapped his fingers around the man's neck. "Ye lie."

Grant's pulse thrummed in quick, short succession beneath Alec's hands. "Nay, I've no ever touched her, I swear. I'll tell ye the names of every woman I've been with." A cocky grin lifted the corner of his mouth even while his eyes reflected his fear. "All the ones I can remember, aye? But she's no one of them."

Alec watched the man's face closely, waiting for his gaze to dart to the left in indication of his deceit. "Then why do ye see her in the middle of the night?"

"I…" Grant jerked his face to the side and stared hard at the patch of ocean in the distance. "I've got the blisters plague," he whispered. "I dinna want anyone to know."

Alarm shot through Alec and he jerked his hands from the man. "What?"

Grant jabbed a finger toward his codpiece. "On my cock. I have the blisters plague on my cock." He glanced to the street as if he feared someone overhearing. "No all the time, aye? She sees what the blisters look like, 'cause they're different depending on how long I've had 'em and how many there are. She makes different pastes for me to put on it depending on what she sees."

Alec swept his palms against the coarse wool of his kilt and stepped back.

"I dinna ever touch a woman when I've got them—Celia made me promise that." His confident posture melted into humble humiliation. "I dinna want to pass on this disease."

"Ye mean ye were there for healing?"

"I can show ye if ye like." Grant grasped the string of his codpiece and tugged.

"Nay," Alec said quickly. "That isna necessary."

The man shrugged and retied his pants. He looked around and his leg bounced impatiently. "Can I go?"

Weight pressed on Alec's shoulders, knotting already tense muscles. "I shouldna have…" Alec started, hating to apologize to a man like Grant, but knowing the depth of this wrong.

No wonder Celia had let Grant flee. She was protecting an innocent man.

From Alec.

"I shouldna have hit ye," he said finally. "I dinna know…"

Grant held up his hand to stop Alec. "I can see how ye thought what ye thought. Even I'm no fool enough to lie with the laird's mistress."

Mistress.

The word burned into Alec's mind. This was exactly what Celia had been afraid of.

"Can I go?" Grant asked, eyeing the alleyway exit like it

was heaven.

"Aye, go," Alec said. The man needed no second telling and left quickly with the silence of a mouse.

Alec waited for the man to leave before he turned and stared out at the jagged cliffs.

There was much to say to Celia, much to atone for. And for all his renowned bravery, he suddenly felt very much the coward.

• • •

Celia squeezed the sponge and a stream of tea trickled between Duncan's lips. He had still not woken from his deep slumber. She pressed a hand to his forehead and found it slick with sweat, yet only warm to the touch. His fever had come down significantly.

For that she could not be more grateful.

The daylight outside had gone dark with an advancing storm and most of its natural light had been shuttered against the freezing rains of winter.

The thick castle walls pressed in on her, dark save for the flickering candle and the orange glow of the fire. Shadows bobbed and trembled across the thick stone with each greedy lick of a flame.

Sweat beaded on Celia's own brow despite the coolness of the room. She placed the sponge in the now empty bowl beside her and swiped a hand over her forehead.

More sweat prickled where she'd wiped it away. Her breath was coming a little faster now.

Were the walls getting thicker?

She stepped back from the bed and tried to draw a deep breath, but her chest was too tight.

Shadows and flames of firelight danced around her in cruel torment, reminding her of the time so long ago she'd been in a castle.

No, she could not think of it. Her eyes burned with impending tears, but she ground them away with the heels of her hands.

Hadn't she pushed the memory too far down to recall?

Her eyes blinked open to the small room, the wavering red gold light, the stone walls, the prison.

No.

Torches flickered on the wall, providing little light and even less heat. Icy fingers of air curled around Celia, peeling her strength apart, one slow, bitter layer at a time.

Rats darted across the filthy rushes, their fat bodies bumping against her feet where she kneeled.

They waited for her to fall asleep.

Her leg flinched, but she did not pull away from where the rat stood with its beady eyes fixed on her.

Fiona needed her. Celia drew a shaky breath and tried to ignore the metallic odor of blood.

Fiona gave a long, low groan of pain from where she lay on the ground. Her arm lay useless at her side, twisted in an unnatural angle at the elbow. Celia swallowed the burn of bile rising in her throat. If only the memory of Fiona's screams could be so easily cleared.

"Ye'll do little good in here, witch." A man's gravelly voice clawed down her back. "We're protected against ye."

Celia turned toward the cell door. The Scottish nobleman gripped the iron bars, his gray eyes lit with wild insanity. He pointed toward her. "Ye'll be next."

His large garnet ring caught the flickering light and sent shards of red slashing through the room.

Fiona gave a low, grating moan.

Celia blinked rapidly.

The sound came again and she sucked in a deep breath of air to clear the fog from her mind.

No.

Not Fiona.

Duncan's head shifted on his pillow.

The blood thrumming through her veins pounded harder now with hope.

"Duncan," she called softly.

He groaned. Green eyes lined heavy with red squinted up at her. "Are ye an angel?" he croaked.

A smile touched her lips. "No, I'm a healer."

Wynda rushed in with a pile of linens, which she hastily shoved aside. "Is that Duncan?" She pressed her palm to her chest. "Ach, lad, ye've no idea what good it does to my heart to see ye awake."

With a grunt, she sank onto her knees and took his hand in hers. She regarded Celia with tears in her small blue eyes. "Ye work miracles, ye know that?"

The boy looked up at Celia with the adoring gaze of a new puppy.

Something warm blossomed in her chest and though she'd never done such a thing, she had the sudden temptation to reach out and stroke his cheek.

"He'll need to drink his tea from a cup since he's awake." Settling back into instructing the healthy to care for the ill was a far more comfortable place.

She purposefully kept her gaze averted from the boy's doting stare.

Wynda jerked a look up at Celia. "Are ye no coming back now?" There was a pitch of nervousness to the woman's voice.

Celia gave her a reassuring smile. "I will be back to check on him throughout the week, but will not need to come daily anymore."

The thought of not having to come into the castle every day was like cool, sweet air to her still-tight chest. She couldn't afford to have her fear attack like that again, not where someone could see.

Where someone might press her for answers.

Her skin pebbled with goosebumps at the mere thought. Even today had been too close.

With luck, Duncan would make a full recovery in a couple of weeks or so and she could cease her visits altogether. She could make enough coin with her herbs, poultices, and healing to pay a handsome rent.

She could afford rent more than she could afford a growing fondness for the boy or the overbearing cook. There was no room in her life for affection.

There could not be.

Wynda hefted her weight forward and used the bed to hitch herself to her feet. "Ach, no, the laird said ye are to come every day. I dinna think he'll take exception to that."

Alec.

He'd been so drunk the night before, so unguarded, so tortured.

His words had scalded her mind and branded her heart. She'd thought about them for far too long after he'd left.

Celia handed a packet of herbs to Wynda. She needed to leave this place. She needed to breathe fresh air and free herself from the entrapment of the pressing castle walls.

And the possibility of seeing its laird.

Wynda smiled and shook her head. "We've enough herbs for Duncan, but thank ye all the same, lass."

"Laird MacLean did not seem well when I saw him yesterday," Celia said carefully. "These are for him." While she had no desire to see Alec, she could at least aid in chasing away the pain of the previous night's intoxication.

"Ach, that's sweet of ye, lass." Wynda took the herbs and sniffed at them. Her nose twitched. "What's in this?"

"Skullcap for his headache, some ginger to ease any stomach discomfort he might have, and St. John's wort to improve his mood."

"An improved mood, ye say? I think that might be in order after all." Wynda winked.

She glanced at Duncan, who had fallen asleep again, and leaned closer to Celia. The aroma of freshly baked bread hovered around the woman. "Between ye and me, the laird has too much he's trying to take on. He's hard on himself, especially after yesterday. I dinna think I've seen him so upset."

Wynda's eyes shadowed with concern and the line on her brow had returned. "I havena seen the laird drink a drop of liquor since he's been home. No until last night…" Wynda twisted her hands together. Flour clung to the cuticles of her nails. "This will help him relax a wee bit also?"

Celia rummaged through her basket until she found the slender vial of valerian root oil. She'd brought it in case Duncan had been in pain or upset from fever.

"Have him put a drop or two of this in his ale at supper each evening, but not in tea. The hot water will dilute the effect." She set the small bottle in Wynda's outstretched hand. "He'll complain about the smell, no doubt, but it will help."

Wynda tucked the vial into the swell of her bosom and patted her hand over the location, as if to secure it. "He can complain all he wants, but I'll make sure he drinks it."

Celia looked down at her basket to avoid eye contact. "What happened yesterday?" she asked. She shouldn't have, yet she could not quell her curiosity.

The idea of Alec going to visit Laird MacDougall had writhed in her thoughts all night.

It tangled with the events that transpired between them and kept sleep at bay.

"The laird dinna like what he heard." Wynda swiped at a streak on her apron. "But ye can ask him yerself."

Celia regarded the cook with questioning uncertainty.

Wynda nodded toward the door with a cheeky grin. "He's right behind ye."

Chapter Fourteen

Alec leaned against the doorframe of Duncan's room. He couldn't remember the last time he'd been so damn tired.

Celia turned and looked at him with her wide, mystical stare. A spike of adrenaline shot through him.

"Celia." He loved saying her name, even now when it came out low and deep like he'd woken from a long slumber. "Celia, I need to speak with ye."

She tried to keep her face expressionless, but he knew her too well now. He'd watched her too much, had studied her beautiful face too often to not notice her lips tighten ever so slightly.

His heart went to lead.

She didn't want to see him.

A soft, grating groan came from somewhere in the room and both women looked toward the bed.

Alec straightened, his pulse a wild thrumming of a hope he dared not believe.

"Was that Duncan?" he asked.

A smiled bloomed over Wynda's face so wide it bared all the gaps with unabashed obliviousness. "He's awake," she said, and quietly clapped her hands in rapid succession.

Alec stepped into the room and let his eyes fall on the boy. What he'd been expecting was a frail shell, white with the lingering threat of death.

He opened his mouth, but found his throat too clogged to speak.

Duncan's color had returned to a normal pallor. This wasn't the face of a boy near death; this was the face of a boy who would live.

The room faded away and even Celia faded with it.

Alec walked to the bed.

The boy blinked his eyes open. They seemed to take a while to focus before he gave a tired grin of recognition.

Alec's chest was so tight it hurt to draw breath.

He wanted to tell the lad how much he'd missed those incessant questions that had somehow become normal, how life wasn't the same without his little shadow, how never before in Alec's life had he been so scared of a loss.

"About time ye woke up." Alec's voice felt thick in his own mouth.

The boy's smile widened. "Missed me?"

"It's been quiet," Alec confessed. He tousled Duncan's straw colored hair. It slid like silk between his fingers. "Too quiet."

Duncan puffed out his narrow chest. "I'll get better as fast as I can."

"Aye, lad, I know. Ye never let me down." Alec gave him a smile. "But first get some rest."

The boys nodded and his eyes were already closing once more.

Alec approached Celia with slow reverence, this incredible woman who haunted his thoughts, who healed the broken, who brought life to what was almost dead.

What she'd done had been nothing short of a miracle.

She looked up at him, her eyes glassy with unshed tears. "Thank you for your kind words to him. It will help speed his recovery."

"I need to talk to ye," he said in a low voice to keep from disturbing Duncan.

She gave a single terse nod and set about gathering her belongings.

He bent to retrieve her pack, but she stopped him with a slender hand. "I can handle my own bag."

Her words stung. She didn't want his help, even when he needed hers.

And he did need her. Beyond the longing to lie next to her

and stroke the velvety softness of her skin, beyond the desire to listen to her strong voice when she spoke and stare deep into those blue eyes, he needed her aid.

If she could save Duncan, what else could she do?

This was a woman he could not afford to lose with his lust. He would have to keep her on his land no matter the cost—even at the sacrifice of his own desires.

Even if it meant telling her things he'd never told a soul before.

• • •

Celia sat in the chill of Alec's solar. It was significantly colder than Duncan's room and met her overheated skin like a caressing sigh.

Alec did not sit. He stood in front of the empty fireplace with a hand braced on the mantel and his gaze fixed on the gaping hole of blackened stone. His seriousness seemed to strip all joy from the world.

He'd not shaved yet and the dark prickle of stubble on his chin looked more like him than his smoothly shaven face of the previous morning. His hair had come loose from its braid at some point and hung in dark waves.

"I was wrong." The words came out deep and rumbling. "I shouldna have gone to yer cottage last night, I shouldna have threatened Grant, and I shouldna…" His voice tapered off.

He turned toward her, his eyes blazing with such ferocity it burned away his appearance of exhaustion. "I shouldna have grabbed yer arm."

"You didn't hurt me—"

"I scared ye. That's enough." He shook his head.

There was more. It hung in the air between them, pregnant with anticipation.

She did not encourage him, she did not speak, lest he be put off from saying what he intended.

"My da scared me when I was a boy." A humorless smile winked across his lips, one full of self-disgust. "He'd yell so loud it made me jump, and his fist was so large it was as though he had boulders for hands."

He curled his hand into a fist in front of him and stared at it.

"He dinna like my mother. Their union was one between two warring clans, an attempt to bring peace after centuries of battle." He snorted. "The marriage never stood a chance, aye? From the start they were enemies. My mother was a saint with me and everyone else, but with my da..."

He shook his head and smirked. "She was a harpy. She contradicted him in front of his men, she goaded his anger, she challenged him. He dinna take it well and solved the issues with her the way he solved his issues with me."

A deep ache squeezed to life in her breast. It was difficult to picture Alec so young. Even more difficult to imagine him vulnerable.

An unfamiliar longing tugged at her, urging her to go to him. Before she could offer her condolences toward the memories Alec shared, he spoke once more. "I've no ever hit a child or a woman. Last night was the closest I've ever come." He strode toward her.

The heavy fall of his boots on the floor echoed off the walls of the empty room. He stopped in front of her and regarded her with such torture in his gaze, her throat went even tighter.

"Celia, I was wrong and I'm deeply, deeply sorry."

She put her hand on his arm. It was automatic, that foreign movement, and came without pause from somewhere inside her.

"You didn't hurt me," Celia repeated.

He looked down at her hand as if he were as startled as she.

"And I dinna ever want to."

His skin was warm beneath her touch, the flesh firm and the muscle beneath it taut.

Her heart fluttered to touch him so and her mind swam with memories best left forgotten.

Being in this castle, surrounding herself with people and speaking to them at length—it was all breaking down the defenses she'd spent too long constructing.

Though everything in her screamed against it, she pulled her hand from his arm. She wanted to rub her fingertips together, to savor the sensation of his skin against hers.

"What was different about last night?" she asked.

The light dimmed from his eyes and the shadows on his face seemed more prominent. "I drank whisky. A lot of whisky."

She remembered him yesterday, dressed incredibly fine with his hard jaw scraped smooth. Their conversation had not gone well, and he'd been on his way to see Laird MacDougall. The chill of the room finally got to her and made her skin prickle.

"Why?" she asked, but she was almost afraid of the answer.

He stepped back from her and dragged a hand down his face. "Yesterday wasna a good day. No that it's an excuse for any of this."

"Was it your meeting with Laird MacDougall?"

"Apparently walls dinna just have ears, they've tongues too." He smirked and shook his head. "Aye, my meeting with Laird MacDougall."

Her heart beat a little faster and she found herself scrutinizing his face in an effort to see something he might not be saying. She saw only exhaustion.

"Did it not go well?" she prompted.

He gave a noncommittal grunt.

She waited.

He lifted his brow. "It isna yer concern, Celia."

He was right, of course, but the bluntness of his response stung like a slight.

A spike of panic she hadn't known was there jabbed through her and sent her brain whirling faster than her pounding heart. "Laird MacDougall is burning witches, Alec. Those women are mainly healers and midwives. He is the neighboring laird, which means at any moment—"

Her words went to sawdust in her mouth and she found herself unable to swallow around the choking dryness.

"At any moment, it might be me tied to that stake," she finished.

Realization flooded his face. "No, Celia, he isna wanting

to carry his witch hunt to my land. I wouldna ever allow such a thing. I already told ye as much."

He stepped toward her and for a moment she thought he might wrap his arms around her. Those strong, warm arms where she once found passion and from which she now craved comfort.

His body tensed and then he stepped back again, his expression returning to something fierce.

"I'll protect ye no matter what," he said.

His words curled around her like iron and dragged the air from her chest.

She'd heard those words once before.

From Fiona.

The moment they'd passed through the cold stonework of the dungeon, the older woman had hugged Celia to her and whispered fervently to her.

I'll protect you no matter what.

The room spun around her and suddenly the cold of the room was ice at her fingertips while the sweat prickling at her underarms and the base of her neck was too, too hot.

"I don't want your protection." She hadn't meant for it to come out so harsh.

Hurt flashed over his face before a hard look of indifference blocked his expression from her. "I protect all my people. Ye included."

His brows tightened together and he reached for her, but she stepped back. She did not stop until the solid door pressed at her back. The air was too thin, too hard to breathe. White dots spotted her vision.

Alec.

Her heart ached like a massive yawning hole filled with flames and brilliant red embers.

"I don't want your help," she gasped. "I don't want your money or gifts and I don't want your cloth."

He didn't move. "What of Duncan?" His voice was quiet with resignation.

"I'll continue to see him when necessary, but I don't—"

The words swelled in her throat, but she had to say them. To push him away lest he get too close. "I don't want to see you."

When he made no response, she opened the door, bobbed a quick curtsey, like a servant might do, and left.

Chapter Fifteen

Two weeks had passed since Celia had seen Alec.

She often wondered if she would hear the low rumble of his voice in the next room or might catch a glimpse of his proud back, but never did such a thing occur.

Duncan had told her Alec left for the village every day before she arrived and did not return until after she'd gone home.

Alec.

She'd hurt him the last time she saw him and though she knew it was for the best, it made her heart ache in a way she wished it wouldn't.

Celia strode the familiar path to Duart Castle and tried not to think more of the laird or his people. She ignored the cold, merciless wind and pressed onward with only thoughts of what she needed to continue healing Duncan.

He'd improved quite well and chatted with her whenever she came. Truly, he was almost completely well now, but she wanted to continue her visits every other day to ensure he remained in good health.

It had nothing to do with the way Duncan smiled when he saw her or the spindly armed hug she'd finally started to allow him to give or the way Wynda fussed over her.

It had nothing to do with the way they both had worked their way into her heart despite her defenses.

She knew she should break away from them as she had with Alec. She knew that, and yet could not bring herself to.

Swirling threads of clouds dimmed the gray sky above and Celia's ears felt stuffed with the roar of the raging ocean. The air trembled with the anticipation of a storm.

But there was something else. An undercurrent crackled against her skin and left the fine hair on her arms standing on end. Ruadh had been several feet from her the entire journey and now wove in an anxious back-and-forth pattern.

He sensed it too.

Celia hugged her pack to her chest, more for comfort than to keep the wind from tearing it free. The leather was damp with moisture, like her hair and the new dress she'd sewn after trading some herbs for a bolt of homespun cloth from a villager.

A jolt sparked down her spine and her skin prickled.

Someone watched her. Someone near enough to pierce her with the weight of his stare.

She turned slowly to look behind her and her heart slid into her throat, choking the air from her chest.

A man sat upon a great black horse about fifty feet away, but she could make out his face, his eyes. Cold gray eyes that watched her without flinching.

Her mind screamed at her body to run, but her feet would not comply, not with the way her limbs quivered.

His lips moved and the wind ripped the word to her ears.

"Witch."

Ruadh raced a circle around her, breaking her paralyzing fear, before darting toward a patch of trees and low lying brush in the distance. The pack slipped from Celia's fingers and her legs flew into action. She darted away from the jagged coastline, following Ruadh's lead. At least in the trees she had a place to hide.

A scream locked in her throat and her legs burned with the effort of her escape.

The shuddering grew stronger. He was too close.

Several more feet until she got to the forest. Frantic breath rasped from her lips and singed her throat.

It mattered not.

All that mattered was living.

The first branch slapped her across the cheek, but she did not stop. She raced between the narrow trees, hoping his horse would not follow.

Pain lanced through the side of her waist and twisted tight across her chest so she couldn't breathe. Her steps faltered. She could run no farther.

Ruadh darted toward a large bush with waxy green leaves and slipped inside. She followed his lead and dove beneath its cover despite the many sticks and branches stabbing into her flesh. A bird screamed at their invasion and shot upward.

"Witch," the man hissed.

She chanced a look up from within her cover of bushes and found him watching the bird's ascent, eyes wide with deranged fear. His hand tightened into a fist, and that was when she saw it.

The ring.

The dark red stone, like a pool of congealing blood encased in a band of gold.

She knew that red stone.

Her chest burned for air, yet she refused to draw a breath.

Not with him so close.

He stared up at the sky where the bird had flown off. "Ye escaped me this time with yer tricks, witch, but it willna happen again." His gray eyes went wide. "I will find ye and I will kill ye."

He dug his heels into his horse's sides and a command erupted from his lips. The steed propelled forward, leaving Celia curled up on the dirt in silence.

Ruadh pressed his moist nose to the back of her hand where she'd wrapped her arms protectively around herself, but she did not move.

She lay there, trembling, panting, remembering too much of what she had wanted so badly to forget.

Those six months of her youth had been the longest of her life.

That red ring.

Those gray eyes.

He was the man who had locked her up as a child.

Her and Fiona.

A hard sob choked from somewhere deep, deep inside.

Ruadh lay his pointed nose near her cheek and huffed a breath of warm air onto her skin.

The man who'd killed Fiona would track down Celia as well. The man was as tenacious as he was crazed.

If not in an hour, then a day, a week, a fortnight, a month perhaps. But he would be back and he would find her.

• • •

The swirling gray clouds overhead mingled with the onset of dusk and spit flecks of rain at Alec as he strode across the castle's courtyard.

Another day without success.

Another day his people went unprotected.

Why the hell was he biding his time to avoid marrying Saraid when Celia had made it clear she did not want him?

But he knew the truth. He couldn't bear to marry one woman while he thought incessantly of another.

Instead he'd focused his efforts on finding his father's men.

He'd put out word that his father's former men were needed. He'd even offered coin, yet every villager he asked averted their eyes and pursed their lips.

This could not go on much longer.

A tall, thin guard ran up to him when he reached the castle keep. "Laird, I must speak with ye."

Alec's stomach slid lower, but he nodded for Donnell to continue.

"Laird MacDougall came by looking for ye."

Shite.

Alec kept his face impassive. "Did he leave a message?"

The man wrinkled his nose. "He wasna happy and when I told him ye werena here, he said he needs to see ye and wants ye at Aros posthaste."

Alec had taken too long to consider the marriage proposal. He knew that. And now it appeared a visit to Aros was imminent.

"Anything else?" Alec asked.

Donnell shook his head.

A loud clap of thunder rolled through the angry clouds.

"Aye, then go on before the rain starts." Before the words

were out of Alec's mouth, the rain did start—in great, fat drops spattering against his chilled skin.

Alec stayed for a moment, letting the cold water plop against his head and face before seeking his own refuge within the walls of the keep.

MacDougall might be mad with his witch trials, but he was also a formidable enemy and a strong ally.

Alec's time was running out and Laird MacDougall needed an answer.

Tension crushed against Alec's skull.

He'd gone all of five feet within the massive entrance when Wynda came flying at him like a wraith. "My laird, thank God ye're back." She plucked at her fingers. "It's Duncan."

A trickle of rain slid down Alec's back like ice. "What about Duncan?"

"He's missing." Tears rolled down her bright red cheeks. "Celia dinna come today and he kept asking after her. I gave him his tea and told him to rest. But when I went back later to go check on him…"

She pulled her apron to her face and let out a howling sob. Her rasping gasps echoed off the high ceilings.

Alec's heart constricted.

"Did none of the guards see him leave?" he demanded.

She shook her head.

"Did Celia ever come? Ever send word?"

Again, she shook her head. "She's no ever missed a day, hasna even been late once. I shouldna have said I was worried about her." She blew her nose into her apron in a great, loud honk. "It's all my fault."

The rain hissed louder outside and Wynda's gaze slid toward an open window.

Alec knew what she was thinking. Duncan and Celia were out there. In the cold, in the wet, and she was not there to protect them.

Her helplessness tightened around him as well, for he was not there to protect them either.

He placed a hand on Wynda's shaking shoulders and held

fast to his own determination. "We'll find them. Get me Donnell. I'll have him organize a search party."

Wynda nodded and ran off with a speed he hadn't thought the plump woman capable of.

Duncan had been much healthier as of late and would survive the storm. If anything, the lad had most likely ducked under a tree or found himself a cottage to beg a meal from in an effort to avoid the rain.

And Celia.

His stomach clenched at the thought of her. He hadn't spoken to her since she'd told him she didn't want to see him. Since she'd left him after he'd told her he was afraid he might be like his father. He'd scared her away and had never forgiven himself for it.

Perhaps she was warm and safe in her cottage.

A chill rose across his skin.

But perhaps she was not.

Chapter Sixteen

The thick green salve melted against Celia's fingertips and spread across the wound on her cheek like butter. Soon the agrimony and slanlus mixture would ease the throbbing burn of each cut and scrape she'd suffered during her escape.

Something outside her cabin cracked, like a stick snapping beneath a heavy boot. She jumped and her heart agitated in her chest with such force her body trembled.

Her gaze fixed on the door as if she expected it to explode inward.

Had the man with the red ring found her?

Was he back to finish what he'd started?

Someone pounded against her front door. She pressed a hand to her mouth to suppress the squeak of fear and grasped her dagger.

She crept to the wall and flattened herself against it. If she stood motionless, he wouldn't see her. Perhaps he would leave.

A fist slammed into the door again, this time hard enough to rattle it on its hinges.

Her palms were slick against the dagger's hilt where she held it tight.

"Damn it, Celia, open up."

Alec.

The frantic hammering of her heart went from fear to a wash of relief, which quickly gave way to a lurch of unwanted excitement.

She crossed the room on shaking legs, twisted the key in the lock, and pulled the door open. Alec stood with his hand braced against the side of the doorway. Rainwater streamed down his face and his clothing was so sopping wet it glistened black against the glow of her firelight.

The muscles of his neck tensed visibly. "Ye're safe," he said quietly.

"Ye dinna come to the castle today," Alec said, louder this time. More certain. His hand tensed around the doorframe and his head dropped forward.

Several of Alec's men stood behind him, shifting from foot to foot with unease.

Celia did not turn her focus from them. "I was…detained."

"Is Duncan here?" Alec asked.

She shook her head. "No, why would he be?"

"He's missing." Alec raised his face and turned those pale blue eyes on her. Lines carved across his brow.

"Duncan?" Her chest squeezed a gasp from her lips. "What happened?"

His brows furrowed and he stared at her injured cheek. He straightened and caught her face in his palm. "Who did this to ye?" His thumb brushed just under the scrape. "Was this why ye dinna come?" His voice was as soft as his touch.

It felt so right, so comforting. It made her want to lay her head to his chest and feel the strength of his heartbeat.

Instead, she pulled back from him. Hurt flashed in his eyes before his stare went hard once more.

"We must find Duncan," she said, ignoring his question. She grasped her thick cloak hanging beside the door and swung it over her shoulders.

Alec's jaw tensed. Even if he wouldn't admit it, she knew part of him was scared for Duncan.

"He is much stronger now than he was when he first woke," Celia said softly. "He'll be fine."

She glanced behind Alec before locking her door. There had been no sign of the man who'd chased her since she left the forest near Duart.

She knew she'd be safe with Alec, but that thought left her more uneasy than if she were on her own.

Because she knew he would give his life for hers.

And that would kill her as surely as the hard steel of a blade.

• • •

The sounds of the forest chirped and cooed amid the wet splat of drops against leaves. It was very dark now and they'd been looking for hours.

The muscles along Alec's back ached with tension and his fingers were frozen around the iron loop of a lantern.

He'd thought Duncan would have been found by now.

Alec glanced at Celia for the countless time, confirming her existence.

Something bad had happened to her that afternoon.

His stomach wound in tight, angry knots. Whoever had hurt her would die.

"Stop staring at me, Alec."

He turned his gaze from her and looked out to the dark forest.

The dark, empty forest.

"I'm sure he's in the village," Alec said. "Duncan has a way of talking himself into people's good graces."

"Your men are checking all the homes. If he's there, they'll find him, and if he's here, we'll find him."

He nodded.

They had to find him. He couldn't stand the thought of what would happen if they did not.

They walked in silence, but the longer they walked, the more a weight of dread settled over his shoulders, pressing him into the depths of his own emotion.

Something was wrong.

He could sense it.

Something was wrong and he hoped to God it did not mean the boy was dead.

• • •

A thick layer of sodden leaves squished beneath Celia's shoes and rain ticked and tapped against the surrounding forest. The Duart guards had fanned across the coast by the castle while

Alec stayed with her to search.

She was certain the splitting was not coincidental.

The lantern swung in Alec's hand and cast a golden glow against the wet foliage. Her eyes ached from straining and yet she did not stop.

"He had no dagger with him," Alec said, his gaze boring into a large bush nearby. "If attacked, he'll have no way to defend himself."

The meager light cut deep shadows across his face.

"He won't be attacked," Celia said with a reassurance she wished she could feel. "He'll be fine."

"The outlaws are getting more aggressive."

"He'll be fine," she repeated.

Ruadh wound around a bush in front of them with his long, pointed ears flexed high.

Alec froze and put a hand out to stop her.

"You needn't worry about the fox," Celia said before Alec could do something protective and brutish to the small creature. "He's an old friend of mine."

Alec cast her a strange look, but he did not press her to explain. She'd not told anyone of Ruadh before.

"There's a way to get rid of the outlaws," Alec said unexpectedly, continuing onward. "But there is a price."

"What is the price?"

Alec drew a deep, pained breath. "Something I hold verra dear."

She felt his gaze heavy upon her and he spoke again before she had a chance to comment. "What would ye do?"

"What would I do?" she repeated back to him.

"Aye, to stifle the attacks of the outlaws, ye'd have to give up something ye want verra badly and let yerself have something ye dinna want, something ye know ye'd never want. What would ye do?"

She thought about it for a moment before answering. What did she want badly?

Safety, security, a chance to rest without fear of the future or being haunted by her past.

And she wanted Alec.

She wanted the warmth of his embrace, the love he promised to offer.

Her heart beat a little harder.

Was it her he wanted?

"If it's for the safety of all," she answered, measuring her words carefully, "then I think you already know what you must do."

He grimaced and she knew her words hit their mark.

His gaze dragged over her face, then he turned his head sharply to the side. "I do."

Ruadh bumped her fingers with his cold, wet nose. She glanced down to where he'd appeared at her side, his golden gaze fixed intently on her.

She reached down to scratch his ears, but he scampered away, ducking with his usual skittishness.

A quiet desperation hung on Alec and pressed Celia the longer they trudged through the forest. She understood his conversation for what it was—yes, partially a solution to a greater problem, but also a distraction from the fact that Duncan had been missing for far too long in such bad weather.

If Duncan was outside, he wouldn't be well, not with him still being so frail.

Ruadh's nose bumped her hand once more, this time more insistent. She turned toward him and again he darted away. He folded himself onto the ground and laid his head against his front paws.

Something tingled along the back of Celia's neck.

"Let's go back," she said quickly.

Alec's head snapped up. "Did ye see something?"

"Not me. I think Ruadh did."

The eagerness on his face sagged to skepticism. "Yer fox? I dinna think he's exactly a hunting dog."

She brushed off the comment and made her way back to where Ruadh lay watching her with his indifferent stare. Her pulse throbbed with restrained hope.

He rose to his feet and trotted through the trees.

Celia picked up her pace, following him, winding through the underbrush and ducking beneath random branches. The light of the lantern Alec held followed her. Alec was close behind.

Her breath came faster with the excited thump of her heart.

Ruadh stopped in front of a fallen tree, his head craned forward. The bushes to the left shook and a fat brown squirrel bounded across the forest floor.

Ruadh took off after it in a spatter of wet leaves.

Celia's stomach slid low in her belly.

"A squirrel?" Alec asked beside her. He shook his head, irritation evident in the hard line of his lips.

Celia glanced at the forest around them and saw nothing. No flash of the green tunic Duncan wore, no glimpse of his blond hair.

Nothing.

Disappointment crumpled deep inside her chest.

Alec had already started walking away when she heard a low sound, so quiet it was barely a whisper.

A groan?

Her pulse quickened.

The noise came from a large fallen tree to her right. She lowered herself to the wet ground. Puddled rainwater soaked through her already damp clothing, but she paid it no mind.

She had to see. Just to be certain.

Leaves stuck to her palms and the forest floor felt as if it slid with her as she nudged forward and peered into the hollowed out log.

Something showed pale against the deep shadows within.

Goosebumps rose on her skin.

"Wait," Celia said quickly. "Bring back the light."

The breath she'd taken locked in her chest. She arched her back and peered deeper into the rotted out tree trunk. Her breath released in a slow, painful exhale.

There, highlighted in the soft glow of light, was Duncan. His legs were curled up to his chest and his skin was pale.

Deathly pale.

"Duncan," she whispered.

He did not move.

"Duncan," she said again. Louder this time.

Still he did not move, and her heart fell.

Chapter Seventeen

Alec carried Duncan's limp body back into the bed chamber where the boy had only recently risen.

Celia hovered behind him like an anxious mother. She pulled the blanket down to the bottom of the bed.

"Lay him here." Her voice held a calm authority that told him this was her territory now.

Alec lowered the boy to his bed. A foreign surge swelled in his throat, choking off any attempt to speak.

"You have to move back, please," Celia said in a gentle tone. Her face tilted up toward him. A strand of wet hair was plastered against the curve of her injured cheek. "He's breathing and though his heartbeat is soft, it's steady."

Alec stepped back to give her the room she needed. His arms folded over his chest, but the action did little to ease the ache there.

She pressed a hand to the boy's forehead, then his cheek.

Restlessness seized Alec and he paced the room. "Is there no anything I can do?"

"You can hand me my bag." The musty spice of dried herbs wafted from within. She accepted the pack from him with a quiet note of thanks.

"How long have ye had yer fox?" Alec asked. He needed something, anything, to pull his mind from seeing Duncan so weak again.

Celia lifted a vial of clear liquid from her sack, along with several strips of linen. "Ruadh has followed me around for years now. You've probably seen him around my cottage—the day I returned, in fact. You thought I hesitated to get off the horse for fear of him." She sprinkled several drops over the linen and gently waved the strips back and forth.

An acrid scent pricked the air, like pine, but sharper. "Aye, I remember. I dinna realize ye kept him."

She laid the scented cloth over the sheets across Duncan's chest. "I don't. He comes and goes as he pleases, but he never seems to wander far. I healed his broken leg when he was a cub and I think he's viewed me as a protector ever since."

Her fingers skimmed Duncan's forehead, pushing the hair from his face. Alec followed the slight movement with his stare and found himself wrestling against a stab of jealousy.

"He's going to recover," Celia said with determined force.

He glanced again at the boy, whose chest rose and fell with a slight wheeze.

"He's much healthier than he looks," she said. "I think he found the shelter soon after the rain started and we discovered him before the chill settled too deep."

When Alec didn't answer, she rose to her feet. Her fingertips brushed Alec's jaw. He jerked his gaze to her, startled. Her touch was warm, soft, and so welcome he almost groaned. How he had longed for the invitation to claim what he desired.

Her cheeks reddened as if the realization of what she'd done hit her as well. She started to pull away when he cupped his hand over hers, gently pushing her slender palm to his cheek. His lips brushed the underside of her wrist where her pulse jumped wildly.

"I can't keep coming here." Her gaze went wide and pleading.

He steeled his heart against the inadvertent barb. "Because of me?"

"That's part of it." She slid her hand from his grasp and looked away. "I'm scared to be here."

"Ye're scared of me," he stated. "Because I grabbed ye like I did at yer cottage."

"No," she breathed. "No, I've told you countless times you didn't hurt me and I didn't leave because I was frightened of you, nor because I thought ill of you. It's…" Her eyebrows puckered together. "That's not why. It has nothing to do with that day or that night."

The bruise across her cheek had darkened and covered the jagged scratch. He trailed a finger down her cheek, careful not to touch her injury. She was warm silk under his touch. "Because of this?"

She pulled in a sharp breath and stepped away from him. "That is another part of it."

Her skin branded his fingertips with a burn he welcomed. "Will ye tell me what happened?"

An indecipherable emotion showed bright in her eyes. "I would prefer not to talk about it."

She looked smaller than he'd ever seen her, more frail. The weight of life sat on those slender shoulders, a feeling he knew all too well.

"I've told ye of myself. I've tried to be patient, to make ye understand ye can trust me. I want to know about ye, Celia. Why ye push me away, why ye come close only to run, why ye willna trust me."

He reached toward her, but she flinched away. His veins hummed with aggravation. If only she would let him comfort her, stroke her, love her.

His cock stirred at the thought, but he tamped down the rise of lust in his body. The decision had already been made.

Hers and his.

She would continue a life without him and he would marry Saraid.

"Let's talk in the hall."

Together they strode from the room to where Duncan could not hear them. Still, Alec kept his voice low. "If ye want to be released of yer obligation to come every day, I'll allow it. And if ye…" The words stuck in his throat for a moment. "And if ye wanted to be with another man, I willna intervene."

Her chest flushed bright red and bled up to her cheeks. "Grant was not—"

He lifted a hand to stop her. "I know why he saw ye."

She tilted her head. "He told you why?"

"He needed a little persuasion," Alec confessed.

Celia arched a brow at him and guilt pricked his conscience. "I apologized," he added defensively.

A ghost of a smile whispered across her lips.

He stared at her for a moment, committing her face to his memory, for soon she would be exactly that—a memory.

"Leave the herbs we need," Alec said with as much courage as he could muster. "Wynda can administer them. I canna make ye stay when ye're no wanting to be here."

Her eyes lowered and she nodded. "Thank you," she whispered.

Without looking up at him again, she slung her bag over her back and swept past him. The scent of rosemary hung in the air, leaving him with the memories of what once was and what could never be.

But she'd been right. He had to make his decisions for his people, not himself.

The following morning he would see MacDougall again, this time to agree to the arranged marriage.

Chapter Eighteen

Alec found himself once more standing in the great hall of Aros Castle. Only this time it was not his pride he would sacrifice, but his freedom.

His mouth was as dry as the rushes crunching beneath his feet. From what he remembered of the laird's daughter, she was a comely lass.

Comely and spoiled.

He should be grateful for the opportunity. A wife would provide him with heirs and assume management of the castle keep. Yet every time he tried to imagine MacDougall's black-haired daughter holding a child, all he could see was Celia in her place.

He shoved the thought away. He would not accept marriage to one woman with thoughts of another in his head.

Laird MacDougall strode into the room and nodded at Alec. "Ye've come." They locked forearms and embraced before releasing.

There were lines around the older laird's eyes Alec hadn't noticed before. The guard had said MacDougall appeared upset when he was at Duart.

"Ye spoke to my guard and said ye needed to see me," Alec said.

MacDougall nodded slowly. "Aye, there's something important we must discuss, lad." His expression drew grim. "There is a witch on yer land." His upper lip pulled back in revulsion and he spat a thick glob of spit into the rushes.

Alec raised his eyebrows, unwilling to commit to a response. Whereas MacDougall had possessed composure and power the previous visit, he now appeared disconcerted and anxious.

"A witch," MacDougall muttered, and shot a cursory glance around the empty room before leaning closer. "I saw her myself and chased her until she turned into a bird before my verra eyes and flew away."

Alec stared at the other man's expression, searching for a spark of humor. There was none.

MacDougall's face was serious.

He was serious.

"She turned into a bird and flew away," Alec repeated.

MacDougall's eyes narrowed. "Dinna mock me, lad. Ye dinna understand these whores of Satan." His hand curled into a gnarled fist. "They are vile creatures. Vile." His eyes bulged. "Ye needed to know about the witch so ye could cleanse yer land of them the way I have."

Alec knew all too well of the witch trials MacDougall held, where the jury comprised malicious nobles armed with retractable blades to "prove" the witches did not bleed when stabbed.

Women were dragged from their homes in the dead of night, their children torn from their arms, before they were strangled and burned.

They were horrible deeds, full of hatred and heartlessness. The stories left Alec's stomach roiling with disgust. He hadn't wanted to believe them, but the feat was impossible with those scars of scorched earth.

In his youth, he would have charged against MacDougall, gone head to head in a battle to save the innocent.

Age had sharpened his prudence. Alec knew better. MacDougall's forces were too great to take on and if he tried to kill the laird in his own castle, Alec would forfeit his life.

While patience in light of such ugliness was difficult, he knew he had almost no ground to stand on. His best option was to wait and grow stronger.

Once he was restored to the full potency of his power, he would have the authority to provide the necessary aid. Until then, he was almost as helpless as those women.

"I dinna come to talk about witches," Alec said.

He would not discuss them now, but he would offer to spare a couple of men to assist on MacDougall land, men who could secretly spy and help protect the accused witches.

MacDougall's fingers danced against his palms with agitated madness, his gaze distant. "Ye need my help still or ye wouldna be here." His attention refocused on Alec. "And ye have a witch on yer land. Bring her to me and we will discuss marriage and the aid ye so desperately need."

Alec didn't answer for a moment. He couldn't. Not when all the words on his tongue were naught but sharp and scornful. He balled his hand into a fist and squeezed until the heat of his darkness, his rage, ebbed.

"Who is the witch?" he asked with a calm he did not feel.

MacDougall's lips curled back from his teeth. "Ye'd know her if ye saw her. She's got the devil's own glint in her eyes and a body with enough curves to bring a man to his knees. Aye, she's grown into the perfect catalyst for Satan to bewitch the souls from men. Ye need to punish the whore and send her to the fires of hell."

His hands twisted against one another and the lower lids of his eyes tensed. "They come in many forms—beggars and prostitutes and healers. All. Must. Die."

Alec's blood chilled with the man's vehemence. He knew too well who among his people would be subjected to MacDougall's wrath.

Of Celia, his beautiful Celia who practiced healing with such skill, many whispered of witchcraft.

She had been right.

She was not safe.

• • •

There was a specific method to slipping cloth up a broken nose to ease the flow of blood and not cause further harm. Celia held her breath to steady her hand and delicately slid the wad of linen into the villager's nostrils.

The large, red-haired man watched her with crossed,

bloodshot eyes. His mouth hung open while she worked, bathing her in hot, alcohol-sour breath.

His wife stood beside Celia, ready to offer assistance. Their home was warm from the smoldering peat fire glowing against the hearth. Celia ordinarily did not venture to the village to heal, but the woman had been insistent, her glassy eyes so fearful she could not be refused.

"Have the drops begun to take effect?" Celia asked the man.

His eyes were starting to droop, but she wanted to make certain the valerian root affected him before she began. His nose had been knocked so hard it smeared across the left side of his face.

Resetting it would be extraordinarily painful.

"I dinna think it has," he slurred. "I'll be needing another round."

Celia repressed her sharp comment. The man would get no more lest he poison himself. She positioned her fingers against the top of his nose. He did not jerk back from her touch, evidence the valerian worked despite his claim. She pressed her palms against his face to ensure she remained steady. The man's body tightened.

She didn't ask if he was ready, she didn't prepare him. Men like him didn't do well with forewarning. Instead, she jerked her hands downward and the telltale crackling beneath her fingertips shot chills across her skin.

The man roared like a trapped beast. His fist swung out at her, but she leapt back. The wind of its path skimmed her already bruised cheek.

"Damn that fecking laird to hell, the meddling bastard of a whoreson. I'm going to fecking kill that shite the next time I see him." Blood soaked through the linen and dribbled against his lips.

"Laird MacLean?"

She stared at the man's wife, who watched her husband with a wide, terrified gaze.

"Of course it was him," the man bellowed. "Who else could get a hit like that on me and no already be dead?"

"Sit down so I can clean your nose." Celia's voice shook. Thoughts raced through her mind, thoughts she hated.

Had he started drinking liquor again?

Had he gone to the village and picked a fight as he had with Grant?

"I'll need a cloth, please," she said.

The woman cradled her right arm to her waist and handed the linen with her left hand.

Celia thanked her and dabbed the cloth to the man's nose. Blood seeped into the white fabric, staining it a brilliant red. "When did this happen?" she asked.

"This morning," the woman answered for her husband.

"Aye," the man agreed. "And the bastard is still in town. Do ye no hear him?"

The room fell quiet and the gentle tap, tap, tapping of a hammer echoed in the distance.

Celia's hands trembled while she cleaned the rest of the man's face. His nose still appeared slanted, but looked significantly better than it had upon her arrival. The wife carefully packed up Celia's supplies one-handed and pulled a coin from a jar on the hearth.

"Is something wrong with your arm?" Celia nodded toward the woman's feeble limb. "I can look at it while I'm here."

"Nay," the man growled. "Ye've done yer job, now go."

Celia's cheeks burned with offense. "She's obviously hurt. It won't take but a minute." She looked imploringly at the woman, who averted her eyes and lowered her head.

The man pressed a meaty hand to Celia's back and shoved her from the house.

She staggered out the door and straightened herself upright. The husband would not always be around. She would come back at a later date to look at the wife's arm.

Her heart squeezed with the understanding of what had most likely happened to the woman.

The tapping was louder outside, nearby. Her heart pounded in time with the quick beat.

Celia followed the sound through a maze of cottages until

it was overhead. She shielded the sun from her eyes with the back of her hand and searched the side of the thatched roof.

Her gaze caught Alec's broad back. His leine was slick with sweat despite the freezing temperature and clung to his muscular shoulders. He looked powerful, imposing.

Her pulse flickered wild and erratic, like a flame tangling in a breeze.

"Alec," she called.

The hammering stopped, but he did not turn.

"Ye shouldna be in town, Celia."

His response was not what she'd expected. She frowned. What did he mean by that?

She shifted the weight of her bag to the other shoulder. "I'd like to speak with you."

He didn't answer and she thought he hadn't heard her. Then he rose from his position on the roof's edge with the same ease as if he were on the ground. He leapt from the ledge and landed perfectly on his feet.

His cheeks were flushed red from his labor and sweat glistened where his leine lay open. "What are ye doing in the village?"

"I was called to aid a man with a broken nose," she said. "Any idea how it happened?"

He raised an eyebrow, but did not bother to reply.

"Did you do it?" she asked.

"Aye."

Silence settled between them.

"Aye?" she repeated. "I don't understand why you would do that. Had he—"

"Did ye check the wife's arm while ye were there?" His expression held the same flat, disinterested look.

His question stabbed into the tender ache in Celia's heart.

Alec reached into his pocket and withdrew several coins. "They dinna have much. Go tend to her." He glanced overhead. "I need to fix this before the rain starts again."

Celia stepped back from the money he held out, her cheeks burning. "I'll not take your coin. I intend to see her later, when her husband is gone."

Alec lunged at her suddenly and the coins flew from his hand. His weight hit her like a massive rock and sent them both flying to the sandy ground.

Air punched from her lungs.

Her mind scrambled to understand what was happening when something *thunked* into the wall above them.

She looked up and gravelly sand scraped against the back of her skull with the action. An arrow jutted from the side of the cottage.

Celia stared at it dumbly.

She'd been standing right there.

Right where the sharp head of the arrow had sunk completely into the wood frame of the house.

A scream rang out somewhere in the village and Alec loosed a gruff curse in her ear. He shoved off her and crouched low in front of her, his hand held out to the side in silent indication for her to stay down.

The same scream tore through the air before abruptly cutting short. Celia's stomach curled into a hard ball and her pulse drummed in her ears. She scrambled to her feet and plastered herself to the wall.

Alec pulled his sword from behind his back, slowly, silently, until a blade of opalescent black flashed in the late afternoon sun.

She pulled her own dagger from her waist and curled her fingers around the hilt for protection.

"Round up all the women and children ye can find and seek safety," Alec said without turning from the street.

His ice blue eyes met hers with calm determination. He pulled a dagger from his boot and thrust it toward her, hilt first. "Take this."

His gaze searched hers, probing, intimate, conveying all the words she'd never let him say. He reached out and stroked her cheek. "Be safe." The words—no—the command was hoarse with a passion that raked across her heart.

With that, he slipped from their alcove with his black sword bared and ran toward the sounds of shouts and screams and danger.

She looked down at the blade he'd given her. It was almost a sword compared to her own pathetic knife. She gripped the large hilt in her hands, the handle still warm from where it'd rested against his skin.

The alley contained a small haven, affording her a precious few seconds to assess the situation. Shrieks of fear sounded from the village. One in particular was high-pitched with pain and cut off with such finality, Celia's own breath ceased.

People ran in all directions, some fleeing, some chasing, some bleeding. A large man ran past with a massive sword in his hand. Blood shimmered along the slick metal surface.

Everything in her demanded she slip away and return to her small cottage where it was safe.

But Alec was counting on her.

Save the women and the children.

Yes, she could do this.

For the first time in her life, she would be brave.

• • •

Blood and fear stained the moist air with its metallic odor. The once quiet streets swirled with chaos.

Filthy men in tattered clothing descended upon the villagers, at least thirty by Alec's count. An unfair war against the unarmed innocent.

His body burned with the kind of energy necessary to fight a battle.

"Da!" A high-pitched wail sounded to Alec's left. An outlaw's back faced him, sword lifted with purpose.

Alec charged, his muscles flaring. He balled his fists around the hilt and drove his blade into the man's neck. The outlaw stiffened and gurgled the cry of his death.

He fell gracelessly to the sand and revealed a small boy who stared up at Alec with round eyes. Blood spattered the lad's pale face and his lower lip quivered.

"Get inside and bolt the door, lad," Alec said sharply.

Movement at his right caught his attention. He shoved the boy toward the nearest cottage before spinning to face the attacking outlaw.

Alec lifted his blade, deflecting the blow aimed at his neck. A panicked shout tore through the air. Men from the village had emerged from their homes to fight back, to defend their families.

Alec's chest ached at the horrendous imbalance of what they fought with versus what they were up against. The villager's movements were clumsy with desperation and lack of experience.

Despite their bravery, they were cut down all too easily.

Alec lunged left and waited for his opponent to lift his arms for a kill strike. His opportunity came quickly and he drove the blade into the man's chest. The mortal wound would not warrant additional attention, not when every second could mean the difference between life or another death.

The black blade glistened where it sucked from the man's chest.

A woman's cries shrieked above the sound of battle behind him.

He turned and found an outlaw lying atop a woman whose face was hidden beneath her flipped skirts. Her naked white legs kicked uselessly beneath the man's weight. Alec's vision narrowed and everything inside him exploded with hot white rage.

He didn't remember running across the street, but he did remember the wet smack of his blade clearing through the man's skull. The man fell still and the woman's screams pitched. Alec kicked the body off her and tugged her skirts down before turning toward the village center once more.

His heart slammed in hard, steady beats. There weren't thirty outlaws as he'd suspected. There were more. Maybe fifty or sixty.

Too damn many of them against men trained to be fishermen. There were no warriors in the village, no men to offer protection.

Alec tightened his grasp on the blade and jogged toward a bald outlaw attempting to pry open a cottage door. The fight might not be in his favor, but Alec was determined to see his villagers saved.

He brought his blade down toward the man's chest, but the blow was deflected by a hidden dagger. A stale odor emanated from the man's filthy clothing.

"Ye're going to have to do better than that." The outlaw flashed Alec a grin that displayed a gap where he was missing both front teeth.

His sword whipped toward Alec, but he darted back before the tip could bite into his abdomen.

A flash of white blonde hair showed between the houses a distance away. Alec's steady heartbeat flew into an erratic rhythm.

Celia.

The man grunted and pushed the point of his dagger toward Alec, this time catching the fabric of his leine.

Celia was a distraction that could cost him his life, yet he couldn't turn away.

She glanced right and left, then darted toward the door of a cottage with a string of children and women behind her. Alec kept her in his peripheral vision and doubled his efforts against the outlaw, slashing his weapon with all the force his body would allow.

The last child had scurried through the door when the flash of a red kilt showed from the shadows near Celia.

He shoved his opponent with a force that sent the man to the ground and spared Alec a precious second to see a man charge toward Celia from behind. Her back faced her attacker, oblivious to the danger.

Alec called her name over the cries and screams, but she did not turn.

The outlaw on the ground near Alec scrambled to his feet and tore off in the opposite direction, freeing Alec to go to Celia.

His heart swelled in his chest with hammering fear. Reaching her would be impossible, but damn it, he would try.

Her attacker's arm pulled back, his sword lifting over her back. She swept into the door without turning and slammed it closed with an audible smack.

Another sword flashed out from the shadows with lethal speed, disconnecting the outlaw's head from his body with enough force to send it rolling.

A man stepped into the light, as tall as Alec, with dark blond hair. His green eyes tugged at Alec's memory with their familiar glint.

Niall. The man his father once held as his prized warrior so long ago.

He glared at Alec for a moment before shoving past him and running toward an outlaw on the opposite side of the street.

A rough call sounded from deep in Niall's throat and over a dozen men appeared from the alleys, their massive claymores brandished for battle.

They were older than Alec remembered, yet he could recall every one of their faces, every one of their names and those of their families.

Alec sucked in a deep, cleansing breath of air, breathing with relief for the first time.

These were his father's men, the ones he'd been searching for, the ones who'd been missing.

The ones who could save him.

After months of searching, he'd found his father's army.

Chapter Nineteen

Celia pushed her back against the door and dug into the worn wooden floor with her heels. A narrow slit of light penetrated the darkness of the cottage. Mothers cradled their children to their breasts and older children aided the younger ones whose mothers were not there. Soft cries whimpered through the small space despite the constant shushing.

Celia gritted her teeth and pressed against the door with every ounce of strength she could muster. If the man who chased her shoved hard enough, the meager barrier would splinter apart.

She tightened her grip on Alec's dagger, borrowing the strength of a warrior.

The rattling slam from the other side did not come. Not so much as a knock. Still she did not move.

"It's fine," Celia whispered to the children, and cast them a reassuring smile. "We'll be fine."

"Help me." A woman's strained voice sounded from outside the cottage.

Celia squeezed her eyes shut in an attempt to block out the pleas. She could not leave the door open. She could not leave the children exposed.

"Help me, please." The woman was sobbing now. A low, keening cry. "My baby…"

Celia opened her eyes and the room blurred despite her resolve.

"Moira," she called to the eldest girl with bright red hair. "Go to the window and see if there is anyone outside. Mind you, stay far enough back."

The girl nodded bravely and shoved her hair from her brow before tiptoeing toward the window, her little back stiff. Light splashed across her face and brightened the blue of her eyes. "There's a lass on the ground." The thin muscles along her neck tightened. "She's bleeding verra badly."

"Are there any men?" Celia asked through gritted teeth.

Moira shook her head and the wave of unruly hair swept into her eyes. "I dinna see any." She turned her attention to Celia and shoved her tresses away again. "Ye're no going to leave her there, are ye?"

"Please…" the woman's voice cried once more. "Please help me."

Everything in Celia told her to stay where she was, to guard the children, to protect herself. She thought back to Alec, to the way he'd selflessly thrown himself into battle.

He was brave.

Rounding up the children had not been brave. It'd been easier than she thought it might be.

Rescuing the woman outside. Putting herself at risk to do so was brave.

Celia eased her heels from where they dug into the floor and the blood tingled back into the soles of her feet. "Of course I'm not going to leave her."

"Take this." She extended Alec's dagger toward a sturdy woman who sat beside her. Alec's blade would be more effective than her own weapon. "Stand to the side of the door and if anyone but me comes through here, you stab them as hard and as many times as you can."

The woman passed her small child to Moira and rose from the ground. Her eyes were wide with fear and the blade trembled in her hand, but she stood where Celia indicated.

The women and their children bunched toward the back of the small cottage and Celia slid the door open.

Moira had been correct. No man stood in front of the door, save the body of the one who'd pursued her. His head lay several feet from his body.

Her stomach lurched into her throat.

"My baby," the woman whimpered. She sobbed beneath a veil of brown hair and reached for Celia, her fingers smeared with blood. "Please, help my baby." Her other hand clutched her abdomen where a bright red stain showed against the off-white homespun gown.

This time Celia did not hesitate. She darted into the street. Her feet slid in the blood-soaked sand, but she did not allow it to slow her.

Nothing would thwart her purpose.

She tangled her fingers in the woman's dress at the shoulders and threw her weight back, dragging the woman toward the cottage.

Celia's eyes scanned the streets with restless fear. Everything in her was on alert, noting every color, every howl of the wind, every terrifying scent in the air.

Lifeless bodies lay everywhere and blood stained the walls and ground.

At last, she reached the rough cottage and gave a quick knock. The door swung open and the mother tensed in her position by the door.

Celia gave one final heave with a strength she never thought possible and threw both herself and the bleeding woman into the cottage. Into safety.

Moira ran forward and slammed the door shut and the mother slipped the bolt into place with a bang.

Celia directed her full attention to the woman in the blood-smeared dress. She pushed the woman's hair back from her face and the breath pulled from her lungs.

Bessie stared sightless with pupils too large for her glassy brown eyes. Her colorless lips worked in a whispered plea, a mindless chant repeated over and over again. "Save my baby, save my baby…"

• • •

Alec's body moved in steady rhythms, ducking and driving against his opponents, forcing them back with the push of additional manpower at his side.

His father's men might have been disbanded for some years, but their skill had not diminished with time. If anything, it had improved.

Only a handful of outlaws remained. Their defensive maneuvers had gone slow and sluggish with exhaustion.

A shout rose up from the back and they scattered into the forest. Alec charged after them, accompanied by the heavy footfalls of his father's men, and arrived in time to see the outlaws scamper onto the backs of several waiting horses before riding off in a thunderous pounding of hooves.

Four additional horses remained, riderless. The beasts stared indifferently at Alec and his father's men. Even if all the outlaws had lived, most would be without a steed for their escape.

Alec gripped the reins of the first horse and swung up onto its back. The animal flinched beneath his weight. The horse was not trained for war.

"We can catch them if we hurry," he said to his father's band of warriors.

Niall folded his arms over his chest. "Why would we leave the women and children unprotected to follow the son of the arse who cursed us?"

The other men all stared at Alec.

Irritation snapped all his patience.

"Because ye've abandoned them for months. They've protected ye while ye hid away and they've died for it." The horse pranced anxiously beneath him, feeding from the anger firing through his veins. "I've looked for months for ye to help me defend them. Ye used to be men of honor, conviction, and integrity. But now…" He met Niall's stabbing glare without flinching. "Now I see aging men so stung by pride and plagued by stupidity they canna aid the verra people who have helped them."

He held Niall's stare until the older warrior slid his gaze away. Alec caught the reins of his borrowed horse. "I dinna want the help of men who lack honor and I'll no waste my time with ye while the outlaws escape."

It was a stupid plan, but he hoped it was simple enough to work.

Alec pulled the reins to the side, turning the horse before he flicked his heels into her plump sides and sent her galloping over the rolling hills of the coast in pursuit of the outlaws.

With the number of outlaws already killed, Alec stood a chance to handle the rest on his own.

Maybe. With a little luck.

The steady beat of a horse's gallop pounded behind Alec's own steed. A quick glance over his shoulder confirmed Niall was racing closer, the other men not much farther behind him.

Alec grinned to himself.

He would not need luck on his side after all, not when he had the force of his father's men.

• • •

Celia knelt beside Bessie's makeshift bed and held the woman's hand. Her palm was cold to the touch and slick with sweat and blood.

"Have you felt the babe move?" Celia asked.

Bessie's eyes watched the ceiling without blinking. A tear slipped from the corner of her eye and melted against her hairline.

She didn't speak, which was answer enough. The bleeding had long since stopped and Celia had done as much as she could to calm Bessie. Fear of losing her baby would only increase the chances that she might.

The battle had ended shortly after Celia had dragged Bessie indoors. For that, she'd been grateful. She had clean water for Bessie and the woman was in a comfortable bed.

Many other villagers had been injured in the attack and she'd aided them all as well as she could with the provisions she had.

Some had been too far gone in their injuries to be saved. Celia had fought regardless, but in some of her battles against death, she'd lost.

She hovered a hand over Bessie's swollen abdomen. "May I?" she asked.

Bessie's shoulder lifted in apathetic permission.

Celia pressed gently on the firm rise of flesh, her focus trained on her fingertips for the slightest movement.

Her heart squeezed with painful sympathy. Nothing.

"He's dead," Bessie said in a flat tone. "The only thing I have left of my Connor." Her face crumpled and hearty sobs wracked her too-slender body.

Celia blocked out the low keens of Bessie's mourning and concentrated on her fingers, hoping with every fiber of her being the child had indeed survived.

She focused her energy on the woman's stomach and leaned closer, as if wishing with all her might could make such a thing truly happen.

Celia moved her hands over the little mound of Bessie's stomach. She followed the shape of the babe through Bessie's skin, a feat easily done with so little fat on its mother.

"Move," she whispered in a quiet voice. "I want you to move."

The taut skin of Bessie's stomach bounced against Celia's thumb. Bessie's sobs ceased with a choked gasp and she stared down at her belly with tears glinting against spiked lashes.

Celia's body tensed with hope. She rubbed her hand across the woman's distended stomach and a heartier bump nudged her palm.

Excitement sparked across Celia's skin and blotted out all vestiges of sorrow.

The baby's survival marked a beautiful display of life in a day scarred by death.

Bessie stared up at Celia with large eyes set in her narrow face. "Ye brought my baby back to life."

"No." Celia shook her head vigorously and stepped back. "He was resting and the pressure of my hands woke him from his slumber."

She glanced around her and found several wounded villagers staring up at her, their faces mirroring Bessie's shock.

"I heard ye command him to move and he did," Bessie said in wonder. She wrapped her thin arms around her stomach.

Celia opened her mouth to protest.

"I heard it too," said a woman beside Bessie's bed, the wife of the man with the broken nose. She did in fact have a broken arm, which was now bandaged and propped across her body with a sling. Her gaze fixed on Celia with reverence. "Ye gave life to the dead."

An old man nodded his head in rapid succession. "I saw it with me own eyes, the way ye looked at her belly when ye spoke, the way yer hands moved over it."

Fear prickled the hair on her scalp. "No," Celia whispered. "You saw wrong. I'm not...her child was not dead, only sleeping."

Her heart smacked against her ribs.

Her knees softened and the room went stuffy with thick air.

Would they take her to MacDougall land where the bodies of witches tainted the sky with oily black smoke? Would the man with the red ring be there, waiting to give her the same grisly fate as Fiona?

"Ye saved my baby," Bessie whispered in a shaky breath. "Ye risked yer life to pull me to safety and ye protected the only thing I have to live for."

Celia eased back to sit on the edge of the bed lest her legs collapse. "I'm not a witch." Her voice strained with her passionate vehemence.

"I dinna care what ye are." A woman with bright red hair spoke up from across the room. Her arm was locked around little Moira's shoulders. "Ye work miracles and ye saved no only our children, but those wounded in the attack." Her head lowered in gratitude. "Thank ye."

Words of appreciation murmured around the room. The woman with the freshly bandaged arm nodded at Celia, a shy smile on her lips.

Celia regarded them in silence, the shock at their gratitude holding her tongue in place. Their kind smiles and genuine appreciation peeled back the blanket of her paranoia.

But she did not deserve their praise. She was no brave

warrior, no magical healer. She had only done what Alec had asked of her.

The door flung open and a man rushed in. "The warriors have returned."

Celia leapt to her feet in a pop of anticipation.

Alec.

Had he returned with the men?

Her heart pressed so hard against her lungs her breath came in short, enthusiastic breaths.

Several women rushed toward the door and shouts of enthusiasm drifted into the crowded cottage.

Celia turned to Bessie and tried to shrug off the restless urge to run into the streets with the other women. "Sleep now. You'll need a lot of rest and you'll need to eat more."

Bessie's fingertips brushed over her stained dress and a wistful smile touched her lips as she nodded.

Celia wound through the makeshift bedding of the injured and made her way to the door.

Her body shook with expectation.

She'd thought of Alec the whole time she'd been inside. Not doing so was impossible.

What if someone came up behind him and attacked when he didn't expect it? What if he was injured somewhere and no one had found him yet?

What if...

Celia closed her eyes against the thought, as if she could shut it out.

What if he was dead?

She pushed the door open, afraid of what she might not see. Alec.

The chill of the night air bathed her heated cheeks and swept away the odor of blood. At first the contrast of going from the candlelight inside to the cloudy moonlit night outside left her momentarily blinded.

Her gaze searched in front of her before she could fully see. So many faces.

Warrior's faces.

The villagers had said the old laird's army had finally returned. For too long they had hidden from the abusive laird after years of poor treatment and heinous commands. The people saw them as brave.

But Celia saw how the people suffered, and to her, those warriors were cowards.

Her gaze swept restlessly over the shadowed faces and frustration ripped through her. She shifted around the reunited couples, her search suddenly frantic. Her heart beat in her chest like a trapped bird.

"Is Laird MacLean here?" she asked the man nearest her.

The man did not respond at first and then, to Celia's great horror, he lowered his eyes. "I havena seen him."

She staggered back under the weight of the nightmare that might be real.

Alec might truly be dead.

Chapter Twenty

Alec stood beside Niall against the fierce coastal winds. Both men stared out at the landscape of low shrubs and muddy, grass-covered hills. Some of the outlaws had been slain, but some had managed to escape.

The others searched, yet they stayed behind to watch the open area.

To wait for an outlaw trying to flee.

Perhaps if Niall and his men had not paused when the outlaws ran, all would have been captured or killed.

Niall folded his arms across his chest. "Now what happens?"

Alec set his jaw. "We find these men."

"I dinna mean that," Niall said. "I meant to me and the other soldiers."

Alec kept his gaze on the open field before them, seeking out the return of Niall's men who'd been sent ahead to search for the missing outlaws. "Ye think I'd have ye punished?"

He glanced at the fierce older man.

Niall's time in hiding had left his appearance feral. His jaw was grizzled with scraggly gray whiskers and his blond-and-white hair snarled into dull knots.

"Ye think I'd have ye punished for what?" Alec demanded. "For no coming to the castle when ye were needed? For abandoning the verra villagers who kept yer hiding a secret? For all the raids before today where ye did nothing but hide while they were left unarmed and slaughtered?"

Niall's eyes glittered in the darkness. "Ye dinna understand."

Fire burned through Alec and set his muscles ablaze with the urge to knock the other man on his arse. "Aye, I do understand. My da drove ye out and threatened yer lives—then after he died, I came home. Ye thought I'd make good on his threats, so ye ran. Am I wrong?"

Niall's thick body flinched with tension. "It wasna like that."

"Then how was it?" Alec's words grated harsh in his throat. "How was it so awful ye left the innocent to die?"

Niall continued to stare into the distance.

"I asked ye a question," Alec said. "No as laird, but as witness to the horrors of yer failure."

"Aye," Niall growled. "We thought ye'd be like him and so we hid. He used us for cruel deeds, things we'll no ever find forgiveness for."

"That's why ye hid?" Alec said, his gaze once more on the moonlit horizon where no men appeared. "Even when ye knew yer people were being murdered?"

The fight slipped from Niall's face the same way the light faded from the eyes of the dying. "We were too far from the village. We dinna know until too late and then we came. We dinna know…" Niall's voice trailed off.

"Ye know now." Alec shot him a hard look in the darkness. "They need ye. Stay with me and fight for them. I'll pay ye well and I will promise to never make ye do something ye dinna like."

Movement showed against the horizon and several of Niall's men appeared in the distance.

"Aye." Niall gave a firm nod. "We'll fight with ye and we'll protect the people. Now let's see if they've had any success so we can get the hell home. I've no slept in a real bed for far too long."

Alec leapt onto his horse in response. Niall followed suit and together the two rode toward the men emerging, empty-handed, from the woods.

His father's men had been found, yet the knot in Alec's gut did not ease. Niall had claimed the men had not known of the attacks, yet how could they not?

Surely they'd had some contact with the villagers unless they were hiding on the other side of Scotland.

He'd seen the guilt shine in the other man's eyes as sure as stars shone in the sky above.

Niall and his men had known about the village attacks.

They'd known and they'd stayed hidden.

Alec rode forward in silence, accepting the heavy burden of realization.

The men he'd sought to save him, his father's former soldiers, were all broken.

They even looked broken when Alec approached them.

Their shoulders were slumped, their faces lined and weary.

True, it'd been ten years since he'd seen them last, but some had been very young when he left.

They all appeared old and weathered now.

"We found one," said one of the younger ones. His dark hair shadowed his face in the moonlight, but Alec still recognized him by the jut of his massive nose. Lachlan.

Alec looked between the returning soldiers for the captured outlaw. Finding none, he turned his gaze to Lachlan once more.

Lachlan rubbed his neck and shifted with obvious unease. "We had him to question and then he, uh, he escaped."

"Escaped?" Niall asked in a flat tone.

"Well, he escaped, but he dinna get away. We killed him."

Alec pressed his lips together in an attempt to seal in his frustration. Yes, they were supposed to kill the outlaws, but they were supposed to question them first, to find out where they lived, to gain information on how to destroy them.

"So, we've learned nothing," Alec said finally. His voice sounded as heavy and tired as he felt.

Lachlan straightened. "We got him to say one thing before he ran."

Alec arched his eyebrow for the man to continue.

Whether the other man could see the gesture in the dark or not, he did continue. "Aye, he said they were told there'd be a bag of gold to the man who caught a witch."

• • •

Celia jerked from her restless slumber and listened to the stillness of her cottage. No sounds emerged save the soft hiss of the burning embers in the hearth. The meager moonlight from her slatted shutters revealed nothing in the shadows.

Yet her pulse throbbed in short, staccato beats and the air snapped around her with unseen energy.

She closed her eyes and the dream fogged thick in her mind.

A blanket of gauzy mist rolled out across the forest floor, lit a brilliant, glowing white in the full moon. Everything held an unnatural still, the air too balmy for the heart of winter.

Thundering horse hoofs echoed off the surrounding trees and the sedentary mist stirred, shifting with anticipation before breaking apart into graceful curls. Blackness flashed through the trees, fast and determined. It raced toward her, but she was not afraid.

Her eyes flew open and she threw the coverlet from her body. Her breathing quickened. Her muscles fired with the burn of agitation.

Alec.

She could lie in bed no longer.

He'd not returned by the time she left the castle.

The press of time weighed heavy on her shoulders. Her feet hit the cool ground and she crossed the room quickly.

In a run.

She had to get outside, to see if the mist was there, to see if the chilled air had warmed.

To see if her dream was real.

She yanked the door open to a gentle breeze. A balmy breeze.

Her heart lurched into a frenzied beat.

Mist clung to the darkened forest.

And stirred.

Hoof beats sounded in the distance, rushing to her with incredible speed.

She sprinted across the yard, heedless of the wet, cold grass stabbing at the soles of her bare feet. The mist parted in wispy strands and the ground trembled against the great steed flying toward her.

The horse smashed through the veil of haze and sent

tendrils of mist scattering in whirls around it and its rider. Steam fogged around the beast's nose in great white puffs. Its speed increased and Celia caught the musty scent of its sweat on the wind.

She watched it without fear, without moving. The rider remained hidden in the shadows, yet she knew him by the familiar way her body ached.

The horse stopped several feet before her. His hoofs slashed into the tender moonlit grass and the rich scent of turned earth filled the air.

The rider slid from his steed and stalked toward her, shoulders squared with determination.

"Celia." Alec's voice was thick. Beautiful.

His arms went around her, pulling her with desperate hunger against the hard strength of his body. She did not fight his touch, not when she had thought she'd never have this again.

Not when she'd thought she'd lost him.

Not when everything in her cried out for this.

Her fingers threaded around the back of his neck where his braid hung like a thick rope. His skin was warm, firm, and very, very real. She clutched herself to him.

This was no dream.

He caught her face in his hands and stared down at her. Shadows consumed most of him, but she could make out the glint of his eyes, the line of his lips.

"I shouldna be here," he rasped. "But I canna stay away."

She wanted to draw him closer to her, impossibly close so every part of him touched every part of her.

"I want you here." Her voice strained with passion.

His hand slipped behind her head and held her firmly. He lowered his face to hers so the warmth of his breath teased her lips.

"Ye want me?" He said it with ragged, broken hope.

She wanted to tell him she'd feared to never see him again, that she'd wept until she fell asleep, that she'd regretted her ridiculous request for him not to touch her.

But instead of saying any of that, she merely nodded.

It was enough.

His mouth came down hard on hers. His lips were cold from his ride and his jaw prickled with unshaven whiskers.

Never had anything been so delicious.

His hands slid down her back and clutched her to him. She wanted to let herself melt into his kiss and tangle her tongue with the one gently teasing her lower lip.

He gave a low murmured groan.

His tongue ran along the seam of her mouth and she opened her lips, eager for the heady, delicious stroke.

A low growling groan rumbled deep in his chest, a ravenous, primitive sound that gave her an exciting prickle of goosebumps.

His body was impossibly hard against her, solid and so wonderfully real. Her fingers ran restless down his back, sampling and reveling all at once.

His tongue swept against hers, hot and starved and full of a promise that made her legs stop working.

Everything about him was hard and cold, save the soft heat of his mouth.

A gust of wind swept against them and sent the leaves of the forest stirring, though she barely registered either.

"I'm so sorry," she said between frantic kisses. "For staying away from you." Her mouth brushed over his. "For acting as though I didn't want you," she murmured against his lips. "When I did."

He caught her face in one hand, the rough pad of his thumb pressed to the center of her heated lips. "I know." His gaze drifted to her mouth and he swallowed.

Celia's breath caught against the quickened beat of her heart. "I want you," she said. "I want this."

His thumb slid down her chin and dragged her bottom lip lower, parting her mouth. "I know."

The warmth of his mouth enveloped hers and his tongue grazed hers, seizing her in a kiss from which she never wanted to escape.

A thrill of desire charged across her skin and throbbed with delicious heat between her legs.

All the fears fled her mind. Nothing would get in the way of her desires. Not this night.

• • •

Alec pressed Celia closer into him so the length of her soft curves stretched against his body. Her tongue swept over his, just as eager, just as hungry.

Lust fired through him and left his cock straining.

He slid a hand up her back, along the crude fabric of her white night rail to the swell of her breast. Her moan vibrated against his tongue.

She was firm beneath his touch, her nipple hard with evidence of her desire.

For him.

Finally.

He tugged the ribbon of her night rail and freed her breast from the ungainly fabric. She was silk beneath his hands, a beautiful, inviting contrast to the coarse, shapeless dress.

Her sharp gasp sounded in the night air and lured him toward what they both wanted, needed. He locked his hand around her slender waist and swept her legs from beneath her.

Wind pushed against his back, propelling him toward the cottage where the door stood open. The golden light of a fire glowed within and the smoky scent of peat tangled with the sweet rosemary of Celia's hair.

Her mouth trailed across his neck as he carried her, as if she could not stop tasting him in the same way he hadn't wanted to stop tasting her.

But, damn it, he wanted her in that cottage right now more than he'd ever wanted anything in his life.

He crossed the threshold and kicked the door closed. There was a brief pause, a moment of realization of unspoken anticipation passing between them.

The sleeve of her night rail slipped from her shoulder, baring the milky glow of her skin and the gentle curve along the side of her breast.

In one flush movement, he lowered her feet to the floor and pressed her body to the door with his own. A moan sweetened her gasp of surprise, a delectable cry he caught with his lips, his tongue.

She rose up on her toes to meet his kiss, her readiness only serving to further ignite his lust.

He brushed his hands over her shoulders and swept aside useless fabric as he did so. The night rail slipped from her body with an alluring whisper, leaving her bared for his exploration.

He stared down at her, noting every swell of flesh, from the tautness of her nipples where they rose and fell with her excited breath to the flare of her hips cradling the tight heat he sought.

Perfect.

Just as he'd remembered.

And she was his.

He pressed his body to her, eager for the heat of her against him. His cock pulsed an encouraging throb through his core and his fingertips trailed down her body to her breasts.

Her skin rose in goosebumps beneath his touch and her breath came faster.

She gripped his shirt in her fist and drew the hem upward. Alec tugged the fabric over his head, impatient to have the press of her soft, warm flesh against him.

Her body arched toward him and ground against the source of his arousal. The pressure was an agonizing, euphoric reminder of how badly he wanted her.

His tongue dipped into her mouth once more and his hand moved down between their bodies, past the triangle of curling blonde hair to the cleft of her legs.

"Alec," she whimpered without pulling from his lips. Her legs trembled beneath his fingertips, but he didn't stop.

He slipped between her slick folds until his finger dipped into her tight, wet heat.

Her eyes fluttered closed and a soft whimper sounded from her mouth. He curled his finger inside her, touching her where he knew she needed.

Her nails dug into his back and she writhed against his hand.

The delicate scent of her arousal greeted him and his blood roiled with molten desire. One simple push of his plaid from his cock and he would have her.

He groaned at the very thought and rubbed the swollen nub of her sex with this thumb. She leaned her head against the door and cried out, her breath hot against his chest.

He nuzzled the curve of her neck, encouraging her throaty moans in a tormenting tease, not only to her but to his own raging heat.

Her body arched against him with each stroke, closer, more eager.

She caressed his stomach and his body tightened. Her fingers danced lower and the belt at his waist popped free.

It clattered to the floor and the heavy fabric of his kilt slipped from his waist.

She pressed against him then, every inch of her silken body stretched against every inch of him. Including the very hungry, very aching inches of him straining with desperate want.

He was on fire in a way that ached. A tight groan sounded between their lips, a sound he only knew as his by the vibration in his own throat.

She slid a long, slender leg up the side of his rigid body, opening her warmth to him. Her hips arched forward until she brushed the head of his cock.

A tease.

An invitation.

Alec pressed his palms against the cool door and rested his forehead against hers. The sweet scent of her breath brushed his mouth and she flicked her tongue across his lower lip.

"I dinna want ye to regret this, Celia."

She rolled her body, pushing him more firmly against the moist edge of her sex, so he rested just at her entrance.

He thought he'd explode then. The blood pounded in his ears and he almost didn't hear her reply.

"I won't." Her voice was husky with the promise of passion. "Alec…" She undulated against him with a longing frustration he knew all too well.

And he would no longer deny himself.

He caught her lifted leg in his hand and thrust inside her tight heat.

• • •

Celia gasped a deep lungful of air, as if this were the first time in four months she'd truly breathed. Alec's fullness swelled within her and shot tingles of pleasure through every part of her body. The hair on her arms rose and her nipples drew taut.

He drew out and thrust deliciously back inside her. Restrained.

His muscles were so tight beneath her fingers he felt like stone.

Still holding a hand to her leg, he leaned her back against the cool door.

The movement caused him to shift and the hardness of him inside her touched a new, deeper place. She cried out in unexpected pleasure.

"Yes," she whispered hoarsely.

He pressed the full weight of his body to hers, pushing her further against the door, and pumped the full length of him inside her.

His slick skin rubbed across hers with each body-clenching thrust.

Heat and pleasure spiraled around her and danced electric notes across her skin. Every part of her sizzled. Every part of her was on fire.

Alec's beautiful stomach flexed in the firelight with the increase of his pace.

The powerful muscles of his chest and back bunched beneath her hands. Their breath came in hard beats as one. His eyes met hers, no longer an ice blue but warm and clear like an endless summer sky.

And she was losing herself in them.

Something flickered inside her, something jarring and unwanted.

Fear.

This was no simple coupling. There was too much intimacy in the way his arms cradled her, the way they shared the air and watched bliss play across one another's faces.

He quickened his pace with a low groan, as if feeling her disconnect.

Celia closed her eyes to the emotion and leaned her head back, reveling in the pull and thrust of his hard cock.

His hand caught her face in a gentle, firm grip. The heady scent of her arousal on his fingers sent a fresh wave of heart-pounding pleasure coiling through her.

"Damn it, Celia. Open yer eyes."

She gritted her teeth against the command and increased the desperate arch of her hips.

Alec growled and his steady thrust slowed.

"Open yer eyes," he said more gently. "Look at me." He nuzzled his lips to her ear. "Trust me," he breathed.

Her eyes blinked open and found his hot blue gaze fixed on her. His thumb swept her lower lip where he held her jaw. His body strained as he thrust forward, his face soft with pleasure.

A warmth in Celia's belly mingled with the swirl of bliss flowing hot in her veins.

She watched his face with each flex of his hips, the way his brow creased with concentrated pleasure, the way his lips relaxed around his breathing, the way his eyes devoured her own excitement.

He pressed her more firmly to the door, caught her standing leg in his hand and lifted it too.

For one dizzying moment she thought she might fall, but then he pushed inside her again and her legs wrapped around his waist.

His hands cradled her bottom and he thrust, hitting a different spot yet again.

Spots of pleasure danced in her vision.

He groaned and his hands tightened where they clamped against her bottom. His movement increased, faster, harder, more desperate.

Her sex tightened around him with the threat of surrender to him.

Alec plunged faster, stoking her body with the promise of explosive euphoria. "Come with me, Celia."

The heat of Alec's gaze said everything she longed for, but never let herself taste.

She was cherished.

She belonged.

She relinquished herself to the grasp of desire and longing and everything else she ever resisted.

He pumped in short, jerky thrusts and swelled against the clenching of her pleasure. His groan coupled with her cry and their bodies tightened together beneath the embrace of shared release.

Stars spun around Celia and flames of passion licked across her flesh, but never once did she tear her gaze from Alec's.

When their breath calmed and the vestiges of pleasure had waned, he still gazed down at her with an open tenderness that stroked a secret flame of longing within her.

Chapter Twenty-One

Alec trailed the tip of his middle finger down Celia's shoulder. Light from early dawn played across her skin, brilliant gold against smooth cream.

Her moan was languid, as was the way she nudged the curve of her bottom against his well-used cock. The night had been spent making up for the months of separation.

He should be tired.

His lips brushed the sensitive spot just below her ear and his body stirred with renewed vigor.

He slid his fingers through the strands of her hair and marveled at how it separated between his fingers like a silken waterfall.

She'd laid open several layers of softness he'd never seen before.

And he wanted more.

"I wish I could see through to yer thoughts," he said quietly.

She glanced at him over her shoulder. "What of my thoughts do you want to know?"

He let her hair fall through his hands and sift down to the curve of her naked back. There were so many things he wanted to say. He wanted to know why she never spoke of her past, why she was so guarded, why she had run before.

"Why did ye no want me before last night?" It wasn't the most pressing of his questions, but it was the one that emerged from his mouth.

She turned her head from him and stayed that way, just long enough to make him curse his own stupidity before she rolled over to face him. "I thought you were dead."

Her lashes swept down, concealing a flash of vibrant emotion he wished she'd let him witness. "I thought I'd never see you again."

"And before ye thought I was dead?"

A slow smile spread on her lips with the same glorious ease as the sun rises. "You're trying to get me to say I wanted you before."

He couldn't help his own smile. "Aye."

"Because you want to know I wanted you as badly as you wanted me."

"Aye."

"And you want me to sing your praises to make up for all the time we missed together."

"Well, it wouldna hurt."

She studied him a moment longer and her smile faded into a look of seriousness. "When I first met you, I thought you were arrogant and stubborn."

"I am arrogant and stubborn."

The skin around her eyes tightened, as if she should actually see what was there. As if she could see all the things he kept locked away.

She wanted to know him more too, he realized.

But he would not shy from it.

Not with Celia.

"Aye," she agreed slowly. "You are. But you're also so much more. The more I learn about you, the more there is to like, to admire. When we first met, I thought you were going to be just like your father."

Something cold and ugly spiked Alec deep in the gut.

Her eyes widened. "I'm sorry, I know you fear you're like him, but truly, I don't think you are."

"But Celia…" He stopped. He'd never told anyone about the darkness before. It was foolish to do so. He'd only just reclaimed Celia.

Confessing to her might make him lose her forever. After all, she'd run away after his last admission.

Heaviness pressed upon him.

She must know. He had to trust her to earn her trust.

He steeled himself against his own words when he spoke. "I am like him."

Her gaze stayed watchful.

Trusting.

He'd never discussed the darkness, never admitted the tendencies pulling against every fiber of his morality.

Perhaps if she first understood.

He pulled her closer to him so her head lay against his chest, so he could not watch her face.

He didn't want to see what might show in her eyes. Shock or fear—or worse, pity.

His stomach drew tight with unaccustomed nerves. "My father had always taken to whisky for as long as I can remember, and it made him verra angry."

Alec stroked her hair and focused on the way the cool strands slipped between his fingers. "He was cruel to everyone, but my mother received the worst of it, as ye know." He swallowed away the threat of his rising past. "And I hated him for it. I hated it so much it became like a living thing inside me, a growing darkness. It burned and swelled inside me until I couldn't control it and hit him back."

Memories of the day rushed up on him, the metallic odor of his father's blood mingling with the stink of stale whisky.

"I dinna stop hitting him. I couldna make myself stop until my mother's hands covered my fists and I stopped. My father lay broken and pathetic on the floor."

Rage balled inside him with a white-hot burn, as intense as it'd been in his youth. "He dinna strike me again and I slept in front of my mother's door to ensure he didn't attempt to harm her either. But even though I defeated him, even though I won, that darkness never went away."

The anger melted like molten metal, bathing his heart in the weight of loss. "My mother succumbed to sickness later and died quickly, like she dinna have the will to fight. After she died, I left. It wasna my father I tried to flee." He stopped, hating the words he was saying. "It was the darkness. The ugly side of me stemming from him, the part of me raging anger or demanding recompense for wrongs."

He closed his eyes against the shame of what he confessed. "I dinna realize my absence left everyone subjected to his wrath." His hand curled into a fist against the sheet. "I dinna think about the people who needed protection."

Celia sat up with a sheet tucked around her torso. Her eyes were soft when they met his, but held no pity. "After all the years you sacrificed to protect your mother, you are anything but selfish."

"No," he said sharply. "Ye make me sound chivalrous. But a chivalrous man wouldna have left his people. He wouldna have the weakness of his father where one drink leads to ten and the world flies out of control."

The rising sun now filled the room in a brilliant light, a harsh contrast to the darkness of his memories. "That night I grabbed yer arm, I felt him in the darkness inside of me. That ugly, inescapable part of him. All those years I ran only to find out it was a waste."

Celia gave him a pointed stare. "You asked me to trust you last night." Her cheeks stained bright red. "Do you remember?"

Of course he did. His body had been so hot, so hungry, and the way she'd pulled away maddened him. He wanted to be more to her than where she found her pleasure.

She slipped her hand in his. "And I did trust you. I still do. You are a strong man, Alec. You have convictions your father never possessed and you fight for the right reasons."

Her face tilted up toward him so sunshine played across her fair skin and her pupils shrank back into pinpricks of black in her midnight blue eyes. "Would you ever hurt me?"

He stared down at her open expression, all the trust he had asked for shining bright before him. "I would never hurt ye." He traced the delicate bruise on her cheek. It had begun to heal and reflected a deep yellow. "But would easily kill any man who did."

"I believe you," she whispered.

"Tell me who did this to ye." His blood simmered to know who would cause a woman so delicate as Celia such pain.

Something shadowed her eyes and she looked away.

Her look confirmed his suspicions. She was no longer safe. The outlaw's confession prior to his death had proven such. A coil of unease tightened along his back. He'd been with her through the night, but could not always protect her thus, not when he was needed at Duart.

Alec swept his mouth against her jaw. "Ye dinna have to tell me." He traced her lower lip with his tongue. "But do me one favor, aye?"

She closed her eyes and her lips parted with sweet enticement.

"Come to Duart Castle with me," he said quietly.

Her body tensed.

"Just until the attacks cease," he said.

Just until he was strong enough to stop MacDougall's witch trials. The outlaw's final confession echoed in his ears.

A bag of gold to the man who caught a witch.

"And Duncan is fully healed," he added in an attempt to appeal to her healer tendencies. "If something were to delay ye, I wouldna want him to look for ye again. No with all the attacks, aye?"

She pulled in a deep breath and stayed silent before opening her eyes. "You don't know what you ask of me."

"Tell me." He breathed the reply, as if speaking too loudly might frighten her away.

She turned away and he sensed her slipping from him. "If ye willna tell me, then at least come to the castle, aye?"

He cupped his hand over her slender shoulder and rubbed a particularly tight area there. She pursed her lips.

"Please." He was begging.

He, Alec MacLean, was begging.

And he'd continue to do so if it made her agree.

"Yes," she said finally. "I'll come."

It was a bittersweet victory. She'd agreed to come, but all the trust in her gaze had fled and was replaced with unmistakable wariness.

Chapter Twenty-Two

Celia's feet were silent on the cobblestones of Duart Castle's courtyard, her peasant shoes hidden beneath the silk dress Alec had talked her into wearing.

She regretted having made the stupid thing at all, she regretted how it let all the cold flap around her, and she regretted how the fine fabric was so unyielding.

Yes, she already hated the silk dress.

Her palms were slick, but she couldn't wipe them on the fabric and leave sweaty marks. Instead, she balled her hands into wet fists that chilled in the icy air and burned molten hot and moist within.

The entrance to the keep came into view, exquisite stonework scrolling over the open door.

Her feet went heavy and refused to allow her to enter.

Alec stopped beside her. "Are ye well, Celia?"

She lowered her head and cast a discreet glance around them through the curtain of her hair. The guards stared at her from their posts, doubtless wondering why the peasant healer was dressed in the clothes of a lady.

No, they didn't wonder. They knew. Same as any servants who would see her. They would all assume.

And were they wrong?

Shame burned inside her.

"Celia?" Alec took her hand, but she pulled her arm closer toward herself and slid from his grasp.

Did he not realize what this looked like?

Did he not realize they would all think she was his mistress?

"May I address the lady?" a man said on the other side of

Alec. Celia looked up to find a bulky man with graying black hair in front of her.

"I'm no lady," she said quickly.

He bowed regardless.

His eyes were bright and young, but the carved lines on his face were evidence of a hard life. "Ye saved my son yesterday, the same as ye saved all the other bairns. They would have died without ye and we're glad the laird's convinced ye to stay close for yer safety." He cast a quick peek at Alec. "Sorry to have interrupted." He bowed once more and slipped away.

The knot of anxiety in Celia's stomach eased a bit. She glanced at Alec to see his reaction. He gave her a reassuring smile. "They all wanted me to get ye. They've been worried about ye being out in yer cottage by yerself."

She pushed her hair from her face and glanced around once more. The eyes staring back at her were not smug with knowing, but warm with welcoming gratitude.

"They don't think I'm your..."

Whore.

The word stuck in her throat.

"They know I desire ye," Alec said. "And they know to keep their hands off ye. But they dinna think ye're my mistress. Unless ye want them to." He winked down at her.

"Celia." The sound of her name cracked from the entrance.

She gazed in the direction and found Duncan holding tight to the doorframe with his left hand. Standing up, he was almost as tall as she. Had he grown in the two days since she'd seen him or had she not noticed his height while he lay abed?

His shirt hung loose on his thin frame and the belt of his kilt had been drawn so tight the extra fabric puckered around his hips. A wide grin stretched across his cheeks and the sun lit his bright green eyes.

"I'm glad ye're safe. I've been worried about ye," he said in a stronger voice than she expected.

She rushed forward to keep him from walking to her. "If I remember correctly, I wasn't the one wandering around the forest while already sick." She tried to give him a sincere, chastising look, but such a thing was not possible with Duncan.

His gaze cut to her cheek and his lips set in a hard line.

Exactly like Alec.

"Perhaps I was right in coming to help ye when ye dinna show. That wound isna fresh from yesterday." He tilted his head with far too much perception. "Were ye attacked? Did they hur—"

Alec swept between them and caught Duncan by the shoulders. "She's only just arrived, boy. Let her get out of the wind and then ye can ask yer questions." He tugged Duncan into the keep and met Celia's gaze. "I wouldna mind hearing the answers myself."

She looked away, uncertain how to reply, when a high-pitched squeal came from across the room where Wynda ran toward her at full speed.

Celia knew she would be ensconced in a massive, floury hug.

There was a happy warmth inside her, a welcome warmth. This must be what it felt like to have a home, a family. This must be what it felt like to have love.

And for that one moment when Wynda flung her arms around her, she did not push it away.

She welcomed it all.

• • •

Alec leaned his shoulder against the smooth stone wall and bit back a grin. Wynda had enveloped Celia in a crushing embrace he knew all too well.

"Ach, lass, I heard of the brave things ye did," Wynda said against the top of Celia's head. "I'm so glad the laird talked ye into staying with us where ye'll be safe."

Wynda opened her arms and Celia stepped free, her cheeks flushed. "And ye…" Wynda fixed her gaze on Alec and propped her hands on her hips.

Shite.

The wind howled through the doorway and sent his kilt flapping against his knees.

"Ye dinna come back to the castle after the battle." She stalked toward him, her red hair flickering in the wind like a flame. "Nay, instead ye send a guard to tell me that ye're safe and ye'll be back when ye can." She snuffled noisily. "Like ye wanted to rip the heart from my chest. If I dinna love Celia, ye'd be in a fine mess of trouble, do ye know that?" She lifted the corner of her apron and wiped the tears from her eyes.

Celia's joy had gone quiet and her expression was pensive. He hadn't wanted her to know he'd come to her cottage before returning to the castle.

The less she knew, the better, especially with her situation being so dire.

Wynda crossed her arms over her chest and stared at him. "I know ye dinna like it, but I want to hug ye right now." A frown pulled at her lips, but she didn't move.

Alec groaned inwardly. The woman and her damn hugs.

Wynda stared up at him like a pup who'd gone too long without a meal, her eyes glossy with emotion.

"Fine," he grunted.

Gone were the tears and in their place was a squeal and a bone-crushing embrace. If the woman weren't so good at baking bread, he might do well to throw her in his ranks.

"Now, ye've got to see to yer men," Wynda scolded, releasing him. "They've been asking after ye and the stable hand needs to speak with ye as well. And when ye're done with all that, I want ye in the kitchen to help with some of the meal plans."

He opened his mouth to protest, but she wagged a finger at him. "And dinna give me that look. Ye've put it off for long enough."

The weight of responsibility was back like a heavy cloak straining across his shoulders.

He had the men, he had the staff, he had the horses and the blacksmith, and now the cook. And he still needed to go see MacDougall to try to quell some of this insanity.

The darkness flickered inside him, writhing in protest at the burgeoning impossibility of any real accomplishment with so many tasks.

"Can I help?" Celia stepped closer.

Her fingertips brushed his once, subtle as the swipe of a butterfly's wing, and then she stepped away from him.

Wynda clapped her hands. "I'd love yer help in preparing a list of meals. I dinna get much from him." She nodded toward Alec.

"That isna necessary," Alec said. "Ye've got yer healing. I willna take from that."

Celia looked up at him. "I know herbs well and it will take but a moment to provide a list of ingredients I think Wynda is looking for."

She glanced toward the cook for confirmation and Wynda gave an eager nod.

The silk dress made her eyes stand out, complex and beautiful as the dark night sky against her fair face. He wanted to stare into them until he saw the heavens twinkle stars in those blue depths. And then he wanted to stare further still to count them all.

No man could deny a woman so beautiful.

"Go to your men," Celia said. "I'll see you this evening." Her voice was low with an unspoken promise. "At supper," she added quickly. Her cheeks went a brilliant shade of red.

He bit back his grin, lest she see how he took her reply. While he hadn't brought her to Duart to be his mistress, it certainly wouldn't stop him from luring her to his bed.

• • •

Supper came more quickly than Alec had anticipated.

The aroma of spiced sauces lingered in the air, hovering over the savory scent of roasted meat. Duncan sat at the table with a healthy flush to his cheeks Alec hadn't seen in far too long. It was good to see him. His empty seat had cast a shadow on all the meals prior.

He caught a glimpse of pale blonde hair and his heart quickened. Celia stood like a queen among his household, her back straight, her head lifted with the self-assured pride he'd noticed the first day they met.

In place of the silk gown she'd once worn, she had now donned a cloth gown of pale blue. While he'd enjoyed the sheen of silk on her body, so too did he appreciate the way the softer fabric clung to her beautiful body. He longed to glide his palms down her waist, her hips, her sweetly curved bottom.

Her name was on every set of lips in the castle. Not only did they see her as a savior, she was kind and gracious and had spent the afternoon setting up a small room for her healing.

He caught her gaze over the laden tables and a smile spread over her lips. Not the overconfident smile of someone wanting to charm or prove a point, but the shy, careful smile of a person whose heart had opened wide enough to make everything feel tentative and uncertain.

He wanted her, not just in his bed, but beside him. Not just now, but for the rest of their lives.

The desire wrenched within him, so palpable it took his breath for a moment.

He watched her, unable to look away and unable to deny what it was he knew in the depths of his heart.

He wanted Celia for his wife.

Chapter Twenty-Three

Darkness had settled outside and rain lashed against the shuttered windows, but Duart Castle was warm and dry. Comfortable, even.

Celia had not expected comfortable.

"Will ye tell me about when ye saved the children in the village?" Duncan asked from where he lay propped against the headboard of his bed. His lips pursed to blow the steam from the mug in his hands.

She folded her arms in front of her waist. "If I can be honest with you…"

Duncan nodded vigorously.

"I was actually frightened." She paused until he took another sip of his tea. He needed to drink it all before going to sleep. "But Alec was brave. And if it weren't for Alec being so very brave, I might not have made it out alive."

Another sip.

"Did ye make a baby come to life?" he asked.

Goosebumps prickled her skin. "Where did you hear that?" she asked through cold lips.

He took another sip. "They're saying it in the village."

She shook her head. "The baby was already alive, but sleeping. I merely woke it from its slumber."

He set his mug down and seemed to consider this a moment. "But ye saved his mother, aye?"

"I healed her, yes," Celia said carefully.

"And pulled her from the street so no one would kill her," Duncan encouraged her. He took another sip.

"Yes. But I was scared then, too. Between you and me, I

thought of Alec and pretended I was as brave as him."

Duncan drained his cup and Celia took it from him.

"He's no scared of anything, is he?" Duncan asked.

She wrapped her hands around the still-warm cup. "I wouldn't say that." She tucked his blankets around him and smoothed his hair from his face, the way she would do to a child. "I've seen fear in his eyes."

Duncan's mouth opened in slack shock. "At the village?"

"Oh no, nothing like that." She smiled at him. "The only time I've ever seen Alec afraid was when you went missing."

His chin jerked up. "Truly?" His voice cracked with the onset of manhood.

"Truly."

A smile lit his thin face.

"Now you need to get to sleep," she said in a gently firm voice, lest another stream of questions begin.

He nodded against his pillow. His grin still had not faded.

Celia strode from the room and glanced back at him one more time before leaving. Something in her heart warmed, a palpable tenderness for the fragile boy and his open affection.

After bidding him goodnight, she quietly slipped into the hall and closed the door behind her.

"I thought I might find ye here." Alec's voice sounded behind her. Celia jumped with surprise and spun around. His arms came around her, steadying her. "I dinna mean to frighten ye."

"You didn't, I mean…" She smoothed a hand down her hair and regretted not having taken off the bulky apron she wore over her dress. "I mean, not much."

He stepped closer to her and spoke in a lowered voice. "I canna stop thinking about ye."

Her mouth went dry. She'd spent most of her day in a cloud of Alec thoughts as well, her body hot and slick with remembering.

"Ye're so beautiful." He caressed the side of her waist and left his hand on her hip. "Ye're so graceful." With the slightest pressure and another step forward, he edged her backward into an alcove beside Duncan's door.

He cradled her jaw in his large hand and she looked up into his eyes. There was a heat there that singed her core.

He stared at her for a long moment, as if he were savoring her image, then his grip tensed and he lowered his lips to hers.

His mouth was hungry, eager.

Celia rose on her toes to meet his kiss, wanting all of him. She arched her body forward so the strength of his body burned through her clothes.

His hands slid through her hair behind her head and his hot tongue swept against hers.

He leaned over her neck and the wet warmth of his tongue trailed down the curve of her ear.

A delightful shiver tingled down her back.

"I want ye," he said in a velvety voice.

A little moan slipped from Celia's throat, an inadvertent confession of wanting him too.

Alec tugged at something behind her and the firmly tied waist of her apron went slack.

"Come with me," he said against her ear.

She nuzzled her face against his, reveling in the scrape of his whiskered jaw against her impossibly sensitive flesh.

He pulled the apron over her head with the same intense gaze he might give if he were removing her gown.

"Where?" she whispered.

His chin brushed hers. "To my room."

She parted her lips to speak, but the warm caress of his tongue stroked the protest from her mouth.

"Come with me." His lips moved over hers as he spoke.

"I have my own room," she said on the exhale of a sigh that belied her protests.

"I know ye do." He nibbled her lower lip, teasing her with warm wet of his mouth. "It was a ruse."

His hand ran up and down the softness of her gown, right over her rib cage, inching dangerously close to her breast.

As if reading her thoughts, he glanced down at her scooped neckline, where her nipples stood hard against the fabric, and swept his thumb against the right one.

Pleasure swept through her in tingling, tightening shivers. Her knees went soft. Her breath went shallow.

"Come with me." He moved back and gently pulled her with him.

She didn't think. She couldn't. Not with her body blazing with a stoked fire and her mind humming with frantic anticipation.

He led her up a private side stairwell leading to a single door—the door to his room.

He pushed it open and revealed a massive stone room with a large bed she could not draw her eyes from. She stepped inside and the door clicked closed behind her.

The air hung thick with moist heat and the scent of a masculine spice.

The warmth of Alec's body behind her pressed through the soft cloth of her gown. They were far enough away from the kitchen to no longer hear the clatter of dishes or hurried calls of the servants. His slow, steady breath sounded quietly in her left ear and the fire popped and snapped in the silence.

"I hope ye dinna mind." He nuzzled her neck. The heat of the room grew more intense.

Thunder cracked somewhere outside, and that was when she saw the large bathtub in front of the fireplace. The sheets lining it draped over the sides like the petals of a flower and steam curled from its glass-smooth surface, promising exquisite luxury.

He hugged her from behind. "I want ye, Celia."

Evidence of his statement pressed against her, nestled at the curve of her buttocks. She arched back against him with a hungry instinct. He groaned, a low, desperate sound that snared her desire.

"You expect me to bathe in front of you?" Her voice was husky when she spoke.

He nudged his face into her hair and his chest swelled against her back when he breathed in her scent. "I expect to bathe together, Celia."

Together.

Her mouth went dry.

Like they'd done at the lake, but instead of a cool caress, they would have sensual warmth cradling their coupling.

"I dinna plan to take no for an answer." His fingertips skimmed over her hardened nipples, once, twice, three times. Her body strained of its own volition toward his touch, eager for more.

"We should hurry before the water cools." He shifted behind her and the heavy thud of his boots sounded against the floor. He strode toward the bath with his back facing her and pulled off his leine. "Ye coming?" The white linen fell to the floor.

He rotated midstep so he walked backward, his chest facing her.

Celia's throat went tight with longing. The firelight caressed his muscular torso, exaggerating the already impossibly hard lines. He grasped his belt and slipped it free. The kilt around his waist spiraled off, revealing his solid thighs and the source of his arousal.

He stood without shame, his body strong in the muted light. She couldn't move, not when he was so beautiful, not when her gaze settled on the proud display of hardened flesh. Every part of the man flexed with raw power.

He stepped into the bath and set the water rippling around his knees. Small waves lapped against the sheet covered sides. Glittering eyes fixed on her, he sank into the water and leaned against the sloping back of the tub.

"It feels verra nice." He stretched his arms out across the ledge and settled deeper back. The muscles of his arms glistened with a sheen of water and bathing oil. "It could feel nicer still."

Any lingering hesitation evaporated like the spiral of steam curling over Alec.

Her fingers trembled as she unlaced the front of her gown. This was not like the time at the lake when she'd wanted to sate a desire. This was not like last night when her fear of losing him had overwhelmed her.

No, this was different, because now she knew she cared.

She slipped off the bodice, the skirt, and, finally, the

chemise. Alec's jaw hardened.

She stared at his half naked body rising from water so still it reflected his glorious physique.

Now she cared too much.

"Get in the water," he said, a command more than an invitation.

And so she took her time obeying.

She walked slowly, purposefully, reveling in a flash of power all woman must feel when they understand the draw of desire.

Alec watched her with intently focused eyes, his chest rising and falling and sending ripples through the water.

She'd never been in an actual tub before. Loch bathing was chilly and turned to a small bowl of meltwater in the winter, but this…

She stepped over the high edge of the tub. The water enveloped her skin in a velvety warmth so decadent it bordered on sinful.

She pulled her other leg into the hot water and eased into its embrace. Everything was warm and comforting and weightless. She leaned back against the soft sheet draped on the opposite side of the tub from Alec, sitting between his ankles.

He watched her through a milky haze of steam, his light eyes dark with desire. The water stirred and his feet brushed against the sides of her lower back.

"I want ye closer." His feet tucked against her and drew her toward him in a smooth surge.

He didn't stop until they were pressed together in a tangle of legs that left her senses suddenly heightened and on edge.

The water caressed her skin and the subtle waves rocked them together with each gentle swell.

"I said closer." He lifted her into his lap and slid his hands to her thighs, guiding her to straddle his waist.

With the way they sat, he could slide inside her with the slightest thrust.

And judging from the way his lips lifted in a grin, he knew it too.

Chapter Twenty-Four

Alec woke to darkness. The sun had not yet begun to glow its outline against the shutters.

There was more time to sleep.

There was more time to love.

He rolled to his side and reached for Celia, desperate for her rosemary scented warmth, the soft comfort of her naked skin.

His fingers slipped against cool sheets. Sleep beckoned, but he held it at bay with a grunt.

He looked to where Celia had lain beside him, but in a world so absent of light, seeing was impossible.

"Celia," he called in a voice heavy with his deep slumber.

His heart slammed hard in his chest.

Not again.

"Celia," he said sharply.

Still no reply.

Alec's blood thundered through his veins, heating his body from the chill of the night with all the frustration, all the rage and hurt only Celia could incite.

He kicked his legs from the bed and bolted across the room while securing the discarded bath linen around his waist. The fabric was cold and heavy with wetness, but he paid it no heed.

The latch shifted against the pressure of his thumb in a clatter of metal and the door swung open.

Soft light bathed the private stairwell.

The rain had stopped.

Perhaps Celia had left. Perhaps she'd returned to her cottage in the woods.

Fear bathed his mouth in something metallic and hot.

Perhaps MacDougall waited for her there, ready to attack.

Alec raced down the narrow stairwell when a bundle of blankets on the thick sill of the window caught his attention.

Celia sat with her legs drawn to her chest and one of the heavy blankets from the bed wrapped tight around her. Her head lay against her arm, her eyes closed with the oblivion of sleep where she lay beneath a veil of moonlight.

He watched her for a moment. Her relaxed features left her face soft. Sweet.

The tender smile warmed in his chest before it spread across his lips.

It would be far easier to coax his slumbering beauty into bed than saving her had been.

Alec eased closer to where Celia slept on the windowsill. Though she was petite, she barely fit.

"Celia," he called softly.

She squeezed herself tighter and whimpered.

This time he reached out and gently brushed a triangle of exposed skin on her back. "Celia."

Her body clenched tighter, flinching from his touch.

She glanced up at him, her gaze hard and cautious. Her eyes found his and widened. "Forgive me," she said, breathless. "I thought…"

She shook her head and cradled her brow with the curve of her fingers.

"Are ye well, lass?" he asked.

She looked up with a smile he didn't believe. "I am."

He held out his hand for her to take. "Will ye come back to bed?" He looked pointedly at his own partial nudity. "I can feel a draft, aye?"

A real smile threatened the corner of her lips. She reached up for his hand and allowed him to lead her up the stairs, toward the darkness of his open door.

Her steps faltered and her pulse quickened against his fingertips.

"I don't…" she started.

He turned to face her. The warmth of her hand had gone

icy cold. "Celia, what is it?" he asked.

She pulled away from his grasp, jerking from him like he meant her harm. Her gaze went wide and luminous.

"I can't." Tears slid silent down her face and shimmered in the soft light. "It's too dark."

• • •

Celia tried to swallow her terror, but found it too large to fit down her throat.

Shadows loomed beyond Alec's open door, waiting to suck her into its eternal abyss.

How could she explain it to Alec, who was so sure, so brave?

Her leg muscles were stiff, but she forced them forward, toward the source of her fear.

She passed under the doorway as if in a dream and the black pressed against her like a hideous demon. It clawed at her heart and ripped her paper-thin bravery to shreds.

Her throat rasped where the demon locked the air from her lungs and held her captive.

She was sliding to a place she did not want to go, where she'd lie in the darkness waiting to die.

The last torch had long since been snuffed.

The darkness was wielded like a weapon in the pits of this prison, this hell.

The quiet sobs of prisoners in other cells whispered in the blackness and a woman newly arrested cried in jerky breaths.

Celia had been spared the inquisition thus far because of her age, but she did not consider herself fortunate. Night after night, she'd sat in the frigid cell with rats tugging her hair in sharp nips, bearing witness to sounds of horrors she was helpless to stop—the sickening crack of breaking bone, the hiss of hot metal to flesh, the raw, animalistic screams of the tortured.

A familiar wail echoed down the hall and sliced deep into Celia's heart. Her body jerked instinctively against the pain. Tears ran warm down her face and soaked ice cold into the fabric of her dress.

Fiona.

Kind, caring Fiona, who had taken Celia in as a child when no one else wanted her, the only mother she had ever known.

They would bring Fiona back at dawn when they returned the others, some bleeding, some broken, some dead.

The guards wanted their souls. Confessions lay at the ready, waiting for signatures, of heinous and cruel deeds and consorting with the devil.

They promised a quick death for signatures.

Fiona wouldn't let anything break her and, judging by the faces that came and went through the bowels of their hell, she hadn't.

A scream ripped through the darkness and the sobs around Celia pitched into terrified keens.

When would they understand?

She was not a witch.

• • •

Alec knelt next to Celia's still form. Her eyes were squeezed shut.

Cold dread coiled in his chest. She'd crumpled so suddenly he hadn't had a chance to catch her.

He gathered her in his arms and carried her back to the stone windowsill where he could see better. Her skin glistened with a sheen of sweat in the pale glow of the moon.

"Celia," he said in a hoarse voice. He'd called her name countless times and still she did not respond.

A strangled cry escaped her lips. "Fiona."

He gathered Celia closer and shushed quietly in her ear.

For all his strength and power, he could do nothing to stop Celia's trembling.

She gripped his arm as if letting go would be her death. Her throat worked in a slow swallow. "It's too dark in your room. I can't…I can't see. Like the prison."

His gut wrenched against her words. People who wanted to escape the law had congregated on his lands. Outlaws, rogues, criminals.

Surely she was none of those things.

"What do you mean, 'prison'?" he asked in a soft voice.

Her gaze turned pleading. "The one in North Berwick. Where they put all the witches." She shook her head and tears gathered at the corners of her eyes.

"That was fifteen years ago," he said, unable to keep the shock from his voice. "How old were ye when they put ye in there?"

Her gaze went distant, staring at the wall and seeing something he could not. "It was sixteen years ago, toward the end of the trials. I was seven."

The hair on the back of his neck stood on end. "Ye were a child?"

She didn't reply. She didn't need to.

Now he understood why she remained so tightly wrapped in the protection of herself. He couldn't imagine what horrors she'd seen there, what she'd experienced.

He wrapped his arms around her and drew her toward his chest. She melted against him, her skin like ice, and buried her face into his chest.

"They would put out the torches at night." Her lips moved against his skin with warm breath. "It would be so dark I wondered sometimes if I'd gone blind. That's when the rats came. They would nibble on clothes and hair. Sometimes they would bite." Her voice went small. "You couldn't see them, only feel the clip of their teeth. I could hear the sounds of torture as they tried to get the witches to confess their crimes."

He flattened his hand over her slender back and rubbed it gently, as if he could soothe away the years of haunted pain. "Did they torture ye, lass?" he asked gently. Perhaps he should not have, but he needed to know.

"Not me." Her voice wavered slightly.

"Fiona," he surmised. "Yer mother?"

She drew in a shaky breath. Her body trembled.

"I had no parents, but she took me in." Her body curled forward. "She loved me." Soft sobs sounded from her. "It was my fault."

He held her, saying nothing, being the rock of support she needed. There was a deep ache in him at his own stark helplessness to undo her hurt.

"Ye dinna need to talk anymore if ye prefer." He drew in

a deep breath of her scent and kissed her head. "I'm here, lass. There's no anything that can hurt ye. I'll light a fire and put a candle by the bed, aye?"

The thought of MacDougall rose forefront in his mind, the other man's insanity, his hatred.

For witches.

Now Alec understood her fear of the trials.

And now he was all the more frightened for her with MacDougall's hunt.

His arms tightened around Celia as if squeezing her might offer her more protection.

She nodded against his chest. "Will you hold me while I sleep?"

She didn't even need to ask. He would hold her for a lifetime. "Aye, love, I will."

So long as there was breath in his body, Celia would never again be harmed.

• • •

Precious candles flickered around the room, lighting it with the brilliant glow of day. Celia curled closer to Alec's powerful body. For this one night, she would allow herself to revel in his strength with the press of his warm skin over the chill of hers.

His arms braced her to him in a solid wall of protection. For this one night, she would allow herself to feel safe.

Exhaustion weighed down her lids and memories scraped through her battered mind.

"You've been here too long, witch. You need to sign your confession and be done with it." The guard's voice carrying down the hall was hard. They all were.

"I'm not...a witch," Fiona rasped.

Celia's heart pounded so hard it made her want to empty the meager contents of her stomach, as it always did when they returned Fiona.

Celia scrambled upright in her cell and ran in two stiff strides toward the door.

There was a pause, a scuffle of feet, a smack of flesh to something hard.

Celia's stomach lurched.

"You'll confess, witch, or we'll start working on the girl."

"She's too young," Fiona whispered, as if she knew Celia listened.

"And you've been here too long." There was no pity in his tone.

Moments later, the cell door screamed open and the guard shoved Fiona's battered form into the cell. Celia caught her and eased her to the floor, a feat easily done with the woman weighing so little now.

Fiona's gaze met hers and watered with tears Celia had never seen and she immediately knew without having to be told—Fiona had broken.

For her.

Chapter Twenty-Five

Celia lay with her eyes closed despite the sunlight on her face. Sleep would come no longer, but savoring it, savoring Alec, still brought great comfort. She rubbed her cheek against the heat of his chest, savoring the intimacy, the comfort of him.

His hand trailed a lazy path down her spine before resting on the curve of her bottom, eliciting an excited shiver from her.

"Are ye awake?" he asked in a gravelly voice.

She opened her eyes to the brilliance of a new day and nodded. "The sun has been up for a while," she said.

"Ach, I know." He rubbed her bottom with his palm before giving it an affectionate pat. "I canna remember being so exhausted."

She turned her face into his chest, as if she could press away the memories of the middle of the night and her confession of her ridiculous fear of the dark.

"Last night, I was foolish." Her face went hot. She glanced around the room to where countless pools of expensive wax flickered with struggling flames. The bath sat before the blackened hearth, cold and still in the daylight.

"I disagree. I dinna know what ye'd been through, I dinna know—"

"That I'm afraid of the dark, like a child?"

His hand caressed her jaw. "Ye were a wee thing, too wee to be in prison."

"You used a fine number of candles on my fears," she said with an embarrassed laugh.

"If ye fear the dark and I can make it light for ye, I will." His gaze narrowed. "I'll always protect ye."

A knot tightened in her chest and welled high in her throat. She'd always known this. Even when they first met, she knew this.

It was why she'd never told him her story. She didn't want his fierce protection.

She didn't want him in danger.

Alec propped himself on his elbow and gazed down at her. His fingertip skimmed over her shoulder and around the curve of her breast.

Her heart pattered faster, much to her chagrin. For all her regrets, she did not wish to give in to her body's desires.

Not now.

His hand dipped lower and brushed across her stomach.

She sucked in a breath in anticipation, but he did not go any farther. Instead, he spread his hand over her belly and held it there.

She glanced up at him and found a slight smile tugging the corners of his lips upward.

"What are you doing?" she asked, curious.

He did not take his eyes from her stomach. "Imagining ye swollen with our child." His gaze dragged to her face. "Ye'd be verra lovely."

The hair on her arms prickled. She would be no less shocked if he had plunged her into the cold remnants of their bath. "You'd have me be pregnant with your bastard?"

His face pulled down in a frown. "I'd have ye as my wife, Celia."

All words fled her tongue. Of all the things he could have said, this was certainly the least expected. Lairds did not marry destitute orphans who'd been to prison, not even honorable ones like Alec.

The hard look on his face melted to something tender, something that tugged at her in a way she'd fought too long to resist.

"I want ye to remain at Duart with me," Alec said. "No hidden away as my mistress, but at my side." His pale blue eyes met hers. "As my wife." His hand skimmed down her stomach once more in a loving caress. "I want ye to be the woman who bears my sons."

Celia opened her mouth, but no words came out. No man had ever spoken to her with such earnest affection. Her heart ached beneath the stroke of his words, foolishly begging for a love she feared.

She shook her head against the emotion warming her face. Her gaze shifted to his hand and she imagined her belly round with his child.

"Dinna answer yet," he said quickly.

She looked up and found him watching her with his brows slightly raised in an almost pleading expression.

"I'm a peasant," she said. "You deserve someone better than me."

His jaw hardened. "There is no better woman than ye, Celia." He removed his hand from her stomach and cupped her cheek. "Please think on this for a few days, aye?"

Deep down, she knew she should refuse him outright, to not give him false hope. To agree with what he asked would put her own crumbling will at risk.

Yet to refuse to at least consider his proposal would be cruel, especially when he'd given so much so freely, when he'd awoken a part of her she thought had long since died.

And truth be told, she wanted this. With all her heart and every selfish fiber of her being, she wanted this.

But not forever. Only long enough to taste it, to build memories to look back on, to placate him.

She could play the part a few more days and use that time to find an undeniable reason she would have to decline his proposal.

"I'll think on it," she answered slowly, willing him to see her hesitation.

His lips stretched in a wide smile and the corners of his eyes crinkled with a joy she'd never seen him express.

Already the weight of guilt pressed heavy to her heart.

She reinforced the wall of her resolve.

She would see him hurt over seeing him dead.

She could not marry Alec MacLean.

• • •

A mighty wind rolled over the high wall of the castle and pushed against Alec. He braced himself in a wide-legged stance, the same as Duncan did beside him.

The boy got stronger with each passing day. If he grew another foot more, he'd be taller than Alec.

Guards gathered in the courtyard below, set in perfect lines as they'd been taught. A hard call echoed off thick stone before being swept away. The men charged one another, their movements fluid and well-honed. Though Alec's force was small, his men were strong and capable.

Duncan stared down, his gaze fixed intently on the movements below.

"Battle always looks different from above," Alec said.

The boy didn't take his eyes from the clash of men. "Different how?"

Memories of Alec's countless battles bled into his mind. "People blur together and men come at ye from all angles. It can be disorienting."

The fierce wind blew against them and pulled Duncan's blond hair until it stood straight up. The boy did not notice. "How is it disorienting? Is it…"

When Duncan didn't finish, Alec glanced over and found the boy's mouth puckered to the right side of his face.

"Is it what?" Alec prompted.

"Scary." Duncan looked up at him with the same wide-eyed innocence as so many men he'd led into war. "Is battle scary?"

Savage shouts pulled their attention to the courtyard once more. A man below whipped his dulled practice blade toward another and his opponent knelt in defeat.

"Battle makes yer heart pound and yer blood burn hot, but ye canna let it scare ye." Alec put his hand on the boy's back, all sharp bones and thin muscle. "Battle can threaten to overwhelm ye with the sounds of men shouting and the pleas of those dying. The first stink of blood will make yer heart go wild. Many men are no strong enough to stomach it and give in to their fear." Alec patted Duncan's back and braced his hands on the rough stone wall in front of his waist.

"What happens to the men who give in to their fear?"

Alec looked at the boy to ensure he understood the severity of the response. "They die. If ye want to survive, ye dinna give in to the fear."

Alec sighed beneath the yoke of his memories. He'd seen too many men die, led too many battles. His world had finally slowed down and he was ready to settle into a life with Celia.

"I'll never be afraid," Duncan said. "I'll survive every battle and fight with bravery like ye."

A soldier approached from the stairs to the right. "Then ye'll survive to fight another day, lad." Alec put his hand around the boy's shoulders. They'd become broader than he remembered. "Ye need to get to the keep now, aye? I need to speak with Niall."

Duncan squeezed a quick hug around Alec's waist and ran down the stairs with a sharp nod to Niall.

Alec grimaced as he watched the boy go.

Wynda had been spending too much damn time with him. She'd make him soft.

Niall approached Alec with an impassive expression. Threads of silver in his hair glinted in the sunlight.

"I hadn't expected to see ye back from Aros Castle so soon," Alec said. Perhaps the warrior's return meant MacDougall had ceased his murderous trials.

Niall considered Alec for a moment. "I dinna go."

Alec's eyes met the aging warrior's and a low, simmering flame licked to life within him. "What?"

Niall kept his pale green eyes fixed on Alec. "I. Dinna. Go."

"Why?" Alec demanded.

"Ye said we dinna have to do anything we dinna agree with." Niall lifted his shoulders in a careless shrug. "I dinna think ye could spare any men and so I dinna go."

Alec stared with disbelief, his hand balled in a fist. "Where do ye get the authority to make such decisions without informing me? Without notifying me of yer refusal to follow a simple command?"

"Do ye have any idea how dangerous it is to be aiding the accused witches in a time like this?" Niall hissed. "If he knows we have a witch here, he might torture me. Kill me."

He stopped and pressed his lips together.

He'd said too much and they both knew it.

Wind lashed around them and filled the heaviness of their silence with the steady flapping of their kilts.

"Ye may go," Alec said through his teeth.

Niall turned and left the way he'd come.

Alec's stomach drew tight around the bitterness of his disappointment.

Niall hadn't gone to MacDougall's territory not because he didn't agree with the task.

He didn't go because he was scared.

The warrior had lost his edge, and with it, Alec knew he'd lost his force of men.

• • •

Celia clutched a stack of blankets against her chest and navigated her way through the crowded courtyard with Duncan at her side. Faces smiled in her direction and nodded in greeting.

A bitter wind swept off the ocean and blew through the heavy cloak she wore. The sky was gray, the castle wall was gray, even some of the people's faces appeared gray.

She scanned the haphazardly scattered tents and crude shelters erected behind the castle walls. "There are more today than there were yesterday," she said softly. Bonfires sprinkled the once green grass and thick black smoke curled above to twist against the fluffy white clouds.

Duncan readjusted his grip on the large basket full of Wynda's bread. "The outlaws have been relentless in their attacks. At least the laird fixed the castle walls so they can stay somewhere safe." He turned to her with an optimistic smile. "I'm happy to have ye here to help."

While she was glad to be able to help the villagers when they needed her most, the task was overwhelming.

After a quiet life of solitude, the constant smells and sounds and voices pulled at her, causing her head to ache and her skin to feel too tight.

Ruadh must have agreed with her, because he had not ventured into the castle walls despite her attempts to lure him. Instead, Alec had given careful instructions to his soldiers on watch to leave the little fox unharmed.

A sigh rose in her chest at the thought of Alec. She wished she had not promised him she'd consider his offer of marriage.

Every night he curled her against the heat of his body and sparked the flame of her desire, slowing singeing away her stoic resolve. For all her determination to avoid wanting the life he offered, she found herself finding convenient reasons to stay.

To help Wynda organize the household, to be there for Duncan's questions so Alec could focus on the war against outlaws, to heal the injured who came into Duart's gates.

All good excuses, but she knew what she was doing.

"Watch yerself, Celia," Duncan said, interrupting her thoughts.

The warning came just as a cluster of children ran toward her. Celia swept to the left to avoid a quick little girl with long brown hair. Though Celia's hand pressed into the thick folds of the woolen blankets, a great wind knocked her off balance.

She staggered across the uneven earth. Blankets flew from her hands and billowed out in the wind like great brown birds fluttering and swooping to the ground. She grabbed at the air in vain desperation to save them from falling to the dirt, but that was exactly where they fell.

Duncan was by her side before she even bent to pick up the first one. A crumple of brown wool was already pressed under the bread basket.

"You're fast," she said with a grin.

His green eyes sparked. "I can be faster." He snatched up the next one. "Faster than ye even, and I've still got my bread."

Celia darted toward the next blanket. "Is that a challenge?"

"Ye know it is," Duncan called out behind her.

She quickly collected three more. Only one remained in

sight, lying between two tents. The wind caught the edge and lifted it from the ground, but she snagged the coarse cloth from the thieving breeze before it could fly away again.

She stood up to call to Duncan.

"The healer has been most helpful," a woman's voice said inside one of the tents.

"Aye, but it's time for her to leave," a man replied. His voice quivered with either age or illness.

Celia's pounding heart shrank into silence in her chest.

She should walk away. She should not be standing there like a child, eavesdropping.

"The laird is in love, can ye no see it?" the woman asked.

There was a pause and Celia's face burned despite the raging wind.

In love.

The very thought pulled at her breath.

"I dinna care if the laird is in love or how kind she has been," the man said vehemently. "The attacks willna stop while that MacDougall bastard knows she's here. I say we spare all our lives and throw him the witches he seeks."

Celia stumbled backward, stupidly clutching the blankets to herself. If the wind continued to batter her clothes and chill her skin, she did not feel it. She felt nothing. Nothing but the savage rending of her heart.

These people were in danger, Alec was in danger, all of them risking their lives.

Because of her.

Chapter Twenty-Six

Alec took a deep breath of the sharp air and let it bite into his lungs. The cold always made his blood pound faster.

Countless villagers swarmed where he stood in the courtyard with Niall, bodies all but pressing against the two men despite many warnings.

"Niall MacLean," Alec said in a loud voice. The crowd stilled, save a few shuffles and the wail of a baby somewhere in the distance. "Ye've disobeyed an order that would have saved lives. Ye once were brave and noble. I fear that is no more." He addressed the crowd. "His weakness makes us all weak."

Several grumbles rose from the otherwise silent masses. Alec's favor with them was held with a thin thread—the taste of his father's wrath was still too fresh in their mouths.

He had to show them. They had to understand.

Alec slid his sword from its sheath. The black blade's edges had long since been nicked silver through the course of many battles, but he would not let the blacksmith grind away the blackened finish.

Niall's back stiffened and he tugged his own sword free with a metallic hiss. He did not wait for a sign from Alec before launching into an attack with the deadly swing of his blade.

A coward he would start and a coward he would fall.

Alec lifted his weapon over his head and a clang rang out. His forearms jerked toward Niall beneath the force of the man's attack. Using both hands on the wide hilt, Alec shoved him back and leapt forward.

The black blade sang as it rent the air with lethal speed. Fear flickered in Niall's eyes. He backed up and threw his weapon up between them in an effort to shield himself.

The blocked hit sent shocks reverberating to the base of Alec's back. Niall would not be unaffected. He would realize Alec was no simple outlaw, easily slain.

The warrior stumbled backward and fell to his knees.

Alec lifted his weapon high in the air.

Niall's eyes went wide. "Dinna do this." He shook his head.

Alec lowered his blade before the first villager could plead for the warrior's life and Niall's face creased with tired resignation, his eyes dull with a defeat extending beyond their simple sparring.

"Let it be known that all who defy me out of cowardice will pay the price." Alec's voice carried over the hushed masses.

This had to be done.

All it took was one man.

One man perceiving Alec as weak, and the heavy tapestry of strength he'd built up would quickly unravel.

He indicated the kneeling warrior. "Is this what ye want protecting yer lives and those of yer children?"

Eyes shifted away.

They agreed, but no one would speak.

"Dinna kill him," said an unseen voice.

Several low murmurs rose up in the crowd in agreement.

Alec shook his head. "His disobedience willna be met with death, but with shame. Niall MacLean, ye are no longer welcome in my guard. Ye may return to yer home."

He grasped the man's forearm and pulled his elder to a standing position. Niall's jaw tensed, but he did not speak. The man was a lifelong soldier. Deep down, he had to know Alec did what any good leader would.

Alec nodded sharply and released the man's arm.

Niall's men gathered around him, as Alec had assumed they would, and together the band of lost men walked slowly through the parting crowd.

The weight of Alec's actions pressed on his shoulders and made his chest ache.

A hand settled on his forearm.

He jerked his head to the left, ready to snarl at the person who dared interrupt him. Celia's wide blue eyes stared up at him and his curt response melted away.

Ah, sweet Celia.

The salve to make everything better.

"I need to speak with you," she said in a low voice. Her tongue flicked over her lips and left them glistening. "Alone."

His cock leapt to attention. She hadn't sought him out during the day before.

They'd both been too busy.

But she was here now, wanting him, and all of Scotland could hold still while his woman saw his day improved.

• • •

The walk to Alec's bedroom, to the room he'd shared with Celia since her arrival over two weeks ago, seemed to take years. Each step there strengthened her resolve.

She was being hunted.

Step.

The village was being attacked because someone suspected she was within the castle walls.

Step.

Leaving would expose her to the witch hunt.

Step.

Staying risked the lives of everyone she loved.

And then they were in the room.

She kept her eyes turned from the massive bed and the memory of too many intimate moments, but she could not keep from breathing in their mated scents nor ignore the way it clawed at her heart.

This must be done.

"Alec…" She turned to face him, but did not have a chance to speak before his arms came around her and his mouth captured hers.

She reeled back and turned her face from him. He pressed hot kisses in a trail down her neck.

This time she pushed gently at his shoulders. "Please stop."

His eyes met hers beneath brows furrowed in confusion. He unwound his arms from her body and stepped back. His gaze went hard. "Did someone hurt ye?"

"I've made my decision," she said in a voice sounding nothing like hers. "I've thought several days, as you asked me to."

His jaw clenched and the rest of his body tightened, as if he were bracing himself for a blow.

A knot of emotion swelled in her throat, but she swallowed it down. "I can't be with you."

"Why?" He shot the question back almost before the words had left her mouth.

Why?

Because the villages are being attacked.

Because you and Duncan and Wynda and the villagers aren't safe while I'm here.

Because I love you.

Her mind scrambled for purchase on an excuse. A viable excuse, the very thing she was supposed to have spent these past two weeks finding rather than enjoying the life that could never be hers.

"This life is too much for me," she answered at last.

"Wynda can resume castle duties." His words were wooden.

"I don't mean the duties. I mean all of it. The silks and the baths and the soft beds, the fine food. I'm no lady. I'm the abandoned child of a peasant couple. You deserve better than me." Emotion seeped into her voice and made it waver.

She pulled in a steadying breath.

He stepped closer and though he didn't touch her, she could *feel* how badly he wanted to. It pulled at her like the tantalizing heat of standing too close to a flame.

"Ye are better."

His desperate gaze tore into her heart.

"What about me?" he asked, watching her carefully. "Am I no what ye want?"

If she said yes, he'd never let her leave.

Everyone would still be in danger.

If she said no, she would wound this iron warrior in the one place she'd found to be vulnerable—his heart.

"I'm used to being alone." She replied with a coward's response by not answering the question at all. "I need to leave."

"Ye canna leave. It's no safe."

Celia lifted her chin, focusing on her resolution. Her being at Duart put too many people at risk. Too many people she had come to love. "I can handle myself. I've lived thus far on my own and survived."

His face went red. "Damn it, Celia, Laird MacDougall has offered a bag of gold for every witch brought in."

Celia tried to keep her face impassive beneath his sharp gaze. "And you think he'd want me?"

Though she tried to sound innocent, she knew better. It had snapped together in her mind.

The man with the red ring was Laird MacDougall. He had to be. And he would not stop looking for her until she was captured.

"All healers and midwives are being brought to the flame." Alec crossed his powerful arms. "I knew I could protect ye if I kept ye here."

"Is that what the offer of marriage was?" She forced bitterness into her tone, latching onto the words he'd meant for caring and turning them flimsy and cruel. "A means of keeping me here?"

His eyes went cold. "Ye know that isna true. I wouldna ask ye to be my wife if I dinna mean it."

She knew too well he had meant it. She'd seen his sincerity every time he looked at her. The warmth of his enamored gaze coiled around her heart and pulled her toward him.

No matter how much she tried to fight the truth, it was there in front of her. It dictated her every decision, including the one she made now.

"I don't want your protection." She stepped back.

"I protect what's mine," he said solemnly.

She needed to do it now. Strike while the iron was hot. "I'm not yours."

His face hardened but it didn't stop the hurt from shining in his light eyes. "Ye dinna want me." He didn't reach for her again, not this time.

Her heart crumpled against the sucking pain in her chest.

She did want him.

She wanted the comfort of his arms around her at night and his steady beating heart against her ear. She wanted to bathe in the warmth of his rare smiles and revel in the way he made her body sing.

She did not want the life awaiting her.

A life alone in an empty cottage without the warm light of love. Without the villagers' smiles and Duncan's questions and Wynda's hugs.

Without Alec's love.

Her decision wavered for one small moment, but then Fiona's burning body flashed in her mind, slumped and covered in wild, licking flames.

"I do not want you." Celia met his stare head on.

"Celia." Alec's voice was hoarse. "Dinna leave me again. Stay. Let me protect ye." His hand reached for her, hovered a moment, then gently caressed her cheek. "Let me love ye."

Every part of her body cried for her to turn toward the heat of his palm.

She jerked away from his touch before she could break. "If you make me stay, you'll be forcing me against my will. Let me go and do not follow."

She did not wait for him to reply and brushed past him.

He did not follow her.

Not to her room where she pulled on the rough homespun dress and left the silk laid out across the bed she had never slept on, not when she gathered her bag of herbs from the kitchens, and not when she rushed through the gates.

Ruadh broke through a patch of brush and darted toward her with an exuberance that only served to feed her pain. Together they raced over the coastline and Celia realized, for the first time in her life, she did not run from danger.

She ran toward it.

Chapter Twenty-Seven

Branches tugged at Celia's skirts and tangles of roots and vines underfoot tripped her, but she did not stop running. Ruadh darted beside her with his usual grace, weaving effortlessly around obstacles.

Thoughts of her home ran through her mind, the comfort of her bed, the silence of the shuttered cottage, the gentle hiss of the fire on cold days such as this.

Familiar surroundings would make being alone bearable.

The face of her cottage came into view. The door gaped open.

Her heart dropped to her stomach and she skidded to a halt in front of the small home.

Shards of wood littered the threshold and the gray skies cast a shadowy light within where chunks of broken furniture lay in ruin. She pulled her dagger from the leather belt at her hip and approached the entrance on shaky legs.

The red fox treaded carefully into the cottage on dainty paws, his tail lowering but never touching the floor. After several seconds he emerged and sat beside the doorway.

Whoever had gone through her cottage was long gone.

That knowledge did nothing to loosen the tension in Celia's shoulders. The wind moaned against the open door and scattered a wave of leaves across her dying garden. Everything she'd toiled over and owned now lay dead and destroyed.

She wanted to lie with the debris on the floor and weep for all she'd lost—both the things taken from her and what she'd just given up. But she knew she could not.

The urge to move on, to press forward and survive,

thrummed insistently in her veins. It forced her into the ravaged cottage, to find what was salvageable.

Ghosts of peat smoke clung to the air and mingled with the sweet scent of fresh lumber. The unique smell had once marked the sturdy hut as home. The aroma now churned in her stomach and brought on a wave of nausea.

She didn't have time for mourning. Whoever had done this would doubtless be back.

She picked her way through the broken drawers, purposefully ignoring the way the once-luxurious bed had been slashed with an angry blade.

Few supplies remained intact, but she managed to recover several needles and a few rolls of linen. The rest would be left for whatever outlaws raided her home later.

Aside from the ravages of winter and abandonment, her garden had remained untouched. For that she was grateful.

She lowered herself to the snarls of weeds and dying plants on legs that trembled with exhaustion. A few pokes and prods revealed the healthy green buds of several herbs trying to live.

The steady crunch of leaves sounded behind her, but Ruadh did not stir at her side. Whoever was there was no enemy.

Celia squeezed her eyes shut against the sting of tears. "I'm not coming back, Alec."

"I'm no Alec," a male voice wavered and pitched behind her. Duncan.

She looked over her shoulder and found his gaze sliding over the cottage.

"If Alec sent you to fetch me back, you've wasted your time." She refocused on the herbs, trying to harvest of the dried leaves what she could. It was easier to work with her hands than to figure out her next move.

She had nowhere to go.

If leaving the Isle of Mull had been difficult in the autumn, it would be impossible in the winter. Despite her better judgment, her gaze shifted toward her broken home and despair stabbed into her heart.

"Alec doesna know I came." The rustling grass grew louder

and marked Duncan's approach. "I came because ye left without telling me ye were going." A pack fell beside her and he folded himself to the ground in a pile of lanky legs and jutting elbows.

Celia looked over at him and found his eyes brilliant green with a sheen of tears. "Ye canna leave us." He swallowed and his prominent Adam's apple bobbed under the skin of his throat. "We love ye, Celia."

His words squeezed at her bruised heart and the plants in front of her smeared in a watery blur.

She swiped at her eyes with the back of her hand. "I can't go back."

"Alec dinna…" he said after a pause, "he dinna…was he no good to ye?"

Celia spun around to face Duncan in horror. "It was nothing Alec did. He was good to me." The very thought made her want to bury her face in her palms and cry until there was no hurt left.

"It wasn't anyone's fault," she shook her head. "It hurts too much to explain."

"Ye dinna have to say yer reason to me if ye dinna want to." His hand settled on hers, hot and sweaty, as if he too had run there. "Ye canna stay here."

Celia nodded, unable to speak around her own anguish.

"I know where ye can go, though." He pulled at the pack he'd thrown on the ground. "And I brought ye some bread and cheese to last ye a couple days."

She stared down at his innocent face and the affection shimmering in his eyes. This boy she'd cared for and nurtured was now trying to care for and nurture her.

Already he sacrificed too much in coming to her. "Duncan—"

"Nay," he said sharply, and his jaw hardened with the same stubborn display of authority Alec's so often did. "I willna send ye to yer death in the middle of winter with no food or shelter. I know where Niall and the other men lived. They told me after they came to live in the castle. I can take ye there." He shrugged. "It isna much, but it's warm. And it's safe."

Celia's protests faltered.

To decline his aid would be her death.

"And I will bring ye food once a week," he added with authority. "I'll no have ye going into the village while MacDougall's men still look for witches, aye?"

Celia shook her head. He put himself too much at risk with what he offered.

"I'll no tell anyone. Only I will know where ye are." He squeezed her forearm. "Ye saved my life. Let me repay ye in this way or I'll follow ye everywhere until ye accept my aid."

Celia sighed. "You're relentless and getting more and more like Alec every day."

A wide grin lit up Duncan's sharp face. "So that means ye'll let me help ye?"

Her shoulders wilted beneath the weight of her decision. Allowing him to help her would keep her alive through winter.

She glanced over at his eager face and also knew he would be true to his word—he'd never stop following her until she accepted his offer. His clumsy tracking could prove more dangerous to him than his help.

She sighed and the dry brown leaves on top of her ravaged garden fluttered. "You don't leave me with much choice."

He hopped to his feet, swung the bag to his back, and hefted her up beside him. "Then let's no waste any more time."

Celia took one last look at the destruction of her life and wrapped her hand around the key in her pocket. It served no value but to remind her of what she'd once possessed.

And everything she'd lost.

• • •

Two days' time wrapped around Alec's heart like stone. He followed the short, stocky MacDougall warrior, trailing Aros's hallways in a way that had become too familiar for comfort.

Celia's absence had torn a hole in Alec's life. Everything once beautiful and pure was gone, and with it his defense against the darkness. It pressed in on him, snagging the edges of his soul.

At least he knew she was safe. Sending Duncan after her had been the only way he knew to protect her. That and what he was about to do.

The shadows of the stone corridor gave way to the muted light of the great hall. MacDougall stood in front of the fire, his legs spread and his arms crossed.

"Laird MacLean is here to see ye," the guard said.

MacDougall turned and opened his arms in a welcoming gesture. "Ah, I see ye've returned. With good news, I hope?" He embraced Alec like an old friend.

"I sent ye a missive last week and havena received a response," Alec said. "I dinna like ye promising the outlaws gold to search my land. We hadna agreed to such a thing."

The warmth melted from MacDougall's face. "I can't just stop the search when I know *she* is there." His jaw twitched as if he were chewing on something.

"Ye mean the one ye spoke of before. The one who turned into a—"

"A bird, aye," MacDougall nodded.

"What did she look like?" Alec asked. Trepidation squeezed at his gut. He knew the answer before MacDougall even spoke, but he had to hear it for himself.

"Beautiful." MacDougall's body was rigid. "Slender but curvy, with long hair so pale it shines like the moon."

No one had hair like that save Celia.

Hot rage went dark within Alec. He flexed his fists at his side to cease the tremble of his hands. Celia's bruised cheek had been a result of whatever MacDougall had done to her.

If they hadn't been in Aros Castle, Alec would have struck the man dead with a single blow of his blade.

The desire to do so regardless strained at his conscience.

But he could not afford the war, not at the cost of his people. Especially not when they were already being ravaged by the outlaws.

"Do ye know whom I speak of?" MacDougall asked, glancing around the room as if she might suddenly appear.

Alec ground his teeth and focused on the chilled air to

slowly cool his anger to a tolerable level. "Aye, I've seen her." He swallowed around the distasteful words he needed to say to protect his people. "I'll agree to help ye, but ye must retract yer offer of gold to the outlaws."

MacDougall stared hard at Alec. "There might be more witches on yer land. Witches to be punished once they confess."

"Those are my terms," Alec said with finality. "And I will help ye find the witch ye seek." MacDougall's eyes flashed with a barely restrained rage. "And my daughter?" Alec swallowed down the bitter taste of defeat. "Aye, I will agree to that as well. I'll marry yer daughter."

Chapter Twenty-Eight

Loneliness numbed Celia's flesh and seeped into her body like poison. A week of long days and even longer nights passed in excruciating time, marked only by the decrease in her food supply.

Sunlight sluiced from a thin line at the base of the door and streaked across the dirt floor. The cottage's crude, whitewashed walls reflected the meager firelight. The small hovel had been carved from a swell of earth and blended with the forest. Unless you knew where to look, it would not easily be found.

It was genius, really, and set far enough away from town to keep outside visitors from stumbling upon it by accident.

Duncan had been right—it was warm and the solid earth walls kept out the merciless cut of wind. Celia's stare wandered to the firelight once more and her mind slipped down a torturous path of memories.

The heat of Alec's body next to hers, the masculine scent of him lingering on her skin after they'd coupled, the deep sound of his voice and the way it grew husky when they were alone.

The door rattled in a familiar pattern, one quick jiggle then three more in rapid succession. The door outside had been dressed to match the forest, but the inside remained wooden.

She ran to the door and unbolted the lock. The simple bit of metal and leather would break under the weakest of kicks, but it was better than nothing.

Duncan came in, and with him a burst of wind and scattering dry leaves. It was the first time she'd seen him since she'd arrived.

The first time she'd seen anyone.

She scanned the forest behind him before she closed the

door, ensuring he wasn't followed.

"Are ye doing well here?" he asked.

She glanced up and everything inside of her squeezed against the ache of solitude. In all the years she'd spent by herself, she'd never felt the pull for companionship so desperately.

"I am, thank you," her voice wavered.

Duncan's mouth pressed into a frown. "Ye dinna sound so well." He set a full sack of food on the lone table. "The witch trials have ceased on MacDougall's land and all the prisoners have been released." His tone was too monotone for such joyous news.

"But?" she prompted.

His brows tucked downward in a pained expression. "But now MacDougall seeks only one witch."

Celia kept her face impassive despite the frantic thud of her pulse. "Me."

Duncan came toward her, his long, thin arms spread in preparation for one of his tender hugs.

Her breath cut off in the swell of her throat. The simple act of being embraced, the very thing her lonely soul cried out for, would crack the delicate wall of will keeping her tears at bay.

If they came, they might never cease.

She shook her head and backed away. "You must return lest someone wonder where you've gone to. No one must suspect you are aiding me."

His hands fell to the side and disappointment showed in the way he cast his gaze to the floor. She'd hurt his feelings, a painful knowledge she regretted.

He nodded and opened the door to the low whistle of wind. His gaze met hers, his eyes glassy with unshed tears. "I just miss ye. And so does Wynda."

And Alec? She hardened her heart against the thought.

"I know," she said softly.

He gave a final nod before easing out the door. The shadows of the room darkened in his absence and curled around her heart.

Once again, she was alone.

• • •

Alec strode down the empty hall toward his solar. The castle was too dark despite the brilliant sunlight shining in through the precious glass. It had taken so long to replace the stink of fear and disappointment his father had left behind.

Brightness and joy had once again filled these halls, but all of that had fled with Celia.

His stomach gave a hard twist.

When Alec agreed to wed Saraid MacDougall, he'd provided his people with a calm they had not known in many decades. The outlaw raids had taken several days to quiet with the aid of MacDougall's men, but once they were done, the villagers returned to their homes and life returned to normal.

For everyone but him.

True, his land was at peace and the restoration of the castle was finally almost complete, but his heart held a perpetual hole where Celia once resided.

His fingers wrapped around the thick metal handle and he pushed open the door to his solar.

The sweet spice of expensive oil met his nose before he saw her. And when he did see her, he found Saraid bent over his desk with a ledger propped open in her spread hand.

"Are ye looking out of curiosity or are ye gathering information for yer father?" Alec asked in a dry tone.

She did not jump at the reproach, nor did she slam the book shut with guilt. Instead, she turned from the open ledger and smiled at him from across the room. Her eyes lit with the same excitement they always did when she saw him. This time, she'd smeared carmine across her full lips. The color stood garish against the red of her gown and called attention to the mass of crooked teeth crowding her mouth.

"Neither," she said with a sly smirk. "Ye know I dinna know my numbers." She sauntered toward him in a hiss of silk. "My education has been directed toward making me a good wife." Her lashes lowered. "Though I'm sure there is much I have to learn still —wifely duties ye will teach me."

She reached out and caressed the fabric of his leine, just over his heart. While he did not pull away, he did not welcome her touch any more than he welcomed the thought of claiming her in bed.

He gave a noncommittal grunt.

Her hands slid over his chest and she pressed the great puff of her skirts against his legs. She gazed up at him with a stare bordering on desperation. "We dinna have to wait." Her breasts swelled with her deep breath.

The scent of her perfume made his head spin, with her so overwhelmingly close. "I'm no that kind of man."

Her eyes flashed with something dark. "Ye're no the kind of man to secure a betrothal with a bit of bed sport, yet ye let yer kitchen staff talk to ye as if they were yer equal and ye lead that pathetic orphan about as if he were yer own heir." She shot him a dangerous glare. "The kind of man who goes back on his word to locate the witch of Duart, the verra one my father has sought his whole life."

Saraid had not changed since they were children. Still spoiled with entitlement.

"We have searched alongside yer father's men for the witch and still no found her," he reminded her.

It was only a partial truth. His men had searched with the MacDougall guards Alec allowed on his land, but nowhere near the crude cottage where Celia hid.

His heart crushed against his ribs at the thought of her.

She might have refused him, but he would not abandon her in her time of need.

Saraid tilted her head up at Alec and thrust out her lower lip. "Forgive me. I know ye've tried to find the witch. Perhaps I can help."

"Help?" Something in her shrewd expression set a coil of unease tensing through him.

"If I find the witch, there will be nothing holding my father back from allowing us to wed." Her brilliant red lips widened into a grin. "Then we can wed."

Saraid strode away with a confident gait. He could have

stopped her, silenced her efforts with the crush of his lips to hers, a feigning of affection.

But he could not bring himself to do it, not while the memory of Celia stayed so strong in his mind.

Celia was well hidden. So long as she stayed that way, Saraid would not find her, nor would MacDougall's men.

For now, Celia was safe.

• • •

The soft ember glow of the hearth was little comfort on the still night. Celia lay in bed, listening to the pull of her own breath, steady, slow, and automatic.

A stick snapped outside. Her breathing stopped and locked in her chest.

The door rattled and her heart leapt to her throat.

Her mind scrambled with frantic haste for a place to go, a place to hide in the open room with almost no furnishings.

The door rattled three more times in rapid succession.

Duncan.

She leapt from the bed and raced to the door, her heart still slamming in her chest. Duncan would never come in the middle of the night if it were not important.

She pulled open the door and found him standing in the icy moonlight, his eyes wide with terror. He staggered into the room and did not speak until the door closed behind him.

"It's Bessie." His words were breathless. "The baby started to come two days ago, but he's still no emerged. She's begging for ye and I held off for as long as I could to get ye." He shook his head, his face stricken in the subtle light. "Then the blood started. There was so much of it. If ye dinna come…"

Celia's throat closed and she knew exactly what he did not want to say.

If she did not come, Bessie and her baby would die.

Chapter Twenty-Nine

Celia's clothes stuck to her skin in the overly warm cottage and fatigue left her limbs heavy. Still, she did not cease her efforts to turn the babe within Bessie's womb.

The graying light of dawn shadowed the woman's pallid face. She'd once again slipped into an exhausted slumber, her body still contracting with the force of labor.

Celia pushed her hands gently against Bessie's swollen stomach, along either side of the baby. It fought back against her ministrations. A good sign.

"I see the bairn's head," Bessie's neighbor, Nell, exclaimed from behind Celia.

Celia's heart slammed hard in her chest and a burst of energy shot through her. Nell had been correct—the baby was crowning.

"Bessie, I need you to wake up," Celia said. "You need to help push the baby out."

The woman gave a soft whimper, but her eyes remained closed.

Her body clenched around another contraction and her legs tensed with such tender effort it tore at Celia's heart.

Bessie was not strong enough to do more than what her body did naturally.

With a painful slowness, the baby's head eased from its mother's body until Celia could tighten her fingers around the babe enough to help.

She tugged, gentle enough to not cause injury, yet firm enough to aid Bessie's next contraction in freeing the baby.

The babe pulled free of its mother's body. The dark eyes

blinked in surprise and the baby's arms and legs threw out wide as if it felt in a free fall.

A boy.

Celia could not stop the smile on her face any more than she could stop the tears welling in her eyes.

A beautiful, healthy baby boy.

The little boy gave a hoarse squall with his new voice and his body showed bright pink.

She quickly tied off the gray cord at his stomach and cut it with a clean knife.

His swollen eyes squeezed shut and his mouth opened to reveal pink gums for another wail. She passed him to Nell with relief.

The babe would be fine. He was healthy.

She quickly cleaned Bessie and knelt at her side to feed her the tea she'd had Nell prepare. Using a sponge, she began emptying the contents of the bowl squeeze by slow squeeze into Bessie's mouth as she'd done with Duncan.

The woman's throat worked around the fluid forced into her mouth. She gave a gurgled cough and her eyes slit open.

"My baby?" The question was little more than an exhale between her pale lips.

Nell carried the swaddled infant and held him out to Bessie's turned head for her to see. "A braw lad, Bessie. Ye did well."

"She'll need rest," Celia said softly to Nell. "But we'll still try to let the babe suckle. Her body will feed him even in her slumber."

Nell's withered hand settled on her shoulder. "Ye canna stay here, lass. It isna safe."

Celia stared down at Bessie's young face and her heart gave a hard wrench. "I cannot leave her."

"Ye must. Tell me what to do and I'll see it done, but I know Bessie wouldna ever forgive herself if ye were captured because ye'd aided her." The baby grunted in the woman's arms, soft sounds of fresh hunger.

Much as Celia wanted to ignore the warning, Nell's words held truth. If Celia stayed, she ran the risk of being captured.

She could do no more for Bessie, nothing Nell couldn't.

Celia nodded and a band tightened in her chest. Nell eased the swaddled infant to her chest and the hungry grunts grew more determined.

"You will have to guide the child to her breast," Celia said in resignation.

Nell nodded. "Aye, I've seen it done before. I'll no let the bairn starve, nor will I allow his mother to die."

"Then let me show you which herbs you will need to use." Celia took a deep breath around the pain and reached for her bag. "And promise to get me should she develop a fever."

• • •

Alec sat in the solitude of his quiet chamber. Night had given way to dawn and dawn had burned into the brightness of day. He'd watched the slow shift of black to rosy gold without moving, only thinking.

Too much thinking.

This kind of morning reminded him of Celia.

She was like the glow of a new day, the way she'd chased away his shadows with her brilliant joy. For those two weeks, she'd represented all the good in his life. Everything beautiful, everything light.

The memory seared beneath his ribs like a ball of fire.

But even with the sun up, he felt no light. Not anymore. Though he tried to ignore it, the darkness rose within him.

His hand curled around the cup at his side, its pewter sides like ice against his fingertips.

He could feel her presence on his land. He knew where she hid. One short ride across the rugged landscape and he could pull her into his arms.

He pressed the rim of the cup to his mouth and paused. She could not stop him if he dragged her back to Duart Castle. The servants would never doubt their laird.

The liquid tipped dangerously close to his lips and the sharp scent of whisky pulled at a ravenous desire somewhere deep within.

Once he had her in his home, he could keep her there—in fine rooms with fine furnishings. She would live like a queen. Safe, protected.

Forced.

He swallowed a mouthful of saliva and drew a deep breath of the hot, heady whisky aroma.

His will fought the same battle that'd raged through the night. And yet now it wavered with exhaustion.

He closed his eyes and imagined Celia as she had looked in the moonlight, her face stricken from a childhood of terror. She had lived through too much for one innocent life.

A rough growl vibrated in his throat and he set the cup to the table with a hard smack, the liquor within still untouched.

Even now, even after these two weeks, Celia burned deeper than his darkness.

• • •

Celia passed through the shadows between cottages in the hopes of remaining unseen. Sunlight flickered overhead, flashing bright before being blocked once more.

Her lungs swelled in her chest in an effort to keep up with her hurried pace. For all the loneliness within her earthen hut, she longed for its oppressive safety.

A splash sounded behind her.

Then another.

Her pulse leapt.

Someone followed her.

She dug out her dagger and slipped around a corner blocked from sunlight, where her shadow wouldn't show. Her back pressed flush to the rough wall. She forced her ragged breath in and out in slow, trembling beats.

Waiting.

The footsteps slapped closer through the puddles. She leapt from the corner, her dagger lifted for attack.

An aging woman with watery blue eyes and frazzled gray

hair screeched in alarm and cowered back, her arm thrown over her face.

"Dinna hurt me." The woman's voice quaked. "My husband is sick. I saw ye and knew ye could help him."

Celia lowered her blade, but her muscles burned with tension and her hands shook with the rush of unused energy.

The woman slowly relaxed her arm and regarded Celia, eyes wide with desperation. "Please. He's all I have." Her puckered chin quivered. She rounded her frail shoulders against the wind.

The woman's shawl was tattered and the rest of her clothes appeared to be in as poor repair.

Celia knew she should leave. Those few extra moments spent to aid another could easily be her demise. While her mind screamed at her to run, she ignored the warning and nodded at the old woman. "Please, show me where he is. I'll do what I can."

The woman did not wait to be told again. She spun around and navigated the narrow alleyways with expertise until they arrived inside a small, tidy cottage.

An aged man lay in a bed at the far corner, his white hair thin and patchy. His breath faintly whispered from his weakened chest and a heartbeat was almost imperceptible. Within minutes, he would be dead.

The weight of that knowledge sat heavy in Celia's chest. She rested a hand to the man's shoulder and his breath scratched a final, struggled exhale. And ceased.

"I'm afraid I'm too late," Celia said slowly. Death was always difficult to acknowledge.

No words of comfort could ever be enough to assuage the force of grief.

"Did ye just…" The woman shook her head vigorously. "I saw ye touch him and he stopped breathing. Fix it. Undo what ye did. Do what ye did to the pregnant lass."

Celia held a hand out to the woman in an attempt to offer comfort. "The child was still alive, just sleeping in the womb. I only—"

"Lies," the woman cried. The desperation in her eyes flickered to wild grief. "Ye lie. Ye dinna want him to live. Ye knew he told the outlaws he'd seen ye and ye'll see him dead for it. I should have known better than to trust ye." Her bony finger curled out toward Celia, stabbing the air with accusation. "Witch!"

"No," Celia said sharply. Her stomach filled with ice despite her strong voice.

This was how Fiona had been accused.

A man she couldn't save.

And she'd paid the price.

The woman stalked toward her, hissing the word as if it were a vile chant.

Witch.

Celia was forced backward until she found herself in a patch of warm sunlight and realized she'd stepped outside.

She turned the way she'd come and ran as quickly as the slick ground would allow her. Where she had been cautious before, now she ran with abandon, paying no mind to her surroundings.

Something hard slammed into her throat and suddenly she stared up at the sky with the ground pressed to her back.

Confusion reeled through her mind.

Pain.

Crushing pain squeezed her throat and kept air from getting to her lungs.

A flicker of panic ran through her, insisting she get up, insisting she run.

Before she could move, someone hauled her upright and something warm and firm clamped over her mouth.

She was too late.

Chapter Thirty

Alec sat opposite MacDougall with an ale in front of him, the appearance of friends who were no longer so given the hard stare MacDougall held him with. Though they might appear as allied friends, Alec knew by MacDougall's hard stare, they were not.

A chill eased in through the partially closed shutters and ruffled MacDougall's white hair against his cheek.

"Ye're taking too long to find the witch," MacDougall said.

"My men search day and night without success. Perhaps she has left MacLean lands." Alec regarded his opponent with careful observation.

MacDougall curled his hands around a goblet, but did not lift it. "Yer men are no looking hard enough."

Alec offered the other man a sympathetic look. "They are."

MacDougall lifted the goblet and slammed it on the table so hard liquid sloshed out. "They could look harder." His voice rang out against the stone walls.

He pulled in a deep breath and smoothed a shaking hand over his hair. "She needs to be found. Let me put more men on yer land to help."

Alec lifted his head with a note of authority he knew the older man wouldn't miss. "I willna allow ye to have so many of yer men on my land. The outlaw attacks have lessened and most have moved on to different territories. My people are finally settled and I willna have them disturbed by the sight of so many warriors."

MacDougall's fingers danced with ceaseless motion against one another, sliding, picking, grinding. "She has to still be here."

He closed his eyes and his red eyelids glistened. "I can *feel* her."

The hair on Alec's arms rose and it had little to do with the black, empty hearth.

The man was crazy.

Crazy and dangerous, an imposing combination.

MacDougall's eyes opened, sharp and determined. "I'll find her, and when I do, she'll pay for all the years she's tormented me, all the pain she's inflicted."

A rap sounded at the door and reverberated off the naked stone walls.

MacDougall paused a moment and his face relaxed into pleasant composure. "What is it?" he asked.

"I have news of the witch, laird." The voice on the other side of the door held a note of pride.

Alec's heart pumped hard in his chest and echoed in his ears. Only the years of warrior's training and squelching emotions in times of stress kept his face impassive.

"Then come in," MacDougall said in a smooth voice.

A guard strolled in, sweaty and thick with more layers of flesh than any respectable warrior should possess. The man's barrel chest expanded with a deep breath. "Yer daughter has captured the witch. *I* was on the team of men to bring her down."

Every organ inside Alec's body stopped. His ears strained to pick up sounds of her voice, of her struggle.

He heard none.

God help them if they brought her any harm.

MacDougall's gray eyes glinted like freshly wrought steel and he smiled at Alec. "It appears yer intended bride has brought ye a wedding present." His hands spread across the desk's surface in a greedy caress before curling into fists. "Bring her to me."

The order hit Alec's gut like a dirty punch. To see Celia dragged in as a prisoner—it was more than he could bear.

The guard shifted on his feet and bits of sand screeched beneath his boot. "My lady still has the witch."

MacDougall straightened. "Then have her come here."

"She isna here yet, laird. We were ordered to stop on the edge of MacLean and MacDougall land. She told us to wait and so we did. I knew ye'd want the witch right away, so I came here at first chance to tell ye we'd captured her." The man's eyes gleamed. "Will we be getting the bag of gold for our efforts?"

Hope beat with a rapid pulse through Alec's veins. If Celia was not already at the castle, she might still be saved. He rose, his muscles firing with renewed vigor. "I'll go get them for ye."

MacDougall turned his eyes toward Alec without moving his head. "Go and find her, bring her to me." His gaze slid back to the guard. "Ye may leave, Laird MacLean."

Alec walked from the room on legs stiff with his restrained gait. He wouldn't consider the guard's reward or fat, not when he had a chance to find Celia, not when there was a chance to save her.

• • •

The wind shoved against Celia's back, but she refused to allow herself to stumble. Five guards glared at her, their faces evidence of how ready they were for an excuse to end her life.

MacDougall's daughter paced in front of her, each step punctuated with the kick of heavy skirts and anger. There had been six guards when Celia was first taken. One guard had gone missing, a sign Celia knew did not bode well.

MacDougall's daughter came to a stop in front of her. A scowl twisted the noblewoman's refined features. "Confess ye're a witch and be done with it."

She lifted her chin. "I've told you before. I'm a healer, not a witch." The same words she'd repeated time and again, but the woman did not seem to hear.

MacDougall's daughter gave a hiss of annoyance and waved her hand toward the guards. "Leave us."

They exchanged uncertain looks. "Are ye sure ye want to be left alone with her?" a towering balding man asked.

Her eyes rolled heavenward before snapping back to him. "It's only for a moment. Go and I will call if I need ye."

The press of their sweaty bodies into Celia's personal space eased and sunlight replaced their shadows. MacDougall's daughter watched them walk away and did not speak until they were out of earshot by the edge of the forest.

She leaned close and her spicy perfume fogged around Celia. "I intend to let ye go."

Celia tipped her head back in order to get a clean breath. "Why would you help me?" she asked, dubious.

"Because witches are powerful allies." The woman settled back with a grin, as if she were exceedingly proud of herself. "Ye have only to make me a simple potion and ye may have yer freedom."

Celia's mind raced. Did the woman pose the option to her as a test? A fake potion could always be made, but what if MacDougall's daughter was merely trying to get proof of witchcraft?

"What kind of a potion?" Celia asked slowly.

The noblewoman's eyes lit up with excitement. "Ye know what I want—a love potion."

Celia frowned and shook her head. "I don't understand. You are beautiful and have the strong MacDougall name in your favor. Why do you need a love potion?"

"Have ye no ever been in love?" the woman asked, her gaze pleading. "Where all ye can think of is the way the man looks and smells and…" Her face fell. "And he canna bring himself to look upon ye. I've been in love since I was a child and he doesna give me the time I deserve."

Alec surfaced in Celia's mind. Tall, strong, ice blue eyes hot with passion. She didn't have to close her eyes to remember how he smelled or how he felt. All of it was locked in a special place in her heart, never to be forgotten.

But to imagine feeling so and not having such emotions reciprocated would be painful indeed.

Celia studied her enemy's young daughter, noting the sheen of tears in her eyes that once glared, the quivering lip on a mouth that spoke so sharply.

For all her nastiness, she was still a girl with feelings and for one small moment, Celia wished she had the power to make her man fall in love.

"Please," the woman said. "After all these years, I want Alec to love me."

Celia's heart crashed erratically against her breast. "Alec?"

The noblewoman's chin rose with an arrogant lift. "Aye, Alec MacLean, of course—my betrothed."

Nausea squeezed Celia's stomach and left her cool skin prickling with sweat.

Alec, betrothed.

To the daughter of the man who wanted Celia dead.

Pain sluiced through Celia with the memory of how she'd rejected him.

He'd obviously gotten over her quickly.

The thought ripped through her mind, but even as it did, she knew it as false.

Obviously he didn't care for this woman if she went to such lengths to secure a love potion, and doubtless this would be an advantageous match for Alec.

The night from the forest flashed through her mind, when Alec stated there was a way to save his people, but that he would have to give up something dear.

Had he meant her?

Had he meant *this*?

"Will ye do it?" MacDougall's daughter asked, drawing Celia's attention to her determined blue gaze.

"Forgive me, my lady, but I am no witch. I am a simple healer who works with herbs from the ground." Celia lowered her gaze lest the other woman see the show of emotion in her eyes and suspect the reason for Alec's disinterest. "You ask what is not within my ability."

Silence followed her declaration. The wind whistled across the thick grass and sent the trees chattering.

"Hamish!" the noblewoman shrieked.

Celia looked up to find a balding guard answering his mistress's call at a full run. MacDougall's daughter turned away, but not before Celia heard her orders. "The witch has confessed. Kill her and we'll return her body to my father to be burned."

Celia's pulse raced and every sense in her body became

more in tune with her surroundings. The chill of the breeze on her face, the odor of the man's sweat as he approached, the cry of a seagull in the distance.

The guard's step faltered. "But, my lady—"

"Do it!" The woman's voice carried on the wind like the crack of a whip.

The man slipped his blade free of its sheath and stalked closer, his gaze fixed on Celia.

Chapter Thirty-One

Celia froze beneath the advancing guard's stare. Her fingers went to her belt on instinct and met the empty sheath where her dagger had once been.

"Forgot we took it, did ye?" he asked.

Her heart lodged in her throat. She was unarmed and at his mercy.

She took a step back. And then another, and another. True, she was prolonging the inevitable, but she was also purposefully pulling herself further from the other guards' view. If she was out of their vantage point, they wouldn't see if she managed to escape. *If* she were able to escape…

The man did not stop her backward progress. He watched her with a glint in his eye, like a cat observing a mouse.

Her muscles tensed to run, to fight, to do whatever it took to survive. The men were clustered together in the distance and paid her no attention. They didn't appear to notice the way she was slowly slipping from view.

Her heel found purchase on an uneven bit of something and her foot rolled to the right. Her balance swayed and she stumbled.

It was all the guard needed.

He pounced at her, the sharp edge of his blade flashing toward her soft, unarmored torso.

A snarl sounded above the wind and the man cried out in surprised pain. His sword fell away at the last second before it could pierce her flesh.

Celia's body froze, her limbs locked with the fear of death. Her brain reeled to understand what had happened.

The man turned away from her and a flash of russet red showed against the straw colored grass.

Ruadh.

Wet red glistened on the man's arm.

In one motion, he swiped his blade from the ground and attacked the little fox.

Celia staggered upright and ran, knowing Ruadh would follow closely behind.

He always did.

She had sprinted the several dozen feet to the coast where numerous caves could provide shelter when a high-pitched yelp cut through the air.

The world around her shrank to nothing and her feet planted into the ground.

Ruadh.

She spun around and found for the first time in years he was not behind her.

He'd stayed to fight.

To protect her.

Tears stung her eyes and something inside her breast withered with despair. She had no dagger, no way to fight, but she would not leave him to die.

The rain started then. Hard and stinging, lashing with the bite of a thousand needles.

She fought through it to get to where the soldier had been, when Ruadh came running toward her at his full speed.

She choked in a great exhale and her knees went weak with relief.

He did not even limp.

Together they ran for the cover of the coast, not stopping until they were concealed inside a cave with little more than a narrow wisp of light trickling in. It was enough.

She curled Ruadh's warmth against her. He did not protest her affection.

The metallic scent of blood tinged the air.

She worked her fingers through his thick fur, seeking the injury until she found the smear of blood where the tip of his ear had been shorn off.

The bit of skin would never grow back, but he would certainly live. Her grasp on him tightened, but still he did not growl or try to skitter away.

He nuzzled closer to her and his hearty sigh fluttered the hair against her neck, as if he were truly grateful for the affection.

And so they huddled together in the semi-darkness, waiting out the threat of danger.

• • •

Alec scanned the coastline once more, his eyes trained for anything out of the ordinary. The gray, angry sky cast a darkness over the low-lying brush and left the yellow and green terrain mixed in a blend of shadows.

"Do ye see anything?" Duncan asked at his side. The boy's horse pranced nervously beneath him, doubtless feeding off his anxious mood.

Frustration tightened along his back and threaded into his brain. "Nothing."

Even Saraid's guards hadn't been visible within the last hour.

The mission had thus far been unsuccessful.

"I dinna understand it," Alec muttered.

Duncan leaned in his saddle. "What'd ye say?"

Alec sighed, deeply regretting having let the boy come along. He was in no damn mood to talk. Not when he knew Celia was somewhere on MacLean or MacDougall land with an army of men looking for her.

"I dinna understand how they found the cottage. It's no like it's a location easily stumbled upon."

Quiet followed his statement.

The boy was never silent.

Something tingled along Alec's spine. "Is there something ye need to tell me?"

Duncan's cheeks flushed bright red. "Bessie had the baby stuck inside her. She'd been trying for two days to get it out." He shook his head, eyes wide. "She was going to die."

Alec narrowed his eyes and every muscle in his body tightened. "What does this have to do with Celia?"

The boy sank a little deeper in his saddle. "I went and got her to help Bessie." The boy's straight back did not waver and he met Alec's hard glare. "I dinna mean to put her in danger, but I couldna let the woman suffer either. What would ye do if Celia had a babe stuck in her womb and faced death?"

Alec ground his teeth until his jaw ached. Celia was not Bessie. Celia was supposed to be in a cottage where she was safe.

He gave a low growl of frustration and looked away, his gaze once more finding the darkened landscape. "I havena seen MacDougall men for a while."

Unease niggled his nerves. He glanced at Duncan and found the boy's eyes squinting into the wind.

"Do ye feel it too?" Alec asked.

Duncan's nostrils flared and the muscles at his thin neck stood out. He nodded.

It was all Alec needed. He snapped the reins of his horse to a full run and ice spiked his blood.

The pounding of hooves filled his ears—those of his own horse and Duncan's behind him. Wind rushed against them and the damn rain started to pour down, but nothing would dissuade him from getting to Aros Castle. Not with the apprehension coiling in his gut.

Chapter Thirty-Two

Celia's clothes hung heavy on her shoulders, soaked through with a mix of sea water and misting rain. Her back pressed against the closed door. She'd never been so grateful for the flimsy lock and solitude. She'd never been so grateful to be home.

Or what was home now.

Ruadh had eased inside the cottage behind her, something he had not yet done with this new place. He sat on her with his furry wet bottom resting against her sodden shoes.

"That was too close, Ruadh."

The hearth had gone cold and a chill settled in her bones, but she didn't dare light a fire. She would chance a precious candle when night fell, but for now the slice of light under the door would have to do.

"You saved my life today, Ruadh," she said in the same gentle voice she used for sick children. "If it weren't for your sacrifice, I would have been killed."

He stepped close to her, his shiny black nose twitching with each delicate sniff.

"You fought valiantly and will forever bear the mark." Her heart hung on her words and she realized she spoke them for herself as much as for him. "I need to tend to your wound because if you become sick after what you did for me…" Her voice cracked and his head cocked to the side.

"I'd never forgive myself." The tears came freely now, flowing down her cheeks. They choked from her clogged throat and poured from her heart.

Ruadh edged closer to her and slid his warm muzzle under her hand. She dabbed some clean linen into an herbed vinegar mixture. "Forgive me if this hurts," she whispered. The cloth touched the wound and a high-pitched whine sounded deep in his throat.

But he did not run from her.

She blew a gentle stream of air on the wound where the vinegar mixture stung the tender skin, but he flicked his ear and gave her an irritated look.

"Too brave for childish coddling?" She gently rubbed the fur at his neck with one hand and reached for the juniper ointment with the other. "This will keep your wound clean so you heal faster."

She gingerly brushed the salve over his torn skin until the fur around the wound glistened. Her heart winced with each gentle stroke, feeling the pain he bravely did not show.

She capped the jar of ointment and set it aside. Ruadh followed the action with his amber eyes, then rested his chin on her leg. Her fingertips skimmed the top of his soft head, caring, soothing. His eyes closed.

She gazed down at him and the knot returned to her throat. She had come so close to losing him.

Pain squeezed her heart, her stomach, her whole being. She'd been irrational all these years to think she could avoid relationships. Shunning people had not kept her free of implicating others—she'd just fooled herself into thinking such.

And Alec had shown her what could happen when she did open her heart and allow someone in.

She closed her eyes and embraced the ache swelling in her throat. He had shown her the beauty of love, everything wonderful and sweet she could experience in life.

Everything she had denied herself.

In leaving, she'd thought she was saving him.

And now she realized she'd sacrificed for naught.

• • •

Alec's shoulder skimmed the stone wall as he wound his way up the narrow staircase behind the guard at Aros Castle. Duncan followed behind, his steps echoing off the stone with a hesitation indicating he didn't feel any more comfortable following the guard than Alec did.

"Ye're no going to tell me what this is about, then?" Alec asked for the fifth time.

The guard, once again, did not answer.

The clench of unease in Alec's gut tightened and he let his fingertips graze the cool hilt of his blade for reassurance. If this was some kind of trap, surely they would have made him remove his weapon.

They could defend themselves still.

He glanced behind him and raised his eyebrows at Duncan. The boy curled his fingers around the dagger at his side and nodded.

The guard halted and opened a thick banded door. The clacking of the handle echoed around them and curled down to the blackness below. Golden light from the other side splashed onto the stairs.

"This way," the guard muttered.

Alec strode into the room with an edge to his confidence, fully prepared to fight.

And fully unprepared for a feminine room of lavender silks filled with MacDougall and his men, all gathered around Saraid's writhing form on her bed.

Everything inside of Alec snarled for him to back out of there and leave.

Living a life of a noble after so many years of being a warrior was still a difficult adjustment to make, but going to the room of a woman who was not family—even he knew such a thing was indecent.

A scream pealed through the crowded room, so high-pitched it made Alec's inner ears wince. The bed creaked and the silk curtains trembled. Saraid's body jerked and she loosed another horrible shriek.

The guards shuffled away from the bed and exchanged looks of concern. MacDougall's face paled beneath his white beard.

Alec stared down at Saraid where she still thrashed and

wailed on her bed. Her lady's maid perched on the edge of the bed and smoothed Saraid's skirts down.

"She's been poisoned," MacDougall said in a gravelly voice. "She caught the witch I bade *ye* to find." The harshness of his tone stressed his apparent accusation.

"And where is she now?" Alec asked, his voice normal despite the tightness in his throat.

"Escaped," MacDougall snarled. His pale face bled to a purple-red. "She got away. Probably crawled back onto yer land."

The clamp around Alec's chest eased and air rushed to his lungs once more. His heart thumped with wild relief.

She was still alive.

This time he would bring her to Duart.

And this time he did not think she would protest.

Saraid gave a low, keening cry. "I trusted her and she poisoned me." She gave a dramatic roll to the side, flashing a length of her calf before the maid hurriedly covered her up once more.

Alec watched the display with distrust. While Celia's escape relieved him immensely, it did not surprise him.

She was resourceful and intelligent. But to poison Saraid…

No, his gentle Celia would never bring harm to another. Not even to her enemies.

MacDougall approached the bed and stared at his daughter with a sneer of disdain. "What do ye mean ye trusted her?"

Saraid stared up at him with a look of terror shining through the throes of her sickness. "I sought her out for a potion to…" her voice trailed off and her dark gaze dragged to Alec before regarding her father once more. "I sought her for a potion to make me more fertile when I wed so I could bear strong sons." Her arms clenched around her stomach and her mouth fell open with a hiss of agony.

The coincidence of the well-timed pain did not sit well with Alec. The way she'd had the presence of mind to look at him before she finished her reply did not sit well with him. And the accusations toward Celia damn well did not sit well with him either.

MacDougall, however, straightened and approached Alec.

"She put herself in harm's way to be a good wife to ye and how do ye repay her?" He grimaced in disgust. "By hiding the witch."

Alec's fists clenched. "If we were helping ye, why would we hide her?" He let a warning tone slide into his voice.

"It doesna matter why, but I know yer lie for what it is." MacDougall grinned. "And I have men marching there right now to get her."

A chill slid down Alec's back, despite the obviousness of the older man's tactic.

It was a test to see if Alec would run to Celia's side. The MacDougall men would secretly follow him and then they would know what MacDougall said was true.

Alec had seen it done before and was not about to give in to the lure. MacDougall's gray stare flicked behind Alec.

"Then wherever they are marching, they will be disappointed," Alec said in a level voice. "I'm no harboring a witch."

Saraid moaned pitifully on the bed.

"Is that so?" A slow smile curled across MacDougall's thin lips. He nodded to someone behind Alec and a soldier's heavy boots thumped across the floor and echoed down the hall.

Something prickled at the base of Alec's skull. "I dinna appreciate the accusation," he growled.

Much as he wanted to, he did not glance around the room to the guard who'd taken his leave. Nor did he look down at Duncan. Doubtless the boy would need reassurance, but to do so would give them both away. He'd been silent at Alec's side thus far. He could not have chosen a better time to tame his tongue.

MacDougall's shoulders eased lower and his posture became more relaxed. "Ach, well, when ye get to be my age, ye dinna trust easy, aye?"

Alec grunted his agreement, but the knot in his gut didn't loosen. Something still did not sit comfortably with him.

Saraid cried out in the bed, her thrashing aggravated and

restless. "I need ye," she whined.

MacDougall turned from Alec and approached the bed. She shook her head against a matted pile of curls beneath her. "Laird MacLean."

Alec bit back a sigh and grudgingly strode toward the bed. Just a few more minutes and he could leave. Then he could send someone to get Celia, in the cover of the night where they would be unseen.

"Ye'll find the witch, won't ye?" She grasped his hand and squeezed it hard. Her fingers were moist and icy cold. "And make her pay for poisoning me. She gave me belladonna instead of the fertility potion I'd asked for. I know it."

He stared down at Saraid's wide eyes. Though her cheeks were flushed, her pupils were not dilated. Her pulse did not race against his hand.

She had clearly not been poisoned. "Of course," he murmured, and glanced to his right to find Duncan in the crowd of men.

His unease in his gut tightened and shot up against his heart. Duncan was not there.

He released Saraid's hand and turned to look behind him, his pulse firing with panic.

Still no Duncan.

A hand curled over Alec's shoulder and MacDougall's voice sounded in his ear, silken with victory. "Missing someone?"

Chapter Thirty-Three

Celia lay curled on her side, her body stiff from holding still for so long in the cool room. She'd lit a candle for at least some warmth and kept it safely perched in its holder by her abdomen. Its heat was scant, but better than the press of cold.

Ruadh had woken and become restless within minutes of falling asleep on her knee earlier. He'd paced in front of the door until she set him free.

Once more, she was completely alone.

Alone, but safe.

She should be grateful.

Her demise had come too close.

Something slammed into the door, hard enough to rattle the hinges. Every nerve in her body leapt and for a split second she remained frozen with uncertainty.

"Celia," Duncan said from the other side of the door. "Ye have to leave now."

She jumped from the bed, careful not to upset the candle. Blood flowed hot in her body. Limbs once chilled now tingled with sweat.

She fumbled with the lock until it finally slipped free and the door swung open.

Duncan all but fell into the cottage and grabbed her arm. "They know ye're here. Alec and I were in Saraid's room. She's claiming ye poisoned her and now they are coming for ye."

Celia's mind raced while she slipped the lock back into place. "What are you talking about, Duncan? How did they find me?"

He raced around the room, gathering her small collection of herbs and ointments, stuffing them into the bag draped over his arm. "Laird MacDougall's daughter. She said she captured ye and ye poisoned her." He stopped what he was doing and ran toward her. His arms came around her in a tight embrace. "Thank God ye're safe. I'd feared…"

Celia shoved him back. "Duncan, leave. If they're coming here and know you helped me, they'll kill you."

He shook his head and widened his stance in that stubborn Highlander way. Like Alec. "I'm no going to leave ye defenseless."

"I can defend myself." She grabbed her bag from him and hurried to the narrow shelf.

Her feet tangled against the hem of her skirt in her haste and she pitched forward. She braced her fall with the shelf, but it shifted under her weight and she landed hard on the ground.

She scrambled to her feet before Duncan could reach her side. "You promised you'd be safe," she said. "You can't be here while there's so much danger."

She threw the bag over her shoulder without packing the rest of her items. They could be regrown, remade.

A life could not.

If Duncan wouldn't leave without her, then they both needed to leave.

Now.

Leaves crunched outside.

Duncan's eyes met Celia's and fear flashed in the bright depths for a split second before giving way to the spark of determination.

He slipped his sword free of its sheath. The blade appeared overlarge in his slender arms, but he held it without wavering. His lips set in a grim line. "Get behind me, Celia."

The baritone of men speaking in low tones murmured from outside the thick walls.

Her breath came so fast it set the room spinning. The harder she breathed, the more starved she felt for air.

She balled her hands into fists and pulled from the bravery she'd seen Alec exhibit. The same Duncan now demonstrated.

Alec would never surrender without a fight and neither would she.

She curled her stiff fingers around the hilt of her paltry eating knife and stood beside Duncan, shooting him a warning look that told him he'd have to deal with her aid. Before he could protest, a voice sounded from outside. "I think I found a door."

Her muscles ached with the force of her grip on her weapon. The small blade would not be enough for what they were up against.

She glanced behind her in search of another form of weapon and her breath caught in her throat. The shelf she'd fallen against was pulled out from the wall and revealed not an earthen wall behind it, but darkness.

A tunnel.

A means of escape.

• • •

Alec navigated his beast through the darkening forest with dangerous speed. The gray skies were slowly filtering to black.

He didn't need to worry about MacDougall's men following him. They were already at least ten minutes ahead. Approximately how long it'd taken him to convince the aging laird he had nothing to do with Celia's hiding place.

Alec ducked to avoid a branch. If he could get there before MacDougall's men, he could swipe Celia onto his steed and race back to Duart where they could lock the castle down. She would be protected.

It was a risk, a stupid one, but it was all he had.

His horse's breath huffed hard with effort, as if he sensed the urgency. The rolling hill housing the cottage came into sight, exactly where Duncan had told him it would be.

Alec's heart pounded in his chest. Horses stood out front, at least three dozen. Some riders still sat in their saddles while others stood at the front with their blades at the ready.

Too many to fight on his own.

Perhaps Duncan had gotten to Celia in time, perhaps by now they were both on their way to Duart.

Every natural instinct in Alec knew that wasn't the case. The impossible ache in his chest told him that much.

He pulled back on the reins and his horse slowed.

MacDougall's men hadn't seen him yet—an advantage he needed. The hill was far larger than the humble cottage Duncan had described. Any man hiding who had a lick of thought in his head would never build a safe home without a trap door.

Going around the back could cost him time he didn't have, but it might pay off. No matter what it took, no matter where she was, he would find a way to rescue Celia.

• • •

Celia cupped her hand around the candle and focused on the warm glow it cast around them. Even with its soft light, the threatening grip of darkness squeezed around her. The dank smell of wet earth hung heavy in the air.

She pressed her lips together and clamped them between her front teeth. The walls around them were carved through the hill and braced with a complex series of wooden beams.

A muffled bang came from behind the closed trap door.

Celia's heart hammered so loud in her chest she thought surely they could hear her.

Surely they would find the secret passage and capture them.

Someone shouted. The words were too blocked by the shelf-door to be understood, but the tone sounded like an order. Duncan's hand against her back became more insistent, pushing her forward.

The path ended in a thick stone slab. Duncan rushed forward and patted around the edges. His fingertips trembled despite his bravery.

A quiet click melted into the earthen walls.

Duncan pushed his body weight against the rock, his narrow shoulders squeezing together. Slowly the blockade moved and the sweet scent of fresh night air swept in. The candle flickered and went out.

Duncan grabbed her hand before the fragile wall of control

could give way to panic and he tugged her into the moonlight.

Together they ran from the tunnel and out into the night.

A horse snorted nearby and they both went still. Celia's pulse tapped an anxious beat.

The musty scent of the beast tainted the night air and slid a cord of unease down Celia's back. She chanced a look up and her heart caught against her ribs.

Staring down at her from the great black beast, his face fierce in the shadowed light, was the very man whose image had haunted her for the whole of her self-imposed captivity.

Alec MacLean.

Chapter Thirty-Four

Alec's chest crushed with relief. Celia stared up at him in the moonlight, her face gleaming like a pearl, her hair shining like precious white gold.

He remembered her being beautiful, but still her image robbed him of breath.

Hoof beats pulsed low in the distance and broke into the dizzying swirl of his thoughts.

"Celia."

He leapt from his horse in a smooth movement and reached for her.

He wrapped his fingers around her smooth hand. It trembled against his palm.

"Great job, MacLean," a grating voice said from the darkness of the surrounding forest.

Celia snatched her hand from Alec with a sharp gasp. Laird MacDougall emerged from the shadows with a force of men appearing behind him. Too many men.

A sardonic smile spread over the man's grizzled chin. "I knew ye wouldna let me down."

Alec turned to Celia. If he had his men with him, fighting would be an option. A risky one, but still one he would be willing to take.

For the boy.

For her.

Right now to protect them would cost them all their lives.

There was only one way to save them.

The thought left a sour taste in Alec's mouth, like the bile remnants after having been sick.

He looked at Celia one last time in the moonlight, trying to convey his love for her, trying to let her understand there was no other way to save her but betrayal.

"Duncan," Alec said sharply without taking his gaze from her. "Did ye aid this witch?"

She sucked in a deep breath, as if he'd hit her.

"She's no witch," Duncan said vehemently. The boy lifted his blade and moved beside Celia.

"What do ye think?" Alec demanded sharply. "That ye could outrun these men? That ye could save the witch with all of Scotland seeking her?"

He glared at the boy and hoped like hell the lad would understand what he was trying to say. But the boy glared back with more hatred than Alec knew was possible for Duncan.

MacDougall swung off his horse and approached them. His armor clanked and clattered beneath his heavy cloak. "So, it was the boy and not ye, MacLean?" Skepticism carved deep lines on his aged face.

Duncan tensed and moved in front of Celia.

"Stand down, boy," Alec growled. "Ye've gotten yerself in enough trouble as it is." He looked to MacDougall. "The boy fancies himself in love with her."

MacDougall's stare fixed past Duncan to where Celia stood. "I hear he was not the only one."

Alec hardened everything in him for the words he had to say. "Aye, she bewitched me."

"And now?" MacDougall said in a snarl. "Are ye still under her spell?"

Celia pulled in an audible breath, but Alec could not look at her lest his lie become apparent to his enemy.

"Nay. It broke when I made her leave my castle."

MacDougall grinned. "I'm glad to hear as much." The men from the front of the hill had now made their way to where everyone stood and gathered around MacDougall, but he held up a hand to stop them.

"Laird MacLean," he said. "I'll let ye have the honor of arresting this witch."

"Only if ye let me keep her in my castle." Alec spoke too quickly, too ready with his opportunistic response.

MacDougall's head snapped toward Alec. "Ye fell weak to her once and may verra well fall weak to her again. Nay, she'll stay in my castle." His hands clasped and rubbed together. "Where I can keep an eye on her."

"Like hell ye will," Duncan yelled. He charged forward without thought, without finesse, with nothing more than the impulsiveness of youth.

Celia screamed and reached a hand out to stop him, but it was too late. The boy was already lunging toward MacDougall.

Alec acted on instinct, protecting Duncan the only way he knew how. He stepped between MacDougall and the lad and swung his fist, connecting precisely beneath Duncan's jaw.

The boy's head popped to the side and he collapsed to the ground, unconscious.

Celia screamed, but Alec did not turn to her. He stared down at where Duncan lay still on the moonlit ground. The boy's jaw would smart in the morning, but at least he was alive. If he'd attacked MacDougall, one of the men would have cut him down without a thought.

Better a sore jaw than dead.

MacDougall patted Alec on the shoulder. "Perhaps I underestimated ye after all. Guards, seize the lad."

"Nay," Alec said. "I'll handle him."

MacDougall opened his mouth to protest, but Alec spoke again with all the passion he could not hide. "I said nay."

"Verra well," the older laird said, and pressed a pair of cold metal shackles into Alec's hands. "Arrest the witch and let this night be done." His gaze settled on Celia the way a hungry man eyes a hot meal.

It made the skin along Alec's neck prickle.

"You hit him," she whispered, her lips not moving with her words. "You hit Duncan."

"The lad gave me no choice," he said.

Her rosemary scent teased the earthy musk in the air. He wanted to brush his hands over her hair, to rub the cold from her chilled arms, to cradle her face in his hands and explain he had to do this to save her.

To save Duncan.

But all the eyes in the forest right now settled on him with the weight of a blacksmith's anvil.

He moved behind her and shifted her arms against her back. She was so thin and delicate in his large hands.

She did not fight his touch.

"I did not bewitch you," she said in a voice clogged with carefully fought tears.

Her words jerked at his heart.

He snapped the manacles around her slender wrists, careful to not put them tight enough to hurt, yet not loose enough to arouse suspicion in his enemy.

"Bring her to me," MacDougall demanded.

Celia stiffened. "Please don't. Not him." She looked at Alec over her shoulder, her eyes wide with a fear he'd only ever seen that first night she'd slept at Duart.

"Don't do this, Alec. I can't go with him. Not again." The breath rasped from her and she didn't stop shaking her head.

He gently nudged her and her feet staggered forward. "There are no other options."

It was all he could say and even still, it might have been too much.

MacDougall's breathing grew ragged when they neared.

Alec looked between them. The savage possession in MacDougall's eye, the raw fear in Celia's.

I can't go with him. Celia had said. *Not again.*

When had she gone with him before?

MacDougall ran his hand down Celia's hair. Alec squeezed his hand around the hilt of his blade, fighting the urge to cut the man's hand from his body.

"It's time to finish what we started now that ye've grown, my little witch. But this time no on yer land, but in mine."

A shard of icy realization shot through Alec.

This man was the one who'd captured Celia when she was young. The one who'd caused her such torment.

Celia turned her eyes toward Alec, her gaze full of hopelessness, hot with accusation, and he knew.

He knew he had just delivered her into the hands of her nightmare.

• • •

Celia sat in front of Laird MacDougall on his horse through the journey back to his castle.

His hands were spotted with age, but clung with strength to the reins. If she tried to escape, he would stop her.

Instead she stared at the ring, the blood red now an eerie purple in the dark of night.

She should have left when she saw him near Duart. She'd known he was a Highlander all those years ago when he'd come to North Berwick to help with the execution of witches.

No Lowlander spoke Erse. No Lowlander had such a strong brogue.

She should have fled when she saw him, but she hadn't and now she paid the price.

Without Alec's ready help.

At first, she thought he had feigned his betrayal, but then he'd struck down Duncan. She winced at the way the adolescent had fallen to the ground. He'd been trying to protect her.

The poor boy had been taken away by one of Alec's soldiers and sent back to Duart to be handled when Alec was free.

She looked to her right where he rode beside them.

Her heart flinched at the sight of his stoic gaze fixed straight ahead. He sat with a straight back, his body confidently relaxed with the sway of the horse. All as if he felt no guilt for what he'd done.

Had he truly betrayed her?

Was this the price she paid for rejecting him?

A massive castle came into view, dark and menacing in its overwhelming size. It stretched so high its top blended somewhere unseen with the night sky.

Wide circles of blackened earth stood out against the

moonlit grass and Celia's pulse went into a wild, erratic thrum.

She knew what those circles meant.

There'd been fire there.

Women accused of witchcraft had been burned there.

"Ye know what those are, aye?" MacDougall whispered in her ear with a reedy voice. "And ye'll join them."

They stopped in the courtyard. Fear blotted out logic and comprehension. The clattering of too many horses filled her ears, the night air blew cold against the sweat plastering her hair to her brow, the rough lurch of being pulled from the horse.

She was shoved toward the entrance of the castle, to a place where stairs did not go up but down.

Dungeons were down.

Her panicked breath echoed off the stonework around her, high-pitched and fast.

Her feet were forced down the stairs curling down into hell, the hand on her arm like a grip of iron, forcing her where she never wanted to go again.

Then the smell rose up, and with it too many memories to fight off.

The choking odor of burning tallow, the stink of unwashed bodies and excrement, the stink of impending death.

"No," Celia said sharply.

The men did not listen.

They pushed her ever forward, making her stiff knees bend with each stair descended.

"No," she said again.

Everything wiped from her mind, save the memories. Blood, rats, torture, starvation, cold.

Fiona.

Being taken out only to watch the woman she loved get burned at the stake.

The prison came into view—cages lining as far as she could see in the flickering torchlight.

Women cowered inside the cells, their eyes wide and haunted in faces gone too thin, too dirty.

A scream loosed from Celia then, so savage it felt as though her throat would bleed.

She screamed for the women in there, the memories she could not escape, the fear she now possessed. It was wild and feral and fierce.

And for all that was in her, she could not bring herself to stop.

• • •

Shrieks of terror spiraled up from the gaping darkness Celia had disappeared down. They coiled around Alec's heart.

He stepped toward the yawning entryway where another animalistic scream met his ears and scratched into his mind.

"MacLean, are ye going somewhere?" MacDougall asked.

A warning went off in the back of his brain, a clanging reminder he was surrounded by MacDougall's men. Yes, he could run down there with his sword bared, and he might save her for a moment before they were both run through.

Alec spun around and regarded MacDougall. The other laird wore a massive fur over his shoulders, making him look part man, part beast.

"I dinna help ye capture her to torture her." There was a savagery to Alec's voice he almost didn't recognize.

"She's a witch," MacDougall said by way of explanation. "And no one can touch her but me."

A choking sob sounded now where the screams had come from, a breathless, gasping sob of someone not in control of their own emotions.

His Celia, down there in the dark, in the hell she'd had nightmares about. And he was here with his enemy, unable to do anything to save her.

He stared back at the hole. It would hurt less to stand idle and watch as someone sliced open his chest and drew out his frantically beating heart.

Celia.

His throat was tight and such powerful rage racked through him he felt as though he could kill a thousand men with one swing of his blade.

But he knew that wasn't the case.

He knew he'd have to wait and suddenly he wished someone *had* cut out his still beating heart rather than have to endure another second knowing Celia was down there.

MacDougall clapped him on the shoulder. "Come, boy, let us get some wine and celebrate the capture of the witch. For tomorrow we shall watch her burn."

Alec's heart dropped into his stomach like a gut punch.

Tomorrow.

He hadn't intended to wait until tomorrow, regardless, but the suddenness was surprising still.

Just another hour or so, he said silently to himself. To Celia.

Just another hour or so and he could rescue her.

Alec turned from the doorway and followed the laird to the great hall. But while they celebrated their disgusting victory, he would watch and he would plan.

Celia would be rescued.

Tonight.

Chapter Thirty-Five

Sounds of revelry swept in from the stairs on an icy current of wind. Celia wrapped her arms more tightly around herself and paced the small cell.

If she kept her body moving, she kept her mind moving.

Because she could not sit and think and *feel.*

It was too dangerous.

If she fell back in a place of terror, she might not ever emerge.

Her jaw ached where she'd been struck by the guard, but at least it had snapped her to her senses.

Somewhere in another cell a woman began to cry, a low, wailing, mourning sound.

Her voice was joined by several others until the chorus of their fear echoed all around Celia.

A sharp ache clutched her stomach. It should have been hunger, but she knew it was not. It was the hurt radiating from her heart, the piece of her so shattered it caused every part of her pain.

In all the years she'd been so alone, she'd worried loving someone would only leave them open for hurt.

Never once had she feared for herself, for the hurt love could cause.

She had trusted him, loved him, sacrificed for him, and he'd betrayed her.

Or had he?

Her mind raced with conflict. Not wanting to believe, yet unable to deny his acts.

Something shifted in the rushes below and her heart caught.

Rats.

Please, no. Not rats.

Her arms squeezed tighter against herself.

She was alone.

Without help, without love.

Without hope.

No, no, no, no.

She shook her head.

But it was too late. Her mind slipped somewhere she could not escape.

• • •

Alec sat at MacDougall's right, a position of great honor, and he loathed himself for it.

The older laird put a hand on Alec's shoulder and squeezed. "Ye're going to be a fine son to me, lad. I'm proud of ye."

Alec nodded mutely and tried to keep the revulsion from showing on his face.

"I've been wanting this witch for years," MacDougall continued in a gravelly voice. "Years." He settled back in his seat and stared out at the drunken revelry going on before them. "King James and his weak stomach dinna agree with killing a child, but a witch is witch. And children grow to adults."

Alec pressed a cup of whisky to his lips.

And did not drink.

Temptation didn't lace the heady vapors, not like it had before. The darkness held no place where Celia was concerned.

His chest ached to even think of her down in the dungeon, afraid and in the dark, blaming him for having put her there.

He pushed himself toward the torment within, reveled in the pain. The feeling part of him pushed the darkness away.

He should have kept her safe.

He should have kept her protected.

But he had failed.

His gaze swept the room once more. Some men had left. Over fifty now remained, all in various stages of intoxication.

Still able to fight.

He balled his hand in a fist.

"Her mother took too long to confess because of her. It was long and arduous for both of us." MacDougall gave a sigh, deep and heavy, as if it were weighted with regret. He tilted his head back with his drink.

No sooner had the cup been clapped back onto the table than it was filled again.

Alec knew the woman's name. Fiona.

She hadn't been Celia's mother, but she'd cared for her as one. He could imagine Celia as a young girl in the dungeon, her face set with the same determination it held when Duncan was sick, relentless in her attempt to heal the only woman she'd ever known as mother.

MacDougall rubbed his forefinger absently over his lower lip. "The only way I could finally get her to confess to her crime was to threaten her daughter."

Her daughter.

Celia.

MacDougall looked out at the band of drunk, rowdy men, his eyes seeing something different than what lay before them, something Alec did not want to see. "I couldna touch the little witch, of course, but I made her watch her mother go in the flames and stay until she was ash."

Alec gripped his cup so tightly it would have shattered had it been glass.

He wished it were glass and that it would break into long shards he could use to cut this bastard's throat. Alec's breathing was ragged now.

He needed to control himself before MacDougall noticed.

"I hear when people are starving, the smell of bodies burning is like the scent of roasting meat." He drew a long, deep sip from his cup. "I've often wondered if the starving girl salivated as she watched her mother burn." MacDougall looked to Alec, his expression pensive before he shrugged his fur-laden shoulders and turned his attention toward the crowd of soldiers once more.

Bile singed like acid in the back of Alec's throat.

Celia, his Celia.

What she'd been through, the torment she'd suffered at the hands of this beast.

Alec gritted his teeth against words thick and painful in his throat.

Damn it, time moved too slow.

Every second that passed, she was down there, alone.

Scared.

Saraid entered then, pulling her father's attention toward the front of the room, along with the gaze of every other person. Her hair was brushed smooth and her face was bright in a manner suggesting she'd never been sick a day in her life, let alone with belladonna poisoning only a few hours prior.

She wore a silk dress so brilliantly red it reminded Alec of glistening blood.

Though all stared at her as she entered, she kept her gaze fixed on him.

"I see ye're much recovered," Alec said when Saraid approached the table. Keeping the bitterness from his tone took serious effort.

She cast him a charming smile. "Indeed. She must not have given me enough to cause serious harm, just enough to have distracted me so she could escape."

Her eyes widened to an innocent expression and she regarded her father with the look of a child who'd done something bad.

Like let his prized prisoner slip through her fingers.

And suddenly Alec understood.

Saraid hadn't known of his affair with Celia and wanted to make him question her integrity. Certainly she'd not become sympathetic to Celia's plight.

Celia had outwitted Saraid, and to keep her father from finding out, Saraid had outwitted him.

"Where's the witch?" Saraid asked with a toss of her head. "Why is she not here on display for us?"

Fear curled icy cold in Alec's heart.

"I'll no have her casting a curse in this hall," MacDougall said before tearing off a bite of bread.

"But father, she poisoned me." Saraid's pout deepened.

Alec reassessed the room.

It was only a matter of time before Saraid convinced her father to bring Celia out to view and then Alec might not get another chance.

A good number of guards remained in the hall, most staggering with drink.

The noises around them were loud with banter and celebration, for when a laird was pleased, so too were his men.

The situation was not ideal for Alec to rescue Celia, but if Saraid got her way and had Celia brought to the hall, there would be no rescuing her.

Ever.

Alec drew in a deep, steadying breath.

He got to his feet and let exhaustion pull his balance slightly off in an effort to appear drunk.

MacDougall turned and looked up at him questioningly. "Going so soon, MacLean?"

Alec shrugged. "Tired."

MacDougall snorted. "Drunk, more like." He swiped his hand through the air in a show of dismissal. "Off with ye then—ye've earned a good rest."

Alec nodded once to the other laird and Saraid before winding his way among the revelers from the great hall.

The time had come to save Celia.

Chapter Thirty-Six

The weight of Alec's sword was reassuring against his back. Solid, thick, Scottish-forged steel, ready to taste the blood of his enemy and save the woman he loved.

Each footstep closer to Celia left his body sizzling with power.

He wandered down the hall toward the room meant for him, but instead of turning right, he turned left. Toward her.

His breath came faster and his heart pounded so damn hard in his chest his hands shook from it.

Never had he been so fraught with emotion before a battle. Not since the first time he stood up to his father.

Alec tried to pace his steps, to appear as though he wasn't hurrying.

But he was hurrying. Every second passed was another second Celia sat in Aros's dungeon—cold and scared, thinking, no doubt, of his betrayal.

The last thought quickened his step.

MacDougall's men be damned.

If they suspected him, he'd kill them before they could raise an alarm.

He swept quickly down the hall where the warmth of the fires was no longer present and the chill of the frosted air blew against his face and hands.

Fortunately, no guards had emerged.

The pungent scent of human waste and death tainted the air now and he knew he neared the dungeon.

He followed the path he'd taken earlier with MacDougall until he got to the dark, gaping stairwell leading down into the pits of hell.

Where his beautiful Celia lay.

It was dark below. Too dark. As if all the torches had been snuffed out.

He would be at a disadvantage to the guards down there. They would be used to such darkness.

But if he used a torch, he would alert them of his presence before he arrived.

A woman cried out from the black depths, a sharp, urgent sound.

Alarm spiked through Alec and his blood turned molten hot in his veins.

Whoever made her cry out, he'd kill them too.

He grabbed the torch from its sconce and slid his blade free of its scabbard, careful and slow to ensure he remained as silent as possible.

The woman below did not cry out again, but her whimpers drifted on putrid air and assaulted his ears and his psyche.

He took the stairs quickly, hating the way the flame glowed off the walls like a beacon. The deeper he went, the more wet the chill became, until it felt as though it permeated through his skin and penetrated his bones.

"I thought we agreed no light so we wouldna have to see how filthy they are." The masculine voice came from below.

Two more steps. Alec cleared them and came to an open area with a row of cage-like cells as far as his light extended. The odor hit him like a punch, the overwhelming stench of human degradation.

A man stood in the nearest cell, eyes squinted against the light, with a woman held tight in his hand. Her dress had been unlaced and sagged from her shoulders, her breasts bared and stark white where grime and dirt did not touch them.

Alec surged toward the gaping doorway. The man was no longer squinting against the light and his recovered gaze lowered to the drawn blade.

He never had a chance to cry out.

Alec moved without thought and shoved his blade through

the man's throat—one clean punch forward with his sword until the sharpened tip bit into bone and stopped.

The man choked, once, twice, then his knees buckled and he folded to the ground.

Alec still held the torch in his left hand, his grip so tight he was surprised the fragile bundle did not crumble away.

The woman had collapsed to the filthy ground, cowering. A spatter of blood showed on her cheek.

She gazed up at him with those savagely frightened eyes, as if seeking some kind of answer.

"I'm here to save ye," he said quietly. "But I need yer help."

The man gurgled where he'd fallen face-first into the rushes.

"Save us," a voice whispered unseen from the darkness. Several others hissed the words in repetition.

Alec looked down where blood pooled beneath the man's face and the fury of angry disgust lashed at him once more.

He tried not to think of Celia being touched by this man, but thoughts raked through his mind like nails sharpened to wicked points, scoring deep images in his brain he would never forget.

The rushes rustled around them, metal clinked against metal, and voices murmured among one another.

The woman clawed her gown shut and held it pinched between skeletal fingers.

"Will you help me?" he asked again.

Her gaze never left him. Finally, a slow, hesitant nod.

"Help *us*," someone insisted in a raspy whisper. "Help all of us."

All of us.

How many were in there?

Alec slid his sword into its sheath and knelt beside the guard's body before trailing his hand along the belt.

The band of leather was slick against his fingers, hot where the weight of thick flesh spilled over its constraint.

"Do ye know where Celia is being kept?" he asked.

The woman shook her head vigorously.

Alec lifted the loop of keys from the man's belt and the woman's wide gaze fixed on them like a starving dog eyeing a slab of meat. "She was brought in today, no long ago." He got to his feet.

"I don't know where." The woman's voice rasped from her throat, from either thirst or disuse.

Or screaming.

Alec tightened his stomach against the rush of hurt for her. "She's here, aye?"

This time the woman nodded.

Hope flickered in his chest.

Another woman pressed against the bars from her cage beside the one where Alec stood. Her fingers curled around the metal like stark white bone and the flesh of her face was drawn tight against her skull, turning her eyes into black, gaping sockets.

"I know that one. She was dragged to the back." Her tone was quietly frantic, urgent.

Alec fled the cage and ran down the narrow aisle between the walls of prison cells with the woman trailing behind him.

The women were all the same, all bone and flesh and barely alive. All stared with eyes too large in their frighteningly thin faces.

Alec cursed himself for his inability to save the women before now. He reached the last cell. A small frame huddled in the corner behind a tangled veil of pale blonde.

"Celia." The word came out choked.

She did not answer. She did not move.

Alec fumbled with the keys, suddenly feeling as though his fingers were too fat to push the slender iron into the lock.

The woman he'd saved took the key ring from him and did the task he could not do.

He nodded his thanks and handed her the torch along with his dagger. "Go free the others. Call if ye need me, aye?"

The woman nodded and Alec turned his attention to Celia.

• • •

Blackness enveloped Celia, shrouding and shielding her all at once.

The chill of it bled into her skin, the thick of it clogged her ears and her throat. The weight of it pressed against her eyes until the pressure made her ache. It was as ubiquitous as it was intolerable.

But in this blackness, there was nothing.

No sounds of torture, no fear of pain, no memories.

Something brushed her hand.

A rat, no doubt, with beady eyes and a round belly fat from whatever its sharp teeth could tear and gnaw.

Her fingers flinched and the rat did not return.

Something settled on her shoulder and squeezed.

No rat.

Far more frightening.

A hand.

She shrank into herself and tried to pull the blackness tighter around her, as a child would a blanket, embracing the nothing.

Another hand on her other shoulder.

No.

She was not ready to die.

Her muscles burned with resistance and her mind screamed for her to fight, fight, fight.

She threw her fist in front of her. It connected with something soft and hard all at once and sent a shard of pain lancing up her right arm.

She lashed out with her left, slapping at where her fist had landed, and snapped her head up in the hopes of seeing her opponent.

Light filtered into her vision, brilliant despite its soft glow, and highlighted the shadowed figure in front of her.

She lurched her body toward her attacker with both hands ready to grab and scratch and gouge, but her wrists were ensnared by large, callused fingers.

She struggled back and a whimper clogged her throat.

Not like this.

Not like Fiona.

"Celia, shush, it's me."

The voice penetrated the chaos of her fear. A gentle voice,

the burr low and soothing. Tender.

"Celia, I'm here for ye, lass. I'm here to save ye."

Tears burned in her eyes, as if her body recognized him before her reeling mind could.

Alec.

Her eyes had adjusted to the glow of light behind him and now she could make out the square of his shoulders, the stubborn set of his jaw.

How could she have missed it before?

So many thoughts, so many words, emotions, churned in her head.

"You didn't betray me," she whispered.

His breath hissed out and he caught her in such a sudden and aggressive hug, it squeezed the air from her. The spicy, wonderful masculine scent of him enveloped her like a dream.

"I dinna betray ye. I'd come to rescue ye, but when MacDougall showed up…" He swallowed thickly. "If I'd resisted, we all would have been killed. I bided my time waiting for ye and it felt like a damn lifetime. I feared…"

She pulled back away from him. "You can't stay here. You shouldn't be here. If they catch you, they'll kill you." Her throat tightened. "I can't let you die for me."

His hand stroked her cheek. "Ye're no Fiona and nor am I."

"But…" she stopped, sorting through the powerful surge inside her until she understood. "But I love you."

He gripped her face in his hands and pulled in a deep breath. "And I love ye, my Celia."

His lips pressed to hers, warm and familiar and wholly wonderful.

"But now we must go," he said.

She allowed him to pull her to her feet and silently berated herself for so foolishly sitting on her cell floor in her open prison while they talked.

Talked.

Instead of escaping.

His hand wrapped around hers, strong and reassuring.

The heat of his fingers pressed over hers, soothing the icy

chill from her flesh.

Together they left the cell and headed toward a mass of women in the middle of the aisle. Only then did Celia realize all the cells were emptied.

Footsteps echoed from the front of the dungeon. Clomping boots.

Several shrieks rose up from the women.

"How did ye get free?" a man asked. His voice slurred with drink.

Celia's breath snagged in her chest.

Alec's hand pressed her back, keeping her from walking forward. "Stay here."

Before she could protest, he was already charging with his blade hissing free of its scabbard.

Chapter Thirty-Seven

Alec plunged down the aisle of the prison toward the main area where it glowed with the golden light of the single torch placed in a sconce. Several women cowered on the ground.

A guard stood in the middle of them, massive compared to their emaciated frames.

His arm drew back and he knocked one of the women in the face. She fell to the ground like a sagging rag doll.

A low, guttural growl came from Alec and he hurtled his body toward the man, but before he could reach him, the guard grabbed one of the women and held a blade to her throat.

The woman's gown fell open and Alec realized she was the one he'd saved when he first came down the stairs. The one who had stayed to save the others rather than flee and save herself.

"Dinna come any closer," the man said. "I've no qualms about killing a witch."

The odor of whisky, hot and stale, fogged thick in the air.

He was missing two front teeth and torchlight gleamed off his bald head.

Recognition smacked into Alec with such force it left him momentarily stunned.

He remembered a man with two missing teeth and a balding head.

In the village.

During the massacre.

"Ye were one of the outlaws who attacked the village." Alec stared at the man's clothes, at the tartan worn by most of MacDougall's men.

"Aye, I was." The man gave a hard bark of laughter. Then

his laugh choked off and blood spilled from between his lips.

The woman he held turned toward him and pulled Alec's dagger from his chest with a wet sucking sound. The guard fell backward and the women surged over him like vultures, their hands clawed to strike.

Alec turned his back to the man and let the women have their vengeance. No doubt their retribution was far more than Alec was capable of.

Celia had come closer, watching with such a quiet glow in her eyes he wondered if she wished to join them. Alec grasped Celia's hand and pulled her toward the front of the dungeon, toward the exit.

"We must go," Celia hissed to the women.

They neared the staircase and Alec's heart pounded in great, hearty thuds.

It was one thing to go into battle with a band of armed men behind you, capable and lethal. It was entirely another to be centered in the enemy's castle with a band of starving, abused women who looked to him for protection.

He felt more than saw their presence mass behind him—a wall of thirty or so slender, dirty bodies pressing toward the sweet breath of fresh air sweeping down the stairwell, leaning toward freedom.

He signaled for them to keep quiet, but their large eyes and drawn faces indicated they hadn't needed the warning.

They climbed up the stairs in a slow-moving wave of carefully placed footsteps and held breath. Torchlight flickered in the darkness above.

He motioned for them to stop and went up alone, his sword drawn and ready.

For nothing.

No guards stood outside the entrance to the dungeon. Most were probably celebrating with Laird MacDougall, but Alec knew better than to relax.

Some men always stayed sober.

Some men were always ready to fight.

The night was cold enough to freeze his breath and it was

so quiet he could hear the shushing roar of waves breaking against the cliffs just outside the castle walls.

He scanned the courtyard and saw no one. Uneven cobblestones jutted up like twisted teeth in the pale glow of the moon. Too far away stood the open gate, the only way to enter Aros, and the only way to leave.

It would be a long run and they would be in the open.

It would be risky.

The shuffle of anxious feet sounded on the stairs where the women waited.

Staying would be riskier.

He went back down several steps and motioned for the women to follow.

• • •

The mass of bodies behind Celia surged forward at Alec's signal. The pressure of the crowd pushed her toward the top of the stairs as much as she climbed of her own volition.

Alec reached through the mass and clasped her hand. His grip was firm and warm. With a gentle tug, he caught her in his arms at the top of the stairs. But his gaze wasn't fixed on her. It was focused on the courtyard.

Celia's heart slammed harder in her chest. She wanted to run out into the courtyard, heedless of who saw her, and sprint toward the safety of trees outside the castle walls.

Alec nodded and stepped into the moonlit night. The milky light bathed him so he stood out like a beacon, one they would all follow to freedom.

He gripped her hand and walked quickly along the wall. Without the alcove of protection, icy air ripped at her hair and stung her face and hands until they were numb.

The shuffle of feet behind Celia told her the other women followed. Their breaths huffed in the air, erratic and heavy and disjointed.

Celia's own breath came too quick, too hard. There was so much fear, so much hope.

The muscles of her legs felt weak from lack of food and spending so much time curled below in the cold, damp dark. Alec's form in front of her remained stoic, his shoulders squared, his head swiveling around to keep aware of who might witness their escape.

Suddenly the light around them dimmed. Celia chanced a look upward and noticed the dark threads of clouds sweeping before the moon, blotting its brilliance.

Good.

She looked forward once more. The end of the wall they followed was near. The rest of the area would be open courtyard until they reached the gate.

Alec stopped and pressed his body flush against the castle wall. Celia and the women behind her did likewise. She glanced down the line of women and saw some still walked in the back.

After it appeared every woman had caught up, Alec nodded and they all ran forward, out into the great wide open. Out where they were all vulnerable.

Celia's feet stumbled over the uneven cobblestones, but she did not let herself fall. Alec clasped her hand tight, urging her to run faster than her straining muscles were capable of. She pushed harder, past where her body wanted to let her go.

There would be guards who patrolled the top of the castle who would see them eventually, but how much time did that give them now?

She wanted to turn her head, ached to do so, to see if anyone stood against the night sky at the top of Aros castle.

To do so might be her demise.

They ran until the gate loomed before them and the sound of men's voices came from the other side of the stonework. The small, battered group drew to a stop and huddled against the stonework. Though clouds shielded the moon, its meager light would still betray their location.

A shiver ricocheted through Celia's body. They were too exposed. The women were silent and still. Her heart wrenched for them. Perhaps it was foolish of her, but she wanted their freedom even more than her own. She knew what they'd been through, knew what horrors to which they'd been subjected.

Alec's body tensed and a metallic taste filled her mouth, the flavor of fear.

He pushed his hand back in a quiet signal to wait before he slipped around the corner.

She leaned forward, just far enough to make out Alec's large frame. One guard lay crumpled three feet away with a puddle of blood seeping from his neck and Alec held the other guard against the wall by his neck.

Alec's blade rose to the man's throat and gave a savage jerk. Blood spilled from his mortal wound, an eerie tint of purple in the semi-dark.

Celia pulled back behind the wall, her heart beating so hard it made breathing difficult.

He was killing so they could be free.

He was killing for her.

No, she realized, not just for her.

She glanced back at the line of women behind her. They bunched against one another, their lips pressed tight. Many, she noticed, held hands. Their bony fingers curled tightly against one another.

Together they would live or together they would die.

Alec appeared beside her and gave a nod. The air almost hummed with anxiety. It vibrated through Celia too, and she watched Alec's face with pinpoint intensity, waiting for his signal for them to run.

He nodded and once again, they ran.

The uneven cobblestone gave way to soft, dewy grass. Everywhere around Celia and Alec, the other women sprinted toward their own freedom.

The tree line wasn't home, but it was an opportunity to hide if chased. It was an opportunity to escape.

Some women moved far more quickly than their starved bodies appeared capable of, running on the will of sheer desperation.

Hope pumped through Celia. It warmed her muscles though her skin was chilled by the unforgiving wind. It kept her legs driving forward when everything shook with heavy exhaustion.

Halfway.

They were halfway across the open field now with the rushing sound of waves breaking against the cliffs to the right.

Celia glanced toward the sound. The soft grass ended abruptly there where the cliffs began and the earth dropped off into the sea.

She would rather throw herself from the edge of the cliff and let her body break against the rocks below than let herself be taken to the dungeon again.

Alec's hand tightened on hers. He pulled her forward, but her legs could go no faster.

Almost to the tree line where they would be safe.

And then the scrape of trepidation she'd had earlier gave way to a chill of realization.

She understood why Alec had appeared disconcerted, why he was rushing her though they were not being chased.

Leaving the dungeon had been done with little effort. Seeing no guards had been too much of a coincidence. Making it this far out in the open without a shout of alarm was too improbable.

This had all been too easy.

Impossibly easy.

This was a trap.

Chapter Thirty-Eight

Alec raced toward the trees with Celia in tow, wondering how much time they truly had.

The women around them were starting to slow despite the carve of determination on their narrow faces.

A woman to his right fell with a small scream. He glanced back and found a band of horses heading toward them.

It was time.

MacDougall was going to attack.

No sooner had the thought entered his mind than the clatter of boots sounded near the open gate behind them.

He stopped, but shoved Celia back behind him, toward the trees. "Go, Celia. Run and dinna stop." He watched only long enough to see her stagger a few steps before he whirled forward once more, pulling his blade free.

The woman who'd fallen dragged herself upright and two others ran to her. They hefted her arms over their shoulders and together the three stumbled toward the tree line.

Surely they heard the men coming, yet still they'd stopped to help.

If Niall and his men had the courage of these half-dead women, Alec might not be in so dire a situation.

The wind swept around him, tugging at his kilt and sweeping his hair wildly around his face. Sounds of the ocean roared just over the cliff.

The woman to whom Alec had given his dagger appeared at his side with the small blade drawn. It would be useless against what they faced.

"Go." He said the word sharply.

The woman stared at the oncoming force. "They'll do this again if we dinna stop them now." The blade trembled in her hand, from fear or exhaustion or cold or all of it combined. Her breath puffed in fast, white billows of steam and into the wind as soon as they left her lips.

"I'm Laird MacLean of Duart Castle," Alec said. "And ye can be damn sure I'll wage war on him." He jerked his head toward the edge of the forest. "Now go."

The set to the woman's jaw gave way to a tremble and tears glinted in her eyes. "God be with ye," she said fervently before she spun away.

Alec turned and saw Celia standing several feet behind him, her feet planted in the ground like a warrior ready to fight. The woman passed the dagger to Celia, who took it with a nod and met Alec's gaze with a stubborn stare.

"Get in the woods." He said it with all the menace and ice he could pull from his core.

Her chin lifted. "I won't leave you."

He wanted to argue with her, to shove her into the cover of the trees to ensure she would be safe, but he never had the chance.

A band of MacDougall guards approached them with the figure of Laird MacDougall in the back.

"I wish ye'd go," he said still facing forward, knowing it'd do him no good. "I'll no ever forgive myself if something happens to ye."

"Then you understand." The voice she used settled deep within his chest.

The retinue stopped in front of Alec. His body tensed for a fight. He widened his stance and pulled in a deep breath of crisp night air.

His gaze swept over the band of his opponents. Approximately five men, all of average height.

Not a one with his blade drawn.

Was this another trick?

The men parted and let MacDougall walk forward between them.

No, Alec realized as the figure drew its hood back, not MacDougall—Saraid.

She did not stop walking until she was directly in front of him. A sheen of sweat glistened on her skin despite the frigid night.

"Are ye glad to see me, Alec?" There was a slight slur to her words.

Compared to MacDougall, aye, but he wasn't about to tell her that.

"What are ye doing here, Saraid?" he asked.

She licked her lips before speaking again. "Ye should be happy I've done this so you could free all those wretched witches." A gust of wind tousled her thick black curls and blew the cloak back to reveal the brilliantly red dress. "I figured ye'd try to free yer whore, but I dinna think ye'd actually help them all."

"What are ye doing here?" he repeated.

"Helping ye free her, so ye can put all this behind ye and have only me. My father wants these women dead, but all I want is ye." Her hand flopped in the direction of the forest. "Those women were all useless anyway."

Alec let his gaze flick to the men standing a ways back from him and Saraid, their hands folded patiently in front of them.

Without threat.

He lowered his blade and shook his head. "I dinna know what ye're talking about."

Though he hadn't turned to see, he could sense Celia behind him. Their energy linked them like a low hum. If only he could get her to leave, if only he could convince her.

But he knew now that was impossible.

"Those women." Saraid pointed a sharp finger toward the trees. "I asked them all to make me a simple potion and every one of them failed." Her face scrunched and she gripped her stomach with a grunt.

"Are ye well?" he asked.

She swallowed thickly and straightened. "They failed me," she repeated. "And so I had my da put them in the dungeon and kill a few for good measure."

The woman was addled. Alec had never seen her act so strangely. Though he was unsure of her goal, he knew every second he kept her talking was another second the freed women had to escape.

"Why would ye need a potion?" he pressed.

Saraid blinked slowly, the left lid closing and opening before the right. "For ye."

If he was confused before, he was genuinely lost now. "Me?"

Her brows pursed together and her eyes took on a pleading look that made her look as if she were a little girl again. "For ye. So ye'd love me."

She stepped closer and put her hands on his chest in a gesture that felt clumsy and awkward. "Ye're the only man who doesna want me, Alec. Even when my da tried to bribe ye with help against the outlaws ye dinna want me."

The rage swept through him again. "Those werena outlaws," he said through gritted teeth.

Her shoulder sagged. "I know. He wanted yer land for its wealth and he wanted to pursue his witch hunt on yer lands. Yer da wouldna let any other laird step on his lands without promising to wage war. Then I wanted ye and he decided on an alliance instead. But ye took so long to decide…"

Hurt showed in her glassy eyes.

"So he kept attacking to lure me into marriage with ye," Alec surmised.

"I want ye so badly." A little smile curved her lips. "I made my own potion, ye know. From the bag yer witch had."

"What?" Celia spoke up behind Alec and his body flinched to attention again.

Frustration pounded in Alec's temples. Why did she have to stay? Why the hell hadn't she fled?

His heart winced around the truth—she loved him too much.

Saraid started to peer around Alec, but he clasped her shoulder with his free hand. "What did ye take?"

"I learned things from those other witches. Everyone

eventually talks," she smirked. "That whore behind ye is the only one worth a lick of real skill." Her eyes went wide and excitement glittered in her gaze, a strange combination with the way her slick skin glowed in the moonlight. "She brought a babe to life," Saraid whispered. "Did ye know that?"

Sweat from the palms of her hot hands seeped through his leine and left the fabric wet. She tilted her face toward his. Her breathing came labored and uneven, tainted with a sickly sweet something.

"Do ye want me now?" she asked.

He stared down, uncertain what to say.

She looked sad—childlike with hope and altogether desperate.

If he agreed, would that afford him enough time to save Celia?

Celia appeared suddenly at his side.

"What did you take and how much?" she asked without looking at the guards, as if they were of no consequence.

The woman was going to get them both killed.

• • •

Celia tried to ignore the sting of jealousy at the image of Saraid laying her pretty head on Alec's chest.

"My lady," Celia said. "What did you take and how much of it?"

Saraid kept her head on Alec's chest and turned her face in Celia's direction.

Sweat covered the woman's face so it shone like it'd been coated in glass. Beneath, her skin was flushed, her eyes brilliant and glossy.

"Some lavender flowers in tea and some of the herbs from yer bag."

Celia did a quick inventory in her head. None of the dried herbs she'd brought along would have caused such a reaction.

"Along with the bottle," Saraid added with a drunken stagger. Ice prickled in Celia's veins. "How much?"

Saraid looked up at Alec with a little smile curving her lips. "All of it."

Celia's heart slipped into her stomach. "All of it?"

Saraid nodded against Alec's chest. Her full weight sagged against him now.

"That was foxglove," Celia said as calmly as she could. Her heart slammed in her chest so quickly it left her head with a light, dizzy sensation. "You've taken far, far too much."

The sleepy look on Saraid's face indicated she either hadn't heard Celia or was too far gone to care.

"Get her to the ground," Celia said. "We have to try to get her to purge what she can from her stomach."

Alec's gaze flicked to the soldiers and Celia followed his glance. The uncertainty on their faces was evident in the way they looked at one another, as if to confirm whether what Celia requested was fine or not.

"Lay her down, Alec," she said in the sharp voice she used for the stunned family of the sick and injured. "We must get her to purge or she'll die."

He nodded and eased Saraid forward, laying her on the ground with hands so gentle the act squeezed Celia's chest.

She clamped her back teeth together. This was not the time to let jealousy invade her thoughts.

He did not want Saraid.

She knelt beside the woman who stared dolefully up at Alec.

"My lady, you must make yourself vomit," Celia said.

Saraid did not move.

Celia touched the woman's shoulder in an attempt to roll her onto her stomach.

Saraid snapped her face toward Celia. "Unhand me, you wretch."

Her body tensed and she clenched around her stomach with a low, wailing moan.

"Alec, help me turn her over," Celia said.

He immediately complied, easing Saraid over onto her stomach, then stood and crossed his arms over his chest.

Celia tried to pull Saraid's hair back from her face, but the woman stopped gripping her stomach and shoved her away.

"If you don't do this yourself, I'll have to do it," Celia cautioned.

Saraid shook her head vigorously. Strings of saliva dripped in clear strands from her lips.

"Forgive me," Celia said quietly.

Before the other woman could protest or react, Celia clamped the dark head in her arms. After making sure Saraid's head was downward lest she choke, Celia wriggled her fingers along the back of Saraid's tongue until the woman started to cough.

The coughing sounds gave way to a dry gag.

Almost there.

Celia focused on her fingers gliding through thick saliva, trying to go deep enough to induce a purge without causing harm.

A blade hissed free, a sharp, jarring sound despite the quiet whisper of it.

"What is this evil?" A masculine voice broke through her concentration and gripped all her attention.

She jerked her face in the direction of the speaker and all the hope bled from her body.

Laird MacDougall.

Chapter Thirty-Nine

Alec cursed himself for letting his guard down. How the hell had MacDougall managed to sneak up so quickly, so silently?

Saraid stopped choking and slid from Celia's hands. Her head rustled the grass softly where it fell forward.

She was not moving.

MacDougall's hands curled into gnarled fists. "What have ye done?" He jerked toward the guards, who appeared suddenly ashen. "And what are ye louses doing standing there watching when ye should have killed them? Damn it, attack. Attack!"

The men leapt as one cohesive unit, barreling toward Alec. Toward Celia.

Alec had just enough time to place himself between Celia and harm.

The first two men attacked at the same time. Alec lashed out with his own blade, swiping the air in a great arc that cut the path of their swords away from him in a metallic *clang, clang.*

The third man plunged his blade forward while the other two recovered. Fortunately his blow landed high enough for Alec to smoothly alter the direction of his own sword and block the blow.

"Go, Celia," Alec said through gritted teeth.

The three Alec was fighting advanced again, all three blades working in his direction.

Parry.
Blow.
Lunge.
Duck.
Attack.

Alec went through the motions as automatic to him as breathing. His body was fluid, following the rhythm of battle with ease.

The edge of his blade caught the first man under the chin and ripped his throat open. The man crumpled to the ground from where he would never rise.

Unfazed, the other two men continued their efforts. They moved together, cohesive, but their attacks were not enough to get through Alec's defense.

His muscles burned with the pleasure of a good fight, but his mind raced with concern for Celia.

Behind him came the choked sounds of coughing. The groan of someone very sick.

But he had not heard Celia. Had she stayed to help Saraid vomit?

He tightened his muscles.

Focus.

Two more men.

He swung his sword with two hands, knowing it was foolish to do so. His ribs were exposed, but the power of his hit would be worth the moment of vulnerability.

The force of the blade came down on top of one man and he slid to the soft ground with his fallen comrade.

Celia cried out softly behind him.

He flicked his gaze left and saw her in the semi-dark, held tightly between two soldiers. She stared at him with eyes so wild they reminded him of the women he'd seen in the dungeon.

A blade flew into view and his body acted on an instinct that had saved his life far too many times to count. He blocked the blow, but his breath came heavy and a mild pain eked into his conscience.

He turned toward Celia and found the guards dragging her toward the scorched earth where fresh poles had been erected among piles of fresh kindling.

• • •

Celia wrenched her body against the bindings at her wrist. The rough rope cut into her with its hair like splintered braiding, but it did not still her efforts.

The hands holding her were rough, insistent. They didn't wait for her feet to find purchase on the ground before dragging her forward.

She sagged in their arms and tried to make herself as heavy as possible, but they drew her forward with far too much ease regardless.

Her eyes searched the poorly lit field, looking back where Alec had been.

The last thing she'd seen was the guard's blade cutting into Alec's ribs. There were too many sensitive places there.

A lung, a liver if the cut was deep, a curl of intestine, his heart.

A low rumble sounded overhead.

She stared out into the empty, dark landscape of rolling hills devoid of witches and guards alike.

And devoid of Alec.

She wanted to call out, but feared to distract him if he was locked in battle.

The men carrying her were panting now.

She willed herself to be heavier and tried to sink further into the earth. Their heaving breaths grew more ragged, but they did not slow. Not even when she dug her heels into the soft earth and let them rake her across the landscape.

The castle walls loomed into view. Celia twisted her body from side to side in an effort to wrench free of their iron grips. To no avail.

But the rough scrape of cobblestones never came.

Instead the brush of lush grass gave way to the crunch of something dead.

An acrid scent pricked her nose.

Not something dead.

Something burned.

Her gaze shot to her feet where her heels bounced uselessly against charred earth.

Everything tilted and spun around her, flying in a dizzying whirl of a thought too overwhelming to truly comprehend.

Neat piles of dry wood had been placed upon the circles of burnt earth in front of her. From each mound rose a massive, jutting wooden pole.

Fear squeezed her throat, filling it until she could no longer breathe.

They were going to burn her.

Like they'd burned Fiona.

Her body would sizzle like roasting meat and blacken to char before disintegrating.

Pieces of her would float away in wispy fragments of ash, which would sift into the grass and melt into the ocean, and all of her would no longer be.

She would be dead.

Burned.

Her chest rose and fell, frantic and fast with panicked breath.

She did not want to die.

Not like this.

Not without having been held by Alec one last time, kissing him one last time, embracing his beautiful life at Duart one last time.

He'd given her all the happiness in the world and she'd shoved it away for fear of seeing him hurt. She should have relished all of it and now it was too late.

Everything in her screamed to fight and insisted if only she struggled a little harder, all would not be lost.

She screamed and writhed and wriggled until the warmth of dripping blood ran down her wrists and she had no more breath in her body.

"This one struggles too damn much," one of the two men muttered with cold resentment.

"She isna weak like the others were," came the other's reply.

And then they stopped.

Strong arms gripped her shoulders and smacked her up against something hard. Her skull cracked back against it and white spots bloomed and faded in her vision.

It was all the time they needed. Her hands were wrenched painfully behind her back, around the rough surface of a tree not shorn of its scraping bark, and bound once more with the jagged rope.

Their efforts had been overzealous and left her binding so tight her fingers tingled with the prick of a thousand needles.

She closed her eyes and breathed deep the last few fragile breaths of air before the true pain could begin.

Never before had she noticed the wet, fresh scent of dew in the air, nor had she noticed the way even cold air felt sweet and invigorating against the heat of her cheeks.

Grass rustled and waves crashed along a shore so close she could taste the brininess of it on the wind.

Everything in her was alive, feeling.

She wanted Alec's arms around her with this heightened awareness of living. She wanted to die with his scent surrounding her and his soft voice in her ear.

Her nose tingled with the threat of tears, but she blinked them away. Something dark filled her blurred vision and made her jerk backward reflexively. Her head smacked against the ragged bark behind her again, scraping a part of her head that was already too sensitive.

"Are you ready to die, witch?" a voice asked.

Her vision cleared and MacDougall's face came into view, his eyes glittering with excitement.

His fingers curled around her neck, cold and wet and sharp.

Panic flickered through Celia before pain even registered, a frightened awareness. She could no longer breathe.

Then came the pain, brilliant and dazzling.

Her body struggled in vain, her tattered wrists tugging in a pathetic, futile effort against her bindings.

But he did not stop, he only tightened his bony fingers with more zeal.

Harder and harder and harder until everything inside her clawed for reprieve, for one more taste of beautiful, sweet air.

Chapter Forty

Alec staggered to his feet. He felt his injuries now, burning hot at his flesh, the blood beneath molten.

The last remaining guard circled him.

"Ye're too late to save her." He jerked his head toward the castle wall where the shadows of two figures showed atop a small hill.

Alec's mind was thick with thoughts of war and rescue, of sacrifice and love.

Was that Celia?

The man lunged forward, but Alec stopped his blade.

If that was Celia, his time was running out.

"No," Alec growled through his teeth. Every muscle in his body exploded with a reserve of energy he didn't know he possessed. He slammed toward the man, knocking him to the ground.

Before the MacDougall guard had a chance to recover, Alec punched his sword into the man's neck with so much force it severed his head from his body.

Alec jerked his blade free and ran, limping, toward the two shadowed figures.

As he drew closer, he saw a third shadow standing at the edge of the wall near the cliffs—Saraid. She swayed like a drunkard, her glassy eyes distant and unblinking.

Alec's thigh ached something fierce where the man's blade had bitten into it and his side stung. He wouldn't glance at either just yet. It wouldn't do to see the wounds, because then the real pain would start.

There was too much to do to really *feel*.

He limped like a beggar, one crippled inch at a time, making his way to Celia.

When he could finally see MacDougall, the man had moved away from Celia and lit the tinder beneath her feet.

Alec's gaze darted to Celia.

She was still, her head hanging limply to the side.

The darkness swept over Alec as suddenly as a squall can overwhelm the light of a summer day. It pounded in his temples and beat a rhythm through his body he could not ignore.

His stride lengthened, his injuries were no longer felt. He approached the other laird and slammed his fist into the man's jaw.

MacDougall's head snapped back and he staggered in shock.

Alec cocked his arm to hit the bastard once more, but something knocked into him from behind and dropped him to the ground.

He flipped over and knelt on his good leg to stand once more. The remaining two guards faced him now. The wound in his thigh sizzled with pain and left the muscle feeling heavy and exhausted.

His heart was heavier, too. Even more exhausted. It hung in his chest like a sack filled with iron.

The darkness loomed over him, wanting to envelop him like a blanket of black velvet. Even if he had strength enough to fight it, he would not.

He let it sweep over him like the darkened clouds had done earlier to the moon. It blotted out anything light in him, it dulled the hurt of his wounds, it made him mad with the desire to taste revenge.

They would pay. Every last one of them.

The guards circled him with a menacing expression and Alec lifted his blade to fight.

He would die, yes, but he'd drag these bastards down with him.

The first one attacked. The jab was practically offensive in how meekly it was delivered. As if he thought Alec so easily slain.

Alec snapped his blade through the air, not even feeling the wound at his side anymore.

The guard's eyes widened in surprise. His second lunge was more substantial, but also easily blocked.

Alec glared at both men, seeing their deaths before they could even be delivered, and let loose a roar pulled deep from his soul.

They would all die.

• • •

Pain flickered through the darkness of Celia's nothing existence. Something echoed around her, distant and muted, a cry of some sort.

She tried to swallow, but her throat ached so badly. It was difficult even to drag in a breath of air.

Awareness pricked her brain.

Smoke.

The thick, heavy scent of it was everywhere. So strong it stung her nose and clogged in her chest. She tried to move, but found herself bound to an unyielding mass scraping already throbbing skin.

She opened her eyes and a haze filled her vision, stinging her eyes.

"Father, she's still alive." Saraid's voice.

Celia squinted through the smoke. Even in the night, even from where Saraid stood far off, near the edge of the castle, Celia could see her eyes were wide and fixed.

"She willna last long," MacDougall replied.

Saraid swayed on her feet and Celia remembered the poison.

Fire crackled along the edges of the woodpile where Celia stood. Alarm screamed through her. The flames hadn't reached her yet, but they would.

The wind howled and swept the smoke from her vision. The reprieve came with a cost, though, and the flames gave a brilliant glow as they were fanned to life.

A low rumble sounded overhead where the clouds threatened to unleash their fury.

But there was something else. The metallic ring of battle.

Despite her own dire circumstance, her heart flickered with a beat of hope.

Was Alec still alive?

Another gust of wind drew back the curtain of smoke and there, by the castle wall, Alec fought two men, his blade moving, flashing, his body still in action.

Realization deflated her hope.

Dark patches of blood stood out on his white leine and he appeared to be limping.

Fighting two men did not leave an injured man much chance to survive.

She strained to pull in a painful breath of air against the squeezing in her chest.

She could not die knowing he would not live.

Then an idea bloomed in the back of her mind, through the cloud of smoke and pain and fear.

If they thought she was a witch, it could be used to her advantage.

She might be able to help Alec still.

"I curse you," she said, but her words came out meek and hoarse from her injured throat.

The flicker of fire glowed closer, the warmth of its newborn flame almost uncomfortable.

She did not have much time.

She would have to be strong and forceful. She would have to push past her pain.

This was for Alec.

She gathered all the strength from deep within her and shouted for all she had left within her to give.

"I curse you, Laird MacDougall." Her voice rang out, loud, clear.

She swallowed against the flare of pain in her throat.

MacDougall went still and the side of his cheek twitched.

Flecks of rain spit down from the sky and spattered Celia's face, but she paid it no mind.

"I curse you and your land and your people." Her voice

came out scratched, but it only lent an element of menace to her threat.

"No," Saraid said sharply. Her hands raked the air at something unseen.

"Your crops will not grow," Celia continued. "Your child will have no children." The rain came down with more force now and the flames around her recoiled with a hiss. "And you will be haunted by every woman you've ever slain as a witch."

Saraid staggered backward and tripped over the hem of her dress. She cowered where she fell.

"I see them," she cried. "I *see* them!"

The men fighting Alec appeared to slow at her words, but he did not.

Lightning flashed overhead and a peal of thunder clapped so loudly it made Celia's ears wince.

Saraid screamed and even MacDougall cried out in alarm.

The rain came down with great force then, as if the spirits of those they'd killed were truly seeking vengeance. It pelted Celia's scalp hard enough to feel like stones and pummeled her eyes so she had to blink rapidly to clear her vision.

Saraid scrambled to her feet, her arms thrashing wildly as if fending off something.

"I see them," she shrieked again. "They want me dead."

The heat of the fire was dying away now, but the curtain of smoke was getting thicker. Breathing was getting more difficult.

Celia's thoughts thinned to almost nothing. She drew in shallow breaths of tainted air. Her gaze fixed on Saraid, watching with burning eyes the form of the other woman who ran like a drunkard, her footsteps uncertain, her balance wobbly.

Foxglove.

The word emerged in Celia's mind.

Too much would kill Saraid anyway, but for now the hallucinating effects were taking their toll.

"Get them off of me," Saraid howled.

Her hands clawed at the air, her footsteps taking her nowhere.

"Saraid," MacDougall's voice was almost completely

drowned out by the roar of the rain. "Saraid." This time it was louder. This time it was edged with panic.

But he was too late.

The smoke whipped around Celia, but she saw the woman in the shrouded moonlight, and watched as Saraid pitched over the edge of the cliff.

The screaming went silent and left only the hiss of the dying fire and the overloud shush of the rain.

Everything was fading, going in and out, blending reality with thought.

Too much smoke.

So hard to breathe.

"Ye killed her." MacDougall's voice seeped into her thoughts, but he seemed so far away.

Keeping her eyes open took almost more than she could give, but she strained anyway. She had to see Alec one last time.

And he was there, staggering toward her.

Broken. Bleeding.

But alive.

He knocked MacDougall to the ground with a hit she did not hear. His fists repeated a rhythm against the man's face, even though MacDougall was no longer moving.

"Don't," Celia said in a long exhale.

Alec stopped and turned to her with a frenzied look in his eyes. It was then she understood: it was Alec himself she was helping.

"You're better than the darkness." It ached so much to talk, to exist. Everything hurt. "You have enough light in you…"

Breathing was so hard with nothing substantial.

He'd gotten to his feet.

But she had to say it.

She had to try.

For him.

He was limping toward her now.

She wanted to feel him so badly, all of her ached.

"You have enough light in you," she said with the last of every bit of energy in her. "To make me love again."

There.

She had said it.

Death pulled at her before she could revel in the touch of his hand on her skin. It sucked her toward a black from which she'd never emerge.

She would be dead, but Alec would live. He would repair his land and live to be a great laird. His people would love him.

Something flickered in her thoughts, fast and flashing in the final breath she managed to inhale.

Fiona.

This was how much Fiona had felt, to sacrifice her own life so readily.

Celia's heart squeezed final tears down her cheeks to think of how much the older woman must have loved her.

She'd died so Celia could live.

And for those few beautiful days at Duart Castle with Wynda and Duncan and Alec, for those few beautiful days, Celia *had* lived.

Fiona's sacrifice hadn't been for naught.

Chapter Forty-One

Alec had lost her again.

He stared at Celia's limp body. Her hair plastered against the whiteness of her skin.

He'd been too late.

MacDougall's guards filed from the castle, their swords unsheathed.

He had lost Celia. His light.

The wood under his feet was warm, but the flames had been smothered by the rain. He staggered over the uneven surface and pressed his body against the slackness of hers before slicing his blade through the ropes binding her hands.

She fell against him, limp and unmoving.

The guards drew closer.

She said he'd had enough light to make her love again. But she had been his light against everything dark and awful.

He lifted her into his arms and turned his back on the approaching soldiers. She was such insubstantial weight in his arms, the way she always had been. But too still.

Too damn still.

This time he did not blink away the hot wetness from his eyes. This time he let the pain in his chest crumple him to the ground with his love in his arms.

Movement in the tree line snagged his attention.

Another army appeared and ran toward him.

But he did not rise. He curled his arms around Celia, as if somehow he might still afford her his protection.

She was dead.

His mind whispered this, but his heart could not believe it.

Arrows loosed from the retinue who'd emerged from the trees and the grunts of injury sounded behind Alec.

He waited for the bite of a blade, for an arrow to pierce his own heart, for the pain of this loss to end.

But it did not come.

The two forces crashed together in a cacophony of shouts and clattering weapons.

"Celia." A familiar voice sounded above Alec.

He looked up to see Duncan. He looked every bit a warrior with his kilt slung around his hips and a sword clutched in his fist. Tears glittered in his familiar green eyes.

"Is she…" the boy asked without asking.

Alec swallowed, unable to even speak his answer.

Duncan pursed his lips and nodded. His chin quivered, but he spoke anyway. "I know why ye turned her in, why ye knocked me senseless, aye?" He put his hand on Alec's shoulder with more strength than he thought the boy capable of. "Ye couldna save her, but ye can avenge her."

He indicated the battle waging behind him. Shouts and cries and metal on metal sounded from the mass.

Duncan grabbed Alec's blade from the ground where he must have dropped it at some point. The boy held it out to him, hilt first. "For Celia."

Alec eased her from his arms so she rested on the ground like an angel, her hair fanned around her. The rain had stopped and she lay untouched. Peaceful.

Alec grabbed the blade and squeezed the hilt with all the force of his grief. "For Celia."

He nodded to the boy and together they charged into the fray of battle with her name on their lips and her memory in their hearts.

And Alec fought, not with darkness, but with light.

Celia's final gift to him.

• • •

Within minutes of Alec joining the fight, the battle ended with MacDougall's men surrendering their blades. With no one left to pay them, there was no motivation.

Immediately Alec returned to where Celia lay undisturbed. A tight ball of red fur lay curled at her side. Ruadh.

Alec was not the only one who knew the crushing impact of her loss.

He stared down at her, looking peaceful save where a vicious ring of purple-red bruise showed on her slender neck.

The battle had not assuaged the savage ache in his chest.

His people would be safe now, free from attacks from the "outlaws" working for MacDougall.

He could restore his inheritance in peace.

But without her it would never be home.

"She was the most beautiful woman I'd ever met," Duncan said quietly beside him. "And also the most caring. I'd have died were it no for her."

Niall appeared and made the sign of the cross. "She saved my daughter once from the plague. May God rest her good soul."

Alec looked at the other man. He hadn't expected to ever see him again, let alone in battle.

Niall moved and a MacLean man took his place. He too made the sign of the cross. "She eased the babe from my wife's womb after I thought they'd both die. She saved everything I've ever loved. May God rest her soul."

He left and yet another man took his place. Only then did Alec realize a line had formed, each soldier with praise on his lips for the good she'd done and a blessing to offer.

Alec fell to his knees beside Celia and took her small hand in his own. "How can ye die when ye are so loved?" he whispered.

Then he felt it. The gentle thrum of her pulse against his palm.

Hope shot through him with wild elation. "Celia," he said, his voice pitched with excitement. "Celia!"

And then, like a brilliant sun breaking through a thickly clouded day, her eyes blinked open.

A gentle smile touched her lips.

"Alec." His name rasped from her throat and a slight grimace of pain crinkled her brow.

"Dinna speak." He had to blink rapidly to keep her from blurring from sight. "Save yer strength."

Her fingers curled over his and gave a squeeze. Not with the weak pressure of the dying, but the solid grasp of the healthy. The living.

Careful, he scooped his arms under her slender frame and cradled her against him. The scent of rosemary, the most wonderful smell in all the world, teased at his senses. He buried his nose in the fine, silken threads of her hair and breathed deep.

His eyes burned and it was all he could do to not crush her to him. "I love ye." His words came out choked from the knot in his throat. "I love ye." This time he said it louder, with all the fierceness of his affection.

Her fingers touched his face and he pulled back to look down at her, his beauty.

She searched his gaze with tear-filled eyes. "I love you," she whispered in a soft strain. "I always have."

"I dinna ever want to lose ye." Something warm ran down his cheek, but she traced it away with her slender thumb. "Marry me, lass. No because I need ye to be my light, but because I love ye. And because life without ye makes me feel as though I canna breathe."

A tear trickled from the corner of her eye and faded into her hair. She nodded. More tears came, faster now, soaking his shirt and turning the tip of her nose the bonniest shade of pink.

His heart swelled in his chest, filled to the brim with the most grateful joy. He rose to his feet with her in his arms. "Let's get back to Duart, aye?"

Celia rested her head against his chest and nodded. Her eyes slipped closed, but the sweet smile on her lips told him there was nothing to fear.

She was alive and had made him the happiest man in all of Scotland.

He cradled her against his chest and nodded to his men.

They were going home.

Epilogue

Celia made her way slowly down the stairs, a feat not easily done with her belly so swollen with child. She kept one hand on the banister and the other she placed on the mound of her stomach.

The babe kicked within. Healthy and strong.

Duncan appeared at her side with his wide smile. "Let me help ye, my lady." He held her elbow in his large hands. The boy was growing into a man more and more every day.

Celia laughed. "You know I'm perfectly capable of walking down the stairs on my own."

"Aye, ye can, but Wynda would have me strung up by my toes if she knew I saw ye and dinna offer my courtly assistance." He winked at her.

Wynda had been overworried and hovering ever since Celia had almost died.

"The great resurrection," as everyone had called it.

Celia hadn't liked that, but no one called her a witch anymore. They all thought of her as an angel instead.

Which, in and of itself, was an uncomfortable thought.

Celia was certainly nothing divine.

"Thank you, Duncan," she said softly when they neared the bottom of the stairs. Truth be told, his assistance was of great help.

Her breath came a little harder. Some of it had to do with the babe not leaving room for breathing, some of it had do with the way her lungs had never fully recovered from when she'd almost died.

Alec stood at the fireplace below, staring pensively into the flames. He looked fine as always in a crisp, golden-colored leine and a fresh kilt. So fine he made her heartbeat quicken.

He turned when he heard them and rushed over. Concern pulled at his brows and creased a deep line on his forehead. "Celia, ye should be in bed."

He clapped Duncan on the shoulder and gave him an appreciative nod before taking his place at Celia's elbow.

"You know I don't agree with that," Celia replied. "It's good to—"

A deep pain squeezed inside her lower stomach. She clutched her hands to her belly.

Alec's eyes went wide. "Wynda!"

The cook ran in, her hands busily wipe, wipe, wiping on her apron.

She took one look at Celia and pressed her hands against her chest. It was what she did when she wanted to hug Celia after Alec had strictly forbidden any Wynda hugs after having learned of Celia's pregnancy.

"Is it time?" the cook asked.

The pain eased, the way it'd done all morning—coming and going.

Celia nodded. "It's time."

She looked at Alec and all the love and happiness of her life swelled in her heart. "Are you ready to be a father?"

He grinned like a boy. "Let's get ye to bed. This time I'll no have ye walking around, aye?" His touch on her arm was gentle, his fingers stroking the delicate skin inside her elbow. "I love ye too much to have anything happen to ye," he whispered.

"You needn't worry," Celia said just as softly. "Because I love you too much to leave you."

She let him lead her toward the room they'd set up for the birthing. Excitement shot through her and left her fingers trembling and her heart fluttering.

She was going to be a mother.

Her eyes found Alec's anxious gaze.

They were going to be a family.

• • •

Alec paced the room.

It was too damn hot.

It was too damn quiet.

The wait was too damn long.

Ruadh paced alongside him, his tail flicking with mirrored impatience. The fox always came inside now.

Alec stopped and stared at the door to the room where his wife labored to birth their child. A long, low moan sounded from the other side. It grappled at his heart and squeezed.

Was that a good moan?

Did that mean the baby was coming?

Why the hell didn't he know all this already?

He started pacing again.

There were few things he knew of childbirth: it was painful, it was long, and sometimes women died.

The last thought was one he'd been trying to avoid, but now that it'd made its way into his mind, he could not clear it.

The words echoed through him and chilled his blood.

He could lose her.

Another glance at the door confirmed it was still closed. The birthing still continued.

He had nothing to distract him, nothing to occupy his thoughts with anything but her.

His castle was restored, the witch trials had been stopped, and there was peace on his land.

All good things, of course, yet now more than ever he wished for some form of distraction.

Everything in him ached to be in there with her. He wanted to hold her hand through the pains, he wanted to offer encouraging words, he wanted to stroke her head and tell her he loved her.

And why should he not?

He was laird, damn it. He should be able to do what he wanted.

Mind made up, he shoved his way through the door.

The room was warm despite the open window and Celia lay on the bed they'd prepared. Wynda's head snapped toward Alec.

"Ye canna be here."

But he didn't care about Wynda's chastisement. He rushed to Celia's side and grasped her hand in his. Her palm was slick and hot, her hair was pasted to her forehead, and her cheeks were flushed red.

She smiled at him. "It's almost time, my love."

"I'm staying," he said firmly.

Her smile broadened. "I want you here."

His heart warmed at her words.

She wanted him there and he stayed. He did everything he'd longed to do outside. He stroked her hair, he told her he loved her, and when the babe finally came, he endured her bone-crunching squeezes like the warrior he was.

Finally, finally at long last, after an extraordinarily painful grip from Celia, a loud squall filled the room.

Alec jerked upright.

Was that—

His throat drew tight.

Was that their child?

After several moments, Wynda came around with a wrapped bundle and placed it in Celia's arms. The crying stopped and the room was suddenly almost too quiet.

"Meet yer daughter," Wynda said. Tears streamed freely down her cheeks.

Alec arched forward to peer at the bundle. An impossibly little face showed through the bundle, pink and swollen. Squinted blue eyes blinked up at him with shiny newness.

She looked right at him and that lingering gaze of hers slipped a loop around his heart he knew would never lose its grip. He stood there, staring into the eyes of his daughter, and realized he could stay so for hours, studying her bonny wee face.

Celia choked out a laugh. "She's so beautiful."

"Aye," Alec said, able to finally speak, but still unable to take his gaze off his daughter. "Thank goodness she takes after ye."

"That hair belongs to ye, laird," Wynda said with a smile. Her face was just as pink as the babe's and her eyes glittered with joy.

She was right. The wee lass had a thatch of dark hair stuck against the top of her head where it was visible from the bundled blanket.

"What will ye name her?" Wynda asked.

"I'd like to name her Fiona," Celia said with reverent softness. She looked up at Alec and tears glistened in her deep blue eyes. "It's because of her sacrifice that I've had the opportunity for such love and joy."

Alec sat on the edge of the bed and put his arms around Celia's shoulders. Her glossy hair still smelled of rosemary despite having labored for hours. "I can think of no better way to honor the woman who saved ye and gave us all happiness, my love."

He stared down at his beautiful family and knew without a doubt: never again would there be darkness in his soul.

Acknowledgments

Books take a lot of work between a lot of people to make them happen—not just the construction and editing, but also support and brainstorming. I'm fortunate to have many who are always there for me.

Thank you to my wonderful agent, Laura Bradford, who is always there for guidance and support. Thank you to my editor, Randall Klein, for finding the most wonderful suggestions to make my writing stronger. Thank you to Trent Hart for the incredible job he's done with getting my book out, and to Sarah Masterson Hally for helping me keep everything in line, and to anyone else at Diversion I may have missed—you're an incredible group who have made my dream come true.

Thank you to the incredible groups of support I have— the Lalalas who are always there, the Fire Breathing Flamingoes who have such wonderful advice and guidance, the First Coast Romance Writers who are so encouraging, and the Celtic Hearts who are so ready to support one another. Being part of Romance Writers of America has changed my life in all the best ways and I'm so grateful for that!

Thank you to the wonderful beta readers who help me through my manuscripts: Alli Searle, who has a heart of gold and is always willing to help someone, Carin Farrenholz, who was the first one to read *Enchantment of a Highlander* and is always encouraging, Katie Couch, who finds the most impossible little misspellings that I need picked out and is a wonderful supporter of my work, Lorrie Cline, whose help has been invaluable— the end of this book would never have been the same without her, and Janet Kazmirski for her constant support, love, and dedication to finding ways to make my books as perfect as they can be.

As always, thank you to my incredible family for their unending support. To the minions for always being so understanding and so heart-swellingly proud of me, to my parents who are so eager to tell anyone who will listen about their author daughter, to John Somar who helps me plot, reads my books, herds minions on nights where I've got a ton going on, and has unending patience and love—even when I go all Type A freak out.

And a big, special, wonderful thank you to the readers who encourage me and get emotionally invested in my characters, who comment on my Facebook and Twitter posts and offer the most incredible suggestions. You make writing truly magical. Thank you.

Madeline Martin lives in Jacksonville, Florida, with her two daughters and a menagerie of pets. She graduated from Flagler College with a degree in Business Administration and works for corporate America. Her hobbies include rock climbing, running, doing Mud Runs and just about anything exciting she can do without getting nauseous. She grew up in Europe and still enjoys traveling overseas whenever she can find the time to get away. Her favorite place to visit thus far: Scotland.

CPSIA information can be obtained at www.ICGtesting.com
Printed in the USA
BVOW08s1403280216

438382BV00004B/60/P